# THE GOLDEN LION AND THE SUN

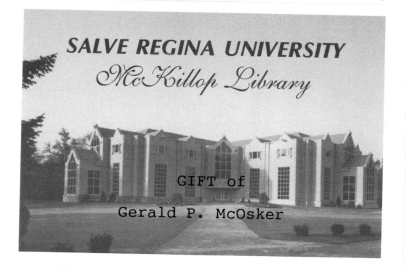

YORAM HAMIZRACHI

# THE GOLDEN LION AND THE SUN

Translated from the Hebrew by Philip Simpson

E. P. Dutton, Inc.      New York

Published in the United States by
E. P. Dutton, Inc.,
2 Park Avenue, New York, N.Y. 10016

Library of Congress Cataloging in Publication Data
Hamizrachi, Yoram.
The golden lion and the sun.
I. Title
PJ5054.H274G6      892.4'36      82–1393
                                  AACR2

ISBN: 0-525-24114-0

Designed by Nancy Scarino

10 9 8 7 6 5 4 3 2 1

First Edition

*In memory of
Harry Herman,
German TV cameraman,
who accompanied me in Iran
and in the Kurdistan mountains*

# THE
# GOLDEN
# LION
# AND THE
# SUN

# 1

The big faded sign bearing the inscription CAFE AND RESTAURANT in Hebrew and European script was rusty and every bit as dilapidated as the establishment it advertised. Below the sign were a greasy green-painted door and a long open window. Cooking smells mingled with the exhaust fumes of cars and heavy trucks passing in the street in a noisy and regular stream. The broad patch of sidewalk between the road and the entrance to the cafe had been eroded by the tires of the trucks that used it as a regular parking place. Pools of oil and brake fluid had mixed with the dust and fragments of asphalt to form a soft brown dough.

The cafe occupied the ground floor of an old stone apartment house in downtown Haifa, in a once-Arab quarter not far from the port. Its proprietors owned the three-story building. They lived on the second floor above and rented out the rest of the building to short-term tenants, mostly young people who came to the town from nearby Galilee, looking for work in the industrial area or the docks, staying for a few months or a year and renting a shabby apartment fitted out with cheap furniture. The cafe was the heart of the building, the place where tenants dined, met, collected mail, answered the telephone and sometimes received guests. Their address was Fishel's Cafe, 10 Sea Road, Haifa.

Fishel's Cafe was busy most hours of the day and night, in fact whenever trucks were on the road, as truckers were its main customers, besides the tenants and other local residents or factory workers. Fishel's was not a place for those of fastidious taste. A dirty refrigerator case with cracked glass panels displayed dozens of varieties of cheese and sausage, tubs of butter and yogurt, dishes of salted fish or homemade pickles, and assorted bottles, all in the state of disarray which seemed to be the hallmark of the establishment. On a marble slab above the case the proprietors worked out their accounts, beside the telephone which had long ago changed color from white to a sticky gray, and there Fishel himself, a bald little man with a perpetual grin, sliced the white and brown bread taken from a wooden bin crammed with rolls, loaves and fresh pita bread. Behind him on old wooden shelves stood dozens of bottles of liquor: wine, dark bottles of local or imported cognac, liqueurs that had stood in their places undisturbed for years, and American or Scotch whiskey beside clear bottles of arak. Tacked to some of the shelves were pinups torn from the pages of *Playboy* or *Penthouse.* There was also a photograph of a smiling Anwar Sadat embracing Prime Minister Menachem Begin, a yellowing portrait of David Ben Gurion, and a 1976 calendar advertising Sony Electronics.

Fishel's customers were a loyal bunch who observed the one rule of the place—not to disturb the other diners. Fishel didn't mind if his customers helped themselves from the fridge, cut their own bread, or even fried their own steaks and omelettes. He never kept a tab on how much his customers ate or drank, or on their phone calls, and when it was time to pay, Fishel never doubted their statement of what they'd taken.

The two men who stood by the doorway of the cafe at noon on a warm cloudless day early in February 1979 were quite unlike

2

Fishel's usual customers. Both wore dark-gray suits and polished soft leather shoes with thick heels, both were in their forties, tall and well built, with fashionable collar-length hair. The blond one wore sunglasses.

The two men stood and looked into the cafe with a mixture of distaste, curiosity and surprise. It was clear that they could not decide whether to go inside or to stay where they were at the door. Fishel left his customary post behind the display counter and walked over, drying his hands on a dirty kitchen towel. He greeted the two men with a sarcastic smile.

"Yes, gentlemen?"

It was the dark-haired man who replied.

"Is this Fishel's cafe?"

"Right the first time!" Fishel's lilting voice bore a distinct East European flavor, probably Polish.

"How can I help you?"

"We were told that Arik Hod lives here."

"Hod?"

"That's the man."

"Have you been upstairs, to his room?"

The dark-haired man nodded. "Yes, but there's nobody there."

"In that case he'll be along soon. He usually finishes about now."

"Finishes?"

"Yes, at the transport depot."

"Can we wait here?"

"Of course!" Fishel smiled broadly, revealing a mouth lined with gold teeth. "This is a cafe after all, gentlemen. Be my guests, there's plenty of room."

He went back to his counter while the two men came inside and chose a corner table from which they could get a good view of the entrance. At this hour the only other customers were two elderly men in blue overalls, eating their lunch and reading the morning paper. From where he sat, the dark-haired man could just make out the headlines: KHOMEINI TO RETURN, CHAOS IN IRAN.

"Shit!" he murmured.

"Did you say something?" the blond-haired man asked in English.

"Nothing, I was just reading the headlines. Iran, of course."

"Of course," the other murmured, "what else?"

"Coffee or tea?" shouted Fishel.

"Coffee please, with milk," the dark-haired man replied. He turned to his colleague. "I've ordered coffee for you."

"That's fine, I'm tired."

"You look it."

The blond man yawned and then took off his sunglasses, folded them carefully and laid them on the table. "If they'd told me a couple of days ago that I'd wind up in Israel in a joint like this, I wouldn't have believed it."

"That's what makes life interesting."

"You reckon?"

"I'm sure."

The American fumbled in the pocket of his jacket and pulled out a silver cigarette case. He lit a cigarette, then leaned back against the gray wall, inhaling. "What kind of a guy is he?" he asked.

"Wait and see."

"Haven't you got anyone else?"

"Your people asked for him." The dark-haired man was on the point of standing up and going to a nearby table where there was a stack of newspapers, but at that moment he saw a heavy truck draw up outside the cafe. A man jumped down from the driver's cab. About thirty-five, powerfully built, he wore faded jeans, a red T-shirt and an army windbreaker stained with patches of engine oil. His big green eyes sparkled above his hollow cheeks and two days' growth of stubble, but deep grooves on either side of his lips gave him a sour expression. The man walked into the cafe and went straight over to the display counter.

4

"Someone's looking for you," said Fishel. "Over there in the corner."

"Arik!" the dark-haired man shouted, rising from his seat at the corner table. "Come and join us . . ."

Arik took off his woolen cap, exposing a tousled mop of thick black hair. For a moment a look of recognition flashed in his eyes, then he nodded without changing his expression. "*You* here?" he said drily, walking across the cafe and holding out his hand to the man in the suit.

"This is Arik Hod," the man said to his blond-haired colleague. The American stood up and stretched out his hand.

"Pleased to meet you," he said in English.

The three men sat down. Arik asked: "What brings you here, Eldad? I haven't seen you for years."

"We have a problem . . ."

"What's up?"

"Do we have to talk here?" asked the American.

"Don't worry," said Arik, "people mind their own business here. What's up?"

The man addressed as Eldad leaned forward. "I'd better introduce our guest," he said. "This is Robin Trenshaw, from the United States."

"What's up?"

"We have a suggestion."

"*We?*"

"You know perfectly well whom I represent." Eldad grinned.

Arik leaned back in his chair. "Listen," he said, "I drive a truck. It's hard and tiring work but it suits me." He took a deep breath and went on. "Before you get down to details you should know that I'm just not interested. I like things the way they are and I don't intend to lift a finger for anyone."

Eldad frowned. "You've got a bloody nerve!"

"Why not?" Arik pulled a crumpled pack of cigarettes out of the pocket of his coat but before he could light one Trenshaw offered him his silver cigarette case. "Be my guest," he said.

"Thanks." Arik took a cigarette and lit it with Trenshaw's lighter. "How did you find me?" he asked.

"Our Haifa section located you. It wasn't difficult."

Trenshaw was studying Arik from head to foot, like a boxing coach sizing up a new pupil. "You drive a truck, Mr. Hod?" he asked.

"Yes, I drive containers from the port to factories around here. It's hard work."

"I guess so." Trenshaw looked at his colleague, as if inviting him to continue the conversation.

"Are you prepared to listen?" asked Eldad.

"I told you. I'm not lifting a finger. I like it here."

"Here, in this place?"

"I love it!"

"I don't believe you."

"I don't care." Arik blew out a long jet of smoke. "Anyway, it's good to know that you haven't forgotten me."

"It wasn't us," said Eldad. "The Americans came up with your name."

"Really?" Arik's expression changed, a flicker of interest showing in his green eyes. "That's something new," he said. "What do they want with a truck driver from Haifa?"

"You said you didn't want to know . . ."

"I've come all the way from Rome just to see you," said Trenshaw.

"C.I.A.?"

"You said it."

"These days it sounds like a curse," murmured Eldad.

"That's fine by me." Arik leaned his elbows on the table, cupping his square chin in his hand, the cigarette wedged firmly between his lips. "I don't mind listening . . ." he muttered.

"We have a proposition," said Eldad. "Something to do with Iran."

Arik coughed, sat bolt upright and threw his cigarette on the floor. "Iran?"

6

"You know the place, don't you?"

"You talk about Iran as if it was a back street in Brooklyn!"

"Do you want to listen?"

"Go on."

"You know Kermanshah and Tabriz?"

"Right."

"That's it then . . ." Eldad emptied his coffee cup and added: "Khorasad is in trouble."

"That bastard?" said Arik with a trace of surprise.

"Yes."

"Is that what you came here to tell me?"

"We want you to go out there, Arik." Eldad spoke in a low voice. He hesitated, then added uneasily: "We have interests there that we share with certain allies. Something's cropped up and the Americans need our help . . . you're the man."

"Bullshit!"

"Not so fast . . ." Eldad lowered his voice still further and leaned forward. "You should hear what Trenshaw has to say."

The American looked around uncomfortably. "Must we talk here?" he asked.

Arik grinned. "No one will understand what you're saying, Mr. Trenshaw, don't worry. I'm baffled myself."

"Khorasad mentioned your name . . . he's in big trouble, Mr. Hod."

"All the Iranians are."

"Khorasad says you'll know how to reach him if . . ."

"If?" Arik narrowed his eyes. "Go on, Mr. Trenshaw."

"If he needs your help."

"Well?"

"According to our latest information he's going to need you a lot sooner than we reckoned . . . in a week at the outside. His life is in danger."

"And why are you so interested in him, for God's sake? There's bigger fish than him in Savak."

"You're right, but you don't know the whole story."

"Okay. Tell me."

"Only if you agree to work with us."

"Go to hell!" growled Arik. "I told you, I like it here." He swung around in his chair. "Get me some sandwiches, Fishel, and a bottle of beer. I'll eat upstairs." Then he turned to the two well-dressed men. "Come up to my room," he suggested. "I want to hear some more before I decide if I want to hear everything."

"Great," said Eldad.

"Not so fast." Arik took a deep breath and licked his thin lips. "I haven't agreed to anything yet."

"This is the telegram," said Trenshaw. He sat down on the big sprung bed with its gray army blankets and leaned back on the embroidered pillow. He pulled a photostated telegram out of his attaché case and handed it to Arik who sat at the table munching a greasy meat sandwich. Arik took the telegram and read it. The room was small, dimly lit and crammed with books, notebooks and documents. A framed photograph on the wall showed Arik Hod and a squad of paratroopers boarding a plane.

Arik read the telegram aloud:

*From Penicillin to Wild Bird.*

*Consider situation desperate. Return to Teheran impossible. Redwood and Nero coming to me. Fastest possible method act through friends in New Deal. Contact Carpenters request Swordfish. He knows how approach New Deal. Further communication three days.*

"Penicillin is Khorasad," said Trenshaw.

Arik grinned and tossed the telegram back to the American. "The poor bastard . . ." he murmured.

"We had trouble identifying Swordfish," said Trenshaw, "but when we'd solved that we checked out the whole thing thoroughly. We reckon you're the only one who's capable of getting to him in time. In fact, you're the only one we have."

8

"I think you're all crazy!" said Arik. "Sending a man to Iran to reach Khorasad? Only a lunatic would go out in times like this to that insane asylum. You've read it for yourselves, the situation's desperate!"

"There's no choice," murmured Trenshaw.

"And anyway, what do you want me to do if I get to him?"

"Get him out, him and the others . . ."

"It's impossible. How am I going to make it to northern Iran? How will I get out again? Bullshit! The whole thing's crazy . . . and anyway, why should I help that bastard?"

"We aren't talking only about Khorasad," said Eldad. "There are others who are more important to us and the Americans."

"Then send in the marines or the Green Berets 'or Richard Burton. Why me, for God's sake? Do I owe you a favor?"

"There's no time for a lot of explanations," said Trenshaw. "Things are moving fast and you're the only one who knows Khorasad and the area around there, which means you're the only one we can use."

Arik stood up and took off his windbreaker. Standing there tensely in his sweat-stained T-shirt he looked more solid than ever. He went and stood by the little window that overlooked the street, his back to his guests. "There's really nothing to discuss," he said. "I finished with this business years ago. Find someone else."

"It's an opportunity . . . ," said Eldad.

*"Opportunity?"*

"You can get back into . . . the business, Arik."

Arik turned to face his guests. "There's nothing to discuss," he said quietly.

"Is that final?" asked Trenshaw.

"You'd better think it over," said Eldad. "We'll see you again tonight, okay?"

"There's nothing to discuss, it's crazy. As far as I'm concerned Khorasad can go to hell. He's no saint, you know."

Eldad stood up and signaled to Trenshaw to join him. "We'll

come back this evening. You think it over. If you're prepared to consider it seriously, we'll tell you the rest."

Arik shrugged. "Suit yourselves," he said.

He accompanied the two men to the door of his room, watched as they descended the dark narrow staircase, then locked the door and sat down on the bed. He took off his battered shoes and sweaty woolen socks and stretched out on the bed, his head on the big pillow, staring into space. From the street outside came the sound of squealing brakes and horns.

"Khorasad," he murmured, "you shitty bastard!" He took a deep breath and cursed softly.

"Do you think he'll agree?" asked Trenshaw as he drove the black Chevrolet with the diplomatic plates toward Mount Carmel, following Eldad's directions.

"I don't know." Eldad chuckled. "Let's find a decent restaurant and wait a few hours."

"Is there no way of persuading him?"

"You saw what kind of a guy he is."

"Yes . . . not at all like his dossier."

"You have a dossier on him?" asked Eldad, surprised.

"Yes."

"What does it say?"

"That he's an expert on Kurdistan."

"That's right."

"That he's brave, intelligent and experienced."

"Right."

"What it doesn't say is that he's a trucker living in a slum."

"I didn't know that either."

"What happened to him?"

"I can only guess."

"Well?"

"When he got back from Iran his army career became a failure. In fact, he was discharged."

10

"Really?"

"Yes, 'unsuitable temperament' or something like that . . . he got himself into fights, turned violent . . . in the end he was sent home."

"If everything I've read about him is true, that was a mistake."

"We've no room for misfits."

Trenshaw parked the Chevrolet outside a smart Carmel restaurant. Inside an elderly waiter in a tuxedo escorted them to a table. Trenshaw took a large manila envelope from the attaché case and handed it to Eldad. "Here," he said, "material that you haven't seen yet. I don't suppose it matters, your reading it."

Eldad opened the envelope and took out several sheets of paper. The pages bore no security classification or name of organization, just the typed heading Information Sheet:

*General Said Khorasad. Born Teheran 1935. Graduated Iranian Officers' Academy and U.S. Army Staff College. Transferred to Savak 1965. Served as District Commandant, Tabriz, and seconded to liaison team for Kurdistan affairs. Liaison officer between Savak, Kurdish Command and Israel. In 1976, special representative of the Shah in the Northern Sector. Recruited 1974. Code name Penicillin.*

*Hobbies: winter sports, hunting, women.*

"What you don't have here," said Eldad, "is that his own people call him the Butcher."

"We don't have to put in everything." Trenshaw smiled.

*Doctor Shah Amiri. Born 1922. Physicist. Graduate of Teheran University, Berlin University. Research fellow London University. Lecturer Teheran University. In 1973 head of Atomic Energy Development Commission, Teheran. Recruited 1974. Code name Nero.*

*Doctor Amin Yasarian. Born Teheran 1930. Mathematician. Graduated Teheran University, Ph.D. Teheran University. Chair-*

11

*man of National Technological Development Committee. In 1973 member of Atomic Energy Development Commission, Teheran. Recruited 1974. Code name Redwood.*

Eldad laid the papers on the table and looked at Trenshaw who had finished his notes and was lighting a cigarette. "The last two are new to me," he said.

"You mean you've never heard of them?"

"We knew about them all right. We've investigated the Atomic Energy Commission but we didn't know you'd managed to recruit them . . ."

Trenshaw smiled. "What's *your* interest in this business?" he asked.

Eldad looked around and saw the waiter approaching with a tray loaded with coffee cups and toasted cheese sandwiches. He waited in silence until the waiter had left them, then he leaned forward.

"Khorasad," he said, "knows a little too much about us. Aside from that, there's goodwill and our readiness to cooperate with your people."

Trenshaw grinned. "My superiors warned me I wouldn't get anything out of you."

When Arik came down to the cafe early that evening, old man Fishel smiled at him and clasped his muscular arm. "Everything all right, kid?"

"Yes."

"Those two guys, the tailor's dummies, they all right?"

Arik laughed. "Everything's fine, Fishel."

The old man shrugged. "How should I know? Two guys wearing suits? That's not your style, Arik . . ."

"Really?" Arik freed himself from the old man's grip and looked past him into the kitchen where the landlord's wife was busy frying an omelette. "Any chance for coffee?" he asked. "Strong and black."

"For you, anytime . . ." the woman mumbled wearily.

Arik turned and leaned on the panel of the display cabinet beside Fishel, scanning the cafe and its occupants. "A bad winter," he said.

"Yes," Fishel agreed. "No rain. Are you on the road tomorrow?"

"On the road?"

"Yes, everything as usual, or not?"

Arik smiled. "Do you sense something unusual?"

"I can tell you're worried."

"Really?"

"Those two guys, I didn't like them."

"I didn't either."

"Black coffee!" shouted Fishel's wife, and Arik turned to the kitchen hatch and took the coffee cup, then went and sat down at the corner table where a few hours before he had met Eldad and Trenshaw. He took a sip of coffee, leaned back and closed his eyes. "Khorasad, you shitty bastard!" he murmured. His thoughts carried him far from the squalid little cafe. In his imagination he recalled the powerful image of Khorasad as he had seen him for the first time on the Iran-Iraq border in Kurdistan. Broad shoulders, thinning hair, a thick black moustache and hairy arms, rounded bronzed face and dark twinkling eyes. When he met him for the first time, the Iranian general was in charge of liaison between Iran and the Kurds who had revolted against the Iraqi government. One of his duties was to escort Israeli advisers across the frontier. Arik was impressed by the enormous energy of the Iranian, by his authority and, most of all, by the total and blind obedience with which Khorasad's men fulfilled his every order.

"I don't know why I like the bastard, but I do," Arik muttered to himself. "All that matters to him is hunting, women and war —and the good life," he reflected, then realized that probably what he liked about the general was precisely that he had succeeded where Arik had always failed.

Arik closed his eyes, remembering the huge mountains which

13

at this time of the year were like shining glaciers, bathed alternately in layers of cloud and patches of mist. It was Khorasad who introduced him to northern Iran and the Kurds. At the start of Arik's first visit to Iran the general had invited him to join in a hunting trip. "Come see how an Iranian general enjoys life!" he had said. They rode in a spacious, well-heated Land Rover with two of the general's bodyguards. Two more bodyguards followed in a jeep with food and equipment.

As they traveled through a green valley on a side road from Kermanshah, Khorasad, very pleased with himself, told Arik how he had just arrested four young men of the underground Azarbaijan Marxist movement. "The Shah telephoned me in person and thanked me," he said in his deep voice. "Just imagine, the Shah himself!" Arik could just imagine the brutal interrogation that the youths might be undergoing at that very moment. He did not want to know. As they drove through the green valley, passing shepherds clad in fur overcoats with black bandanas tied around their heads, he concentrated on the scenery. Khorasad knew the name of every mountain, stream and crevice and as he drove the Land Rover he gestured in all directions and talked enthusiastically of his hunting and womanizing exploits. When they left the valley and began climbing a narrow mountain track, almost on the edge of the chasm, the landscape changed. Here the ground was strewn with massive rocks, piles of fallen stone and sparse vegetation. The valley they had left stretched out behind like a distant green band. The general stopped beside a sharp bend, spoke in rapid Farsi to his bodyguards and then said to Arik, "Come on, from here we'll go on foot."

They had emerged from the warmth of the vehicle into the cold mountain air and Arik was startled by the change in temperature. "Here we can hunt mountain goat," Khorasad said, grinning at Arik. "Are you cold?"

He admitted that he was. The general bared a set of strong white teeth. "Let's go. The exercise will warm you up!"

They had left the mountain track and climbed down into a

huge ravine, following a snaking goat path about half a yard wide. They walked carefully, the general stopping at intervals to inspect the terrain through his binoculars. Finally after an hour of strenuous walking they saw a herd of mountain goats. Khorasad took aim and with a single thundering shot brought down a gigantic ram. He ran toward it, yelling triumphantly, and when he got there he drew out a long knife and dispatched the quivering animal with a few swift, vigorous strokes. When they returned to the car the two bodyguards were sent down into the ravine to retrieve the dead ram.

On the trip back to Kermanshah, the valleys and mountaintops had been shrouded in mist. On hairpin bends Khorasad sounded the horn to warn shepherds or other vehicles. "When heavy mist comes down," he said, "only deer and mountain goats can cope." Suddenly they had come upon a pair of Kurdish shepherds emerging from the mist leading a large and straggling herd of goats. "Look, people do still move around in the mist!" Arik had said.

The general laughed. "In *thin* mist, my friend, and those aren't people in the normal sense of the word. They're Kurds."

Arik stood up and walked to the entrance of the cafe, opened the door and went out into the street. For a moment he shivered in a sudden blast of cold, then he went over to his silent truck and started kicking the tires. Just as he was about to return to the cafe he saw the black Chevrolet approaching. Trenshaw was at the wheel. He waited for the two men to come to him.

"Good evening," he said.

"Have you decided?" asked Eldad.

Arik sighed. "Come on, let's hear what you have to say."

# 2

Khorasad slammed down the telephone receiver and leaned back in his chair. He was afraid—not as panic-stricken as most of his fellow Savak officers, but any fear was a new and unfamiliar sensation to him.

In the room were a writing desk and a long conference table with two smaller tables jointed to it to form a T shape. Khorasad sat at the apex wearing an olive-green winter uniform without insignia or badges. An army Colt-45 was strapped to his waist. Above his head hung a large portrait of Reza Shah Pahlevi, silver-haired, in gray civilian clothes.

Khorasad had been listening on the telephone, without reply, to the voice of a junior officer at Savak Staff Headquarters in Teheran. "They've dismissed them all!" wailed the young officer. "The government has dismissed them all!"

Khorasad remembered Teheran as he had seen it on his last visit to the capital only two weeks before: the thousands of demonstrators, the smoke-filled streets and the soldiers in riot gear. For the first time in the history of the service, Savak officers looked scared and helpless. "Good thing you're going back to Tabriz," a senior ministry official told him. "Things aren't so bad up there—not yet." Some of his friends told him in confidence that they had evacuated their families to Europe. He heard of officers who had delayed their return from overseas missions and he was considering moving his own wife and three sons to Switzerland, where his bank account was, when he heard of the decree issued by Shapur Bakhtiar's government forbidding the departure of official personnel and their families.

His apprehension had mounted when he was summoned before General Hedayat, a white-haired, potbellied veteran Savak officer serving as temporary adviser to the prime minister. "I have been ordered to investigate certain incidents in your sector, Said. Somebody in the Majlis is claiming that our activities in Azarbaijan and Kurdistan have been irregular . . ."

Khorasad slammed his fist on the table. "Irregular activities . . ." He groaned and stared at the big black safe. *Must burn the papers,* he thought. The last thing he had seen in Teheran before returning to Tabriz had been Savak heads of department destroying whole archives, the fruits of years of interrogation and painstaking investigation. "Must burn the papers," he repeated aloud.

Before leaving Teheran he had kept an appointment in Shimran Street outside the National Television Center with a diplomat from the United States Embassy. The man had pressed an envelope into his hand, muttered a few polite words and disappeared into the crowd. Now Khorasad pulled a bundle of papers from his pocket and flicked through them until he found the American's letter.

*Redwood and Nero will join you in Kermanshah within a week. If you require assistance use call sign Alpha Delta 99.*

He tore up the letter, threw the scraps into a big ashtray and set fire to them. He watched the little flames until they died down, then went through his papers again and put them back in the pocket of his tunic.

There was a knock on the door of his office. Hastily he tipped the smoldering ashes into the wastebasket under the table, buttoned his tunic, cleared his throat and shouted, "Come in!"

The door opened with a soft creak and a young man dressed in blue civilian clothes came into the room.

"Good morning, General."

"Come in, Dariush," he said. "Come in and close the door."

"Yes, General." The man obeyed, locking the door and sinking into a chair next to the general's table.

"Well?"

"It wasn't easy," he said.

"Did you send the broadcast?" Khorasad asked.

"Yes." Dariush nodded wearily. "Then I wrecked the transmitter."

"Excellent! What was the answer?"

"Swordfish is coming."

Khorasad stopped short. For the first time in weeks he felt a slight easing of tension. "Say that again!"

"Swordfish is coming."

"Great . . ."

"Is that good?"

"It's excellent! Prospects are improving. Everything ready?" he asked.

"Yes, everything . . . the guests are just waiting for your instructions."

"Good."

Dariush looked up at the general. He seemed to have recovered slightly and his red-rimmed eyes were dry. "Who or what is Swordfish, General?"

"A friend . . ." Khorasad leaned back in his chair. "If these religious fanatics only knew . . ."

"I don't understand, General."

"An Israeli, Dariush. Swordfish is an Israeli."

18

A few hours later Khorasad left his office and made his way briskly toward the small parking lot, the snow cracking under his boots. He now wore a heavy trench coat over his uniform, its collar turned up against the cold. Dariush trudged through the snow close behind him, followed by a driver in civilian clothes who carried the general's attaché case. The three men climbed into the Rambler. Khorasad switched on the radio-telephone in front of him and leaned back, wrapping the coat around him tightly. He looked out at the carpet of bright clean snow covering the buildings of the camp, at the barbed-wire fence with its burden of sparkling icicles and at the low cloudy sky, and gazed lovingly at the snow-covered black Mercedes. He wondered if he would ever again drive such a beautiful, conspicuous car. For now the Rambler would have to do.

Khorasad looked in the mirror and saw Dariush crouching in the corner of the back seat.

"Are you cold?" he asked.

"Pardon, General?"

"I asked you if you were cold."

"Yes." Dariush shivered. "Very cold."

"It has been two months since I've driven in the Mercedes."

"Yes, General . . ."

"There'll be trouble if anyone throws a stone at it . . ."

The driver released the clutch and the Rambler moved forward, toward the gate separating the Savak sector from the rest of the camp. The sentry, a paratrooper, opened the gate and saluted as they passed. Khorasad thought he saw a venomous gleam in the eyes beneath the helmet. *Just my imagination,* he thought. *Hell, I'm getting as jumpy as an old woman.* But as they drove through the camp he stared intently at the passing soldiers and civilian workers and saw more faces full of hatred. Years of experience as an interrogator told him this was not imagination. It was blatant. The intense nausea that he had felt in the morning returned to him now. He might have left the country a day earlier; now he knew he was trapped. Some of his friends had already quit Tabriz, crossing the border into Turkey. Others had chartered a light plane and headed for Pakistan or the sheikhdoms of the Gulf. For the first time in his life, Khorasad had missed the bus.

When he first read and understood the C.I.A. man's brief note, he knew he was in deep trouble. It was he who had recruited Nero and Redwood on behalf of the Americans. It was he who had set them to work and he knew that he could not leave Iran without them. Portilio and Schreiber would not evacuate him to Turkey unless he brought both the scientists with him. He stared out of the window of the Rambler. The snow was not deep and in some places the road and the sidewalks and the roofs of buildings were bare and dry. He inspected the leaden sky, searching in vain for some sign of improvement.

At the hotel, a Savak uniform still commanded respect. The clerks and waiters sprang to their feet as he marched into the tastefully furnished lobby, footsteps muted by the expensive carpets. Walking slightly stooped he crossed the lobby and rapidly climbed the stairs to the first floor. Dariush stayed behind, sinking into a deep leather armchair.

Khorasad knocked on the door of number 12 and without waiting for an answer turned the handle and entered the overheated room. An old man clad in pajamas stood up from the bed on which he had been sitting, putting down an open book. His untidy hair was gray and flecked with streaks of white. He made an effort to smile.

"Sit down, Doctor!" Khorasad said sharply. He took off his coat and threw it down on a chair. "Have you got any liquor?"

"Vodka, General . . ." The old man's voice was soft, and puckered his mouth. "Is there any news, General?"

"Dariush has come back from Tabriz . . . there's no chance of getting out that way." Khorasad sat down in a big red armchair. "All the roads to the north and west are blocked. It's total chaos there."

"Yes, that's what I heard," said the scientist. He turned to the bedside cabinet, bent down and took out a bottle of vodka and two glasses.

"Where's Redwood?" asked Khorasad lightly.

"In his room. He'll be here shortly." Amiri filled the glasses and handed one to the general. "What are we going to do?" he asked.

"If necessary we shall leave by other means."

"How?"

"Let me worry about that, Doctor." Khorasad emptied the glass in one gulp, grimaced and sighed. "I came here to tell you to be ready. Don't leave the hotel, not even for a moment."

"Some of my assistants from the Institute came to see me today," said the doctor.

"Did they suspect anything?"

"No, I told them I didn't feel well. I said I was waiting for my wife."

"And Redwood?"

"He said he had to wait in the town until he was transferred to Teheran."

"That's good."

The doctor sat down again on the corner of the bed. "Do you believe it's going to work?" he asked.

"Have I ever deceived you?"

"Yes."

The general sat up in his chair, frowning. "When, for God's sake?"

Amiri shrugged and forced a smile. "There's no point in regrets now, General. What's done can't be changed. We're in this together and fate has turned against us."

Khorasad pursed his lips angrily. "Listen, Nero," he said at last, controlling his voice with an effort, "you're right. We're in this together. Sometime—today, tomorrow, in another hour—when the mob storms this place, you won't be able to change the fact that you're a scientist and I'm a cop and as far as they are concerned that's the same thing . . . so don't look for a way out.

21

You joined us because you wanted to. You, me, Redwood, we're all in this together. Understood?"

"But I believed . . ."

The general interrupted Amiri, leaning over him until their faces almost touched. "This has nothing to do with belief. When we recruited you we knew exactly what we were doing. Your Swiss bank account is loaded, isn't it? And, my dear doctor, don't forget Paris."

Amiri put down his untasted glass. His shoulders drooped.

"Say something!" Khorasad commanded, slapping the old man's shoulder.

Amiri took a deep breath. "I've nothing to say," he replied softly. "I'm as much involved in this as anyone else, up to my neck, and I'm sorry."

"We're all sorry."

"What about my wife?"

"She must stay in Teheran. There's no choice."

"I understand."

"My wife is in Teheran too, with my sons," said Khorasad. "We'll try to get them out later."

Suddenly the door to the room opened and in walked a bearded middle-aged man, accompanied by the acrid smell of pipe tobacco. He wore a well-tailored pinstripe suit; a bald patch shone through his thinning gray hair. He smiled at the general, who had broken off his train of thought and risen.

"Sit down, General, sit down," he said in a deep voice.

"I didn't stand up out of respect for you," said the general, "I'm just not used to lounging around in chairs. My ass hurts."

Doctor Amin Yasarian roared with laughter. "Rome is burning and you're fiddling with your ass!"

"The general says that the roads out of Tabriz are blocked," said Doctor Amiri.

"Really?" Yasarian sat down heavily on Amiri's bed. "What are we going to do?"

"Don't worry, Redwood," said Khorasad, "I'll get you out."

"My secretary is coming with us," said Yasarian.

"Is she indeed?" Khorasad struck a defiant pose.

"I'm not going without her."

"Is she your mistress?" Khorasad sounded a little surprised.

"She's my secretary."

"What's her name?"

"Janet Simpson."

*"What?"*

"You heard what I said, General. Janet Simpson."

"English?"

"American."

"Where did you dig her up?"

"The United Nations. She works for the U.N. Research Fund."

"Here, in the Atomic Research Center? How come I know nothing about her?"

"She was based in Teheran. I invited her here when I thought that the troubles were beginning to die down."

"Nice?" Khorasad leered.

"Please, General," Yasarian protested. "A little respect, for God's sake!"

"Respect?" barked Khorasad. "What are you talking about, Doctor?"

"She's coming with us," Yasarian insisted. "Otherwise I'm staying here."

"As far as I'm concerned . . ." Khorasad trailed off, shrugged. He knew he could not refuse. "All right," he said at last, "but you haven't answered my question. Is this Mrs. Simpson worth it?"

Yasarian sat down again on the bed. "Yes," he said, "very pretty."

"And Mrs. Yasarian?"

"She's gone to Berlin. She's with relatives."

"Excellent," murmured Khorasad, "just excellent." He picked up his coat and put it on slowly. "Don't leave the hotel under any circumstances," he said. "If there are any problems Dariush will look after you. He's staying here. The poor bastard's probably hungry. I suggest you give him something to eat."

With the general gone, the two scientists were left sitting on the broad bed in gloomy silence. Amiri took out his false teeth, put them in a glass, then picked up his book. As he turned over the pages he coughed. "Don't worry, I believe that we'll get out safely."

"You think so?"

"I'm sure. The general will sort everything out for the best."

Yasarian nodded his head slowly. "Yes," he said, "he has no choice. In the final analysis we're much more use to our friends in Washington than he is."

Amiri smiled wearily. "So there's no need for panic."

"I hope not, but this morning I heard that in Teheran the militants are more powerful than ever. Imagine what would happen if they stormed the American Embassy. If they open the secret files we won't stand a chance."

"It's the mullahs that scare me," said Amiri.

"Them too," Yasarian agreed. He went to the window and looked into the street. Down below, Khorasad's Rambler moved out into light traffic. Yasarian closed the curtain.

"What's the army doing?" asked Amiri.

"Shitting themselves like everyone else," replied Yasarian.

"And Savak?"

"I don't envy their chances."

"What about the general?"

"The Butcher will be the first to get his throat cut, right here! The Kurds and Azarbaijanis will see to that."

Amiri lifted his feet onto the bed. "I'm cold," he said. "If you don't mind, I think I'll go to sleep."

Yasarian treaded softly down the long gloomy corridor. At the door of room 19 he knocked. A key turned in the lock, and a woman opened the door. She was slim but well rounded, her breasts bulging at the neckline of her tightly fitting blue night-gown. The redhead recoiled slightly as Yasarian pawed at her.

"I've talked to him," he said. "It's all right."

"Yes?" The woman sat down on the bed, crossed her legs and lit a cigarette. Her voice sounded relaxed and she smiled faintly through the smoke.

"Are you worried?" he asked.

"Of course."

"Listen, Janet, everything's going to be okay." He took off his jacket. Standing there in his vest with its pocket watch and gold chain he put on a mask of breezy self-confidence. The deep bass voice helped. "Are you hungry? Would you like to go down to the restaurant?"

She shook her head. "No . . . we can have some food sent up here."

"As you wish." He sat down beside her and leaned his head on her bosom. "Don't worry," he said, "I'll get you out of here whatever happens."

She chuckled softly. "Sometimes," she said, "I can't believe that this is all happening to me . . . that Iran is falling down around our ears. I'd never have believed it . . ."

"Regrets?"

She shrugged. "I don't know."

"I love you," he said, suddenly alarmed.

"I know . . . that's something strange too."

"What?"

"Yes, being a mistress."

"You're the woman I love," he insisted.

"And your mistress."

"I've never heard you complain."

"Oh, I have no complaints. Christ, I've got no complaints!" She laughed. "Did you know, I agreed to come out and do this work in Iran just so I could forget someone?"

"I don't understand." He pushed her away and looked intently at her face.

25

"I had an affair with a married man."

"And your husband?"

"It was because of that he divorced me." She shrugged. "What a shitty mess we're in. I'm no starry-eyed innocent, you know, and I did have a good time with you in Teheran. But now I'm scared, really scared."

"I'll get you out of here," he said. "Don't worry."

"Are you sure?"

He looked into her blue eyes, smiled and kissed her.

On his way back to camp Khorasad passed by the Kermanshah City Hall. His driver went slowly, trailing behind a heavy truck laden with building materials. The sidewalks were almost deserted. Here and there stood groups of soldiers, and armed gendarmes paced back and forth in heavy trench coats. An armored car was stationed by the gates of the City Hall. A bored young soldier sat at the gun turret. The Rambler overtook the truck and turned north, passing a block of shops, most of them boarded up.

Suddenly a group of young people emerged from a nearby alleyway. Some carried banners and others waved placards bearing the portrait of Ayatollah Khomeini. A few were armed with sticks and chains. Khorasad reached for his revolver, but at the same moment a brick was hurled at the windshield of the car, smashing the glass and showering the two men with splinters. The driver jammed his foot on the brake and the Rambler skidded to a halt, hitting a curbstone and bouncing back into the middle of the road. Khorasad drew his revolver and flicked off the safety catch. A crowd of youths swarmed toward the car, yelling. He fired a shot in the air, then lowered the muzzle of his pistol and fired two more shots. The solid phalanx of rioters halted, some dived for cover and others fled, but the majority stood their ground. He saw a group of girls huddled over two men who lay bleeding on the wet asphalt. He brushed the glass splinters from his coat and grabbed the receiver of the radio-telephone. His driver pulled out an Uzi submachine gun from under the seat and aimed into the crowd.

Before Khorasad had time to speak into the receiver a Molotov cocktail bounced off the hood of the Rambler and smashed in the road behind the car. Khorasad leapt out of the Rambler and saw other drivers abandoning their vehicles and taking cover. A light truck skidded and squealed onto the sidewalk and crashed into the window of a food store, smashing metal and glass. The mob surged forward again, and he heard the rattle of the driver's machine gun. He aimed his Colt at the mass of demonstrators and emptied the magazine. He saw youths crouching in the road, arms flailing, a bewildered young girl clutching her lacerated stomach, an older man dragging his body across the ground. Placards and portraits of the Ayatollah scattered in the road as the demonstrators fled, leaving the wounded in pools of blood behind them.

Khorasad ripped out the empty magazine and replaced it with a fresh one. It aimed again at the hysterical mob. Another Molotov cocktail exploded not far from where he stood. The Rambler was now in flames; the fire had spread to another vehicle close behind and there was the acrid smell of burning asphalt. Khorasad retreated and took cover behind a stationary car that had been left straddling the road at a peculiar angle, its doors wide open and inside, the contents of a woman's handbag scattered over the seat. He saw his driver standing behind the burning Rambler, still firing into the crowd of demonstrators, who had now turned and were advancing again. More shots were fired; Khorasad watched with horror as the driver was engulfed by the crowd, disappearing under a hail of fists, sticks and chains. He heard screams and then saw a young man leap forward brandishing the captured submachine gun. The mob went wild. "Death to the Shah! Long live the Ayatollah!" they screamed.

Khorasad took slow and careful aim, focusing on the chest of the young man who held the driver's weapon, and pressed the trigger twice. Both bullets found their target. The boy staggered, waving his arms, and then collapsed as the submachine gun fell into the road. At that moment the fuel tank of the Rambler exploded. The blast drove the demonstrators back to the alleyway, leaving the dead and wounded in the street, among the scraps of clothing, broken glass and blood-soaked placards.

Khorasad heard behind him the roar of engines and the wailing sirens of police cars and ambulances. He put away his revolver, left his hiding place and walked toward the burning Rambler. As he passed the boy whom he had shot, he saw that he was still alive, writhing and staring at him with eyes full of terror. A thin stream of blood trickled from the boy's mouth and his blue overcoat was soaked in blood and filth. Khorasad stared at him in disgust for a moment, then walked on to the burning car. The flames had begun to subside and only the rear section and the tires were ablaze. He opened the driver's door and pulled out his attaché case. He glanced at the alleyway into which the demonstrators had fled and walked toward a squad of soldiers and riot police drawn up further down the street.

A pale young police officer armed with a heavy revolver ran to meet him. He stopped and saluted respectfully. "Everything all right, General?" Khorasad returned the salute and pointed to the bodies and the burning wreckage. "You call this all right, Colonel?" The officer licked his dry lips nervously. Behind them the soldiers and the police were advancing, rifles at the ready and bayonets fixed. Khorasad watched the three ranks fan out across the whole width of the street. Not one of the soldiers or policemen spoke. They passed him in silence, breathing hard behind their gas masks and helmets. Eyes stared at him. He shuddered and walked back to the army vehicles. There were no civilians in the street, but a few men and women watched from the windows of apartments and offices, on balconies and rooftops. Most looked on with an air of indifference—as if the ghastly drama did not affect them.

He reached the vehicles and returned the salutes of the elderly police sergeants standing there, then turned to the one who looked the most reliable and commanded: "I want you to drive me to the camp. Now!"

The sergeant saluted. "Right away, sir!"

Khorasad was back in his quarters early the next morning when the soldiers came. Still in his dressing gown, he sat at the table in the dining area of his kitchen, glancing through that morning's edition of *Azarbaijan,* the local newspaper of Tabriz. The account of last night's rioting in Kermanshah took up little space compared with the latest events in Teheran and elsewhere, but the report contained one paragraph, written in florid journalistic style, which troubled him deeply:

> *Savak General Said Khorasad was caught up in a demonstration march by local residents of Kurdish and Azarbaijani origin and opened fire on the demonstrators. Eyewitnesses told our correspondent that the general personally killed three demonstrators and wounded five others. General Khorasad is well known as a keen amateur hunter and an excellent shot.*

He read the report again, then swore softly. He knew what he had to do, but as he stood up to return to his bedroom he heard the sound of boots on the flagstone path outside his door, followed by loud knocking. He went to the door and opened it wide, shivering in the sudden blast of cold air, and found himself confronted by a tall, clean-shaven young officer at the head of a party of soldiers armed with G-3 German automatic rifles. The officer did not salute and Khorasad felt a pang of apprehension. "Well?" he asked.

"General Said Khorasad?"

"Captain, you know who I am. What's going on?"

"Are you General Said Khorasad?"

"Yes."

The officer handed him a typed sheet of paper. "This is a government order, General."

"I don't understand."

"I have been ordered to arrest you."

Khorasad stepped back quickly and slammed the door shut.

As he ran to the bedroom he heard the soldiers shouting and kicking at the door. He hurried to his bed and took his revolver from under the pillow, but at that moment there was the sound of smashing glass and the muzzle of a rifle was poked through the shattered window. Behind it he saw the face of the young officer. "Put down your weapon, General!" The officer's voice was calm but stern.

"Go to hell!"

"Put down your weapon!"

Khorasad threw his revolver down on the bed and watched the soldiers enter the room. The officer ordered him to dress and collect his gear and papers. "I have been instructed not to handcuff you, General, but if you try to escape I shall not hesitate to shoot."

"Where are you taking me?" he asked.

"To your office. You will remain there under camp arrest until we receive further orders."

He felt relieved but was careful not to show it. "Who else is being arrested?" he asked.

"I am not at liberty to tell you."

They marched away from the living quarters toward the office area. He saw detachments of armed soldiers standing guard in the bitter cold over some of the buildings, and in the distance, from the direction of the army camp, he heard loud shouting and bursts of automatic fire.

## 3

Arik leaned back and watched the Anatolian landscape flash past in its sober pastel colors. The earth, the trees, the sugar-beet fields with their thin covering of frost, the peasant cottages and the roadside shelters all seemed to be wrapped in a gray veil. Patches of white mist nestled between the low hills and in some places he saw peasants in East European-style peaked caps warming themselves over little fires that burned in the corners of fields or beside the narrow twisting road.

The big old taxi was painted bright red, its roof a gleaming white, and the nickel fittings were as brightly polished as if the vehicle had just rolled off the American production line. The driver spoke only a few words of English so there was little point in trying to conduct a conversation with him. They passed through a few villages, their streets full of rustics dressed in dark robes, Turkish soldiers in light khaki or the gray-blue of the air force, blue-clad policemen in caps or white plastic helmets. There were noisy, colorful markets wailing with Oriental music, and here and there appeared mosques, with their green domes and minarets adorned with silver crescents. He saw Turkish flags flying above buildings that looked like government offices or schools, and as they drew closer to Ankara he saw as well blood-red wall slogans scribbled in blurred Latin script. In some places the slogans had been erased or covered with a thin layer of white paint. On one wall he saw a hammer and sickle, partially erased, elsewhere a red star or a clenched fist. Army and police patrolled the sidewalks with submachine guns.

Near Ulush Square in the approaches to Ankara they stopped at a checkpoint. The driver presented his documents and Arik handed his false Panamanian passport to the scowling policeman, who glanced in turn at the passport photograph and at Arik's face. Even when he had returned their papers he was in no hurry to let them go. He opened the rear doors and inspected the interior of the cab, then waited as the driver opened the trunk and the hood for inspection.

Beyond the checkpoint sprawled Ankara. Above the city hung a gray cloud, holding down the mist and the tarry smoke that wrapped the brown stone houses in gloom. At last the policeman waved them on, and driving under a railway bridge they soon joined a four-lane arterial highway. Finally the driver brought the taxi to a halt outside a large building which bore the sign HOTEL VICTORIA in big ornate letters. Arik paid the driver and allowed a thin pale youth in blue livery to carry his leather case into the lobby. At the reception desk sat a young woman with blond hair and thick framed glasses. She greeted him with a weary smile in English. "From Panama?" she asked as she took his registration card.

"That's what it says."

"I know," she said.

"Is anyone waiting for me?" he asked.

"Someone came by asking that you not leave the hotel," she replied softly. "They said they would be back later, in the afternoon or the evening . . ."

"Fine," he said.

"What is?"

"I'm tired."

The woman smiled. Behind the thick spectacles her eyes were large and gray and she wore little makeup. "It's a long way from Panama," she said.

"Yes."

"Is this your first visit to Turkey?"

"Yes."

"Don't drink the tap water, it's filthy. In your room you'll find a jug of drinking water and if you like you can order soft or strong drinks."

"Anything else?"

"We have a good restaurant, anyway, if you're not going out . . ."

He took back his passport and picked up his room key, which dangled from an ornate key ring carved from an antelope hoof. "Any other messages?" he asked.

"We have no other guests from Panama, sir . . ."

"Okay. I'll go and rest."

"I'll have your luggage sent up to your room."

"There's no luggage, just this case. I'll manage it myself."

The woman smiled and sat down behind the desk. "Welcome to Turkey," she said.

As he stood at the door of the lift he saw Yosi walk into the lobby, elegantly dressed, with the bellhop trailing behind him carrying a heavy suitcase. Their eyes met for a split second, then parted. He watched Yosi approach the reception desk and as the young woman stood up and leaned forward to take his passport, Arik caught a glimpse of her shapely and statuesque figure. He could not keep himself from sighing.

During the next few hours all five members of the Israeli team arrived at the Ankara hotel. Most of them came via Istanbul and Ankara's Esenboga airport, equipped with false passports and identities. They had little occasion to meet since they mostly stayed in their rooms and waited for instructions, but if they did meet they acted like strangers. The rooms allotted to them had been chosen at random and there was nothing to suggest any connection between them. Arik had a room at the front of the hotel, overlooking a dingy office building, a broad street fringed by small, frost-covered ornamental trees, a taxi stand and a few shops.

He checked the room thoroughly, then inspected the door, the window and the bathroom. Having set his mind at rest he sat down on the bed and stripped off his shoes and socks, then his jacket, sweat-stained shirt and red vest. After a moment's hesitation he took off his trousers and underpants as well. He went into the bathroom and turned on the hot tap.

As he waited for the tub to fill he studied himself in the large mirror. His torso was solid, his shoulders broad, chest hairy and muscular and his legs long and suntanned. A long red scar marred his right shoulder, a souvenir of the Six Day War, of the battle for Sinai where he had served as a junior officer in a paratroop brigade. Another scar, more recent, with stitch marks on both sides, stood out on his right hip. He rubbed the scar thoughtfully and shuddered momentarily as he remembered Kurdistan again and the swift strike of the Iraqi assassin who had leaped suddenly from the doorway of a peasant's hut, long switchblade in his hand; he remembered Khorasad's desperate cry—"Arik, look out!"—the sharp pain, the report of Khorasad's revolver and the sight of the young man frozen with the blood-stained knife poised for a second blow, inches from Arik's chest. "Lucky you jumped aside," said the general quietly, afterwards. "Lucky you were with me," Arik replied.

They never knew why the Iraqi had attacked him. Now, studying his blurred image in the mirror of the steam-filled bathroom, Arik wondered if the young zealot hadn't really meant to stab Khorasad.

When he had finished his bath he wrapped himself in a big

34

soft towel and went back into the warm bedroom, sat down in a comfortable chair and leaned back, closing his eyes. The truck, Fishel and Haifa seemed far away, a different world, and in spite of his weariness he was impatient to hear the knock of a visitor on his door or the ring of the telephone. Since landing at Istanbul airport he had heard nothing of developments in Iran, and this worried him. Perhaps events were moving so fast that there would no longer be any need to go to Khorasad's rescue.

He went to the telephone. "Reception, please," he said to the anonymous Turk who answered him in fluent, lilting English: "Central switchboard, at your service, sir!"

Then he heard a woman's voice: "Reception."

"Is that you?" he asked.

There was a moment's silence, then he heard her laugh.

"Yes, room 32. It's me. How can I help you?"

He frowned, paused for a moment and asked: "Any news?"

"No messages." She put down the receiver and he wondered if he had made a mistake. He knew that he was supposed to wait quietly in his room, but the lack of news worried him. "Damn it," he murmured quietly. In the end he went to bed, climbing between the sheets naked, and began to doze.

When he awoke the room was in pitch darkness. He heard the light tapping on the door, got out of the bed hurriedly, picked up the damp bath towel from the floor and fumbled for the light switch. When the light came on he went quickly to his case and took out a small pocket knife with a blade of Sheffield steel. "Just a moment," said Arik in English. "Who's there?"

He heard the click of a key in the lock, then the door opened and in came the reception clerk with a bundle of newspapers in her hand.

"You forgot that every hotel worker has a master key!"

"I never thought of that," he said.

She smiled when she saw his pocket knife and then she looked him over until their eyes met. "I've brought you some papers," she said.

35

"Thank you," he said. "I'm keen to know what's happening in . . . the world," he added after a pause.

She laughed. Arik looked her over and his eyes rested on the thick, gleaming wedding ring on her left hand. She followed his glance and laughed again, then laid down the newspapers on the table beside the bed and stretched out her hand, waggling her fingers. "I'm married," she said, "and you can stop talking about the world. I know where you're going."

"Really?"

"Yes." She glanced over the exposed parts of his body and their eyes met again. "Aren't you cold?" she asked.

"What about your husband," he said, "doesn't he mind?"

"Mind what?"

Arik took a deep breath before replying. "You running around a hotel with a master key."

"Why should he care?"

Arik shrugged. "Yes, why indeed? I'm sorry, for a moment I forgot myself." To his surprise he felt his heart racing and the blood pounding in his veins. Now that he stood close to her, he noticed the clear sweep of her neck.

"I don't know your name," she said.

"You've seen my passport," he replied.

"It doesn't matter, I'll find out sooner or later." She turned and went to the door, but to his astonishment she locked it and returned to him, taking off her glasses.

"I don't know your name," she said, "but I think I know exactly what you're feeling."

"Yes?"

She smiled. "You give yourself away . . ."

He stepped forward, throwing away the towel, put his arm around her neck and pulled her gently toward him. She let him undress her, helping him only when his hands became confused by the hook of her brassiere. She showed little emotion, and unlike Arik she kept her eyes wide open even when he laid her across the bed and pushed her legs apart, thrusting himself between them

36

hurriedly. When he finished he lay still for a moment, then rolled over beside her.

"I'm sorry," he said.

She laughed and sat up, leaning on her elbow. "You came quickly." He looked at her in surprise and then grinned.

"I can't believe it," he said.

"What?"

"All this business, you . . . who are you?"

"Don't you believe that a woman can want a man just as much as a man wants a woman?"

"Who are you?" he asked again.

"Does it matter?"

He stretched out his hand and gently massaged her nipples, then kissed her stomach and stood up. She waited for a few moments, then joined him and dressed hurriedly.

"You'll find everything you want to know in the papers," she said. "Everything."

"Can't you stay?"

"No."

"Your husband?"

"That's none of your business, understood?"

"Yes, I'm sorry."

"I suggest you put some clothes on . . ." She finished adjusting her corduroy skirt, kissed him lightly on the lips and pushed him away when he tried to kiss her again. "That's enough for one evening," she said and left the room quickly.

Arik watched the door close behind her. Still feeling amazed he went back to the bed, then got up again and groped in the pocket of his windbreaker until he found his cigarettes. He smoked as he read the English and American newspapers that she had brought. He managed to read the headlines but felt too agitated to concentrate on the rest. "Goddamn!" he exclaimed, shaking his head in disbelief, finally returning to the bed which still bore the sweet smell of her perfume.

"I've got to admit I was pretty upset when I received orders to return to Ankara," said Henry Schreiber in a soft voice and smiled. A man of medium height who might well have been a middle-aged bank clerk, he closed the door and leaned against it. "How are you, August?"

"Damn leg's killing me," replied August Portilio, head of the C.I.A.'s Turkey office, a husky but calm-looking man in a well-fitting executive's suit. He got up from the edge of his desk, where he had been waiting since the marine at the Embassy entrance had announced Schreiber's arrival. He limped over to his visitor and shook hands. "Well, happy to have you aboard, Henry."

"Hereabouts it's you who're the boss, August."

"Right. You know what they call me now, don't you?"

"I guess I do. The Turkish sultan?"

"No. Just plain the Sultan." Portilio's smile vanished as quickly as it appeared, and his face screwed up in disgust.

"Something wrong?" asked Schreiber.

"Nothing special. The same old story." Portilio walked back to the desk, where he perched himself again. From the pocket of his jacket he took a small leather case containing pungent Turkish cigars.

"How can you smoke that stuff?" asked Schreiber, wrinkling his face in mild disapproval.

Portilio shrugged, stuck a cigar in his mouth and then lit it, striking a match on the sole of his shoe. "Right, then, we're agreed? If you've got no objection I'll set the process in motion right now."

"No, that's all right by me. I suggest we meet the whole team tomorrow morning."

"Okay. But we should contact the Israelis first. Trenshaw may arrive at any moment and I want to talk to the man he's bringing from Tel Aviv."

"I've no objection." Schreiber looked around the sealed and windowless room. The walls were covered with sketch maps, some of them concealed behind black curtains. The little office with its long line of safes and locked filing cabinets reminded him of other installations in Teheran and Kabul. "Imagine all this falling into unfriendly hands, eh, August?" He indicated the contents of the room with a broad, almost theatrical sweep of his arm.

"We've got the marines."

"A lot of good they are."

Schreiber stood up, buttoning his jacket. "Too bad our offices aren't equipped with self-destruct mechanisms," he said. He looked at Portilio's smiling face.

"Don't laugh. Nothing and none of us is safe."

"I know," said Portilio. "Don't forget, my last assignment was Saigon."

The two men left the room, Portilio taking care to lock the heavy steel door with its wooden frame and leather padding, and went out into a passage. On both sides of the passage similar doors led to the radio and central communications rooms. The suite of offices through which they passed was typical of the Embassy: writing tables laden with papers, modestly dressed secretaries hammering away vigorously at their machines, vases of flowers, a cheap carpet and a few prints of nineteenth-century American landscape paintings. The two men took the elevator to the ground floor and parking lot. Schreiber paused to button his coat and scan the city which sprawled at their feet. "If we're not careful," he said to Portilio who was unlocking the black Plymouth, "we'll lose this place as well."

They drove through the outskirts of Ankara to a half-built concrete warehouse surrounded by piles of rusting scrap metal. Around the building stood a high fence, a combination of chicken mesh and barbed wire, and laconic Turkish soldiers patrolled the exterior of the fence and the surrounding open spaces. A jeep of the Turkish Military Police was parked outside the entrance and close behind it, almost touching, another black Plymouth in which sat three men in civilian clothes.

"For Christ's sake, what is this place?" asked Schreiber. He saw one of the men get out of the Plymouth and walk toward them while a Turkish policeman, armed with an antiquated Thompson submachine gun, watched them suspiciously from the jeep. Portilio wound the car window down and handed a document to the man in civilian clothes, meanwhile answering Schreiber: "It's a sugar refinery. At least, that's what it was meant to be. The Turks lent it to us."

"I don't like it," said Schreiber.

"There was no alternative. The Turks didn't want to entertain us in an army base . . ."

"Them too?"

"Yes."

When they were waved on, Portilio drove to the dark entrance of the warehouse, parking close to the base of a huge green crane. He and Schreiber climbed out of the car. "They're inside," he said, pushing up his sleeve and glancing at his watch. "According to our schedule they should be preparing the equipment now."

"Are they all here?"

"Yes, aside from the Hercules crew."

"Do they know what's going on?"

Portilio shook his head. "Only that the objective is Iran," he said, pausing in the doorway to light a cigar.

They entered a massive, dimly lit hall. At the far end strong neon lamps cast a patch of light in which several men were moving about. Schreiber looked around him and saw piles of machinery, wooden packing cases and big aluminum containers, painted in dark colors and bearing the words TRANS-ASIA AIR TRANSPORT SERVICE in strong white letters.

"Come on, let's go join the boys," suggested Portilio, coughing on his cigar.

The two men advanced briskly, their footsteps echoing through the empty hall as they approached the patch of light where the men were working. They heard the clicking of rifle bolts and a soft murmur of conversation.

A man in blue overalls was checking automatic rifles, shortened versions of the M-16 fitted with telescopic sights and silencers; he tested the bolts and trigger action and finally laid the rifles out on a big trestle work table, alongside an assortment of automatic pistols and Israeli Uzi submachine guns. Another man in overalls was bent over an open crate unpacking hand grenades and arranging them in rows on a blanket spread out on the cold concrete floor. The others assembled a variety of equipment, from gun belts to parachutes.

In the corner of the patch of light, a dark, powerfully built man of about forty was studying an open notebook and talking in a low voice to his bald-headed companion. When they saw Schreiber and Portilio the two men greeted them with a smile. The tall man in overalls stepped forward and held out his hand.

"Henry! Good to see you!"

"It's good to see you, Leonard. I hope you're settling in okay."

"August is looking after us just fine." Leonard's voice had a Southern drawl but was clear and firm. "Meet my assistant Walter." He introduced his companion, then called across the room to three men, who put down the equipment on which they were working and came to join Leonard: one about twenty-five, slim and blond with a boyish face, one an older, stockier man, with red hair, and a third, broad-shouldered black man with fine features and a wispy beard.

"Here they are," said Leonard, "Michael Mackintosh, Thomas Barrett and Glenn Dyer, my team."

Schreiber shook hands with all three. "Good to see you boys," he said. "I hope all the preparations are on schedule." He took a rosewood pipe and plastic tobacco pouch out of his suit pocket.

"Is it definitely going ahead?" asked the black man, wiping his hands on a colored flannel cloth.

Schreiber sucked on his pipe and said: "I reckon you'll be going out within a day or two. All the signs are that that's what's going to happen."

"Iran?"

"This evening, or tomorrow at the latest, you'll get a detailed briefing," said Portilio, breaking into the conversation impatiently, chewing the wet Turkish cigar between his lips. "You'd better get back to work. There isn't much time."

"What's the equipment like?" asked Schreiber.

"First class," said Leonard. "Everything's exactly what we asked for. A-one."

"And the plane?"

"They're making test flights now." Leonard waited until the other three had gone back to their work before proceeding. "It's a real model exercise, flying the same sorts of mountains as those at the objective. And short airstrip landings."

"What's the team like?"

"The best there is, they were with me in Nepal and Tibet."

"You're pretty confident then," said Schreiber. It was a statement, not a question.

Leonard raised his eyebrows and looked doubtful, then he shook his head briefly and said: "I'd better tell it to you straight. August tells me that we're taking three Israelis along with us." He paused for a moment and went on: "I've no objection to that, but he says that in the operational zone one of the Israelis will be in charge."

Schreiber smiled. He knew that the question was going to be asked sooner or later and he preferred to handle it now. "That shouldn't be a problem . . ." he said softly, calmly stuffing his pipe with fresh tobacco.

"It's unprecedented," said Leonard. "What are you doing, hiring us out to somebody else?"

"No! When your hear full details of the operation you'll agree that there's no other way."

"What can they do that we can't, Henry?"

"That isn't the problem."

"Well?"

Schreiber lit his pipe, taking advantage of the interval that this required to prepare his answer. Finally he said: "We are involved in a situation where there is no time for detailed planning and training. We may have to rely on the expertise and experience of others and aside from that, the client, if I may put it like that, issued a . . . a special invitation."

Leonard was not satisfied with this reply. He scratched his square chin, frowned and said: "It'll be hard for me to accept this. I mean, how can we coordinate every step and every action? What happens if at any time or place there's a misunderstanding? How are we going to arrive at a point of agreement?" He glanced around. "I'd like you to try and reverse this instruction, Henry. I think it's unrealistic."

"No chance," said Schreiber, quietly but firmly. He sucked vigorously on his pipe, but otherwise remained calm and relaxed. "You will obey your instructions because that's what you've been trained to do . . ." He paused for a moment and glanced at Portilio, who stood beside them shifting his weight from one foot to the other. He knew that Portilio was also unhappy about this aspect of the operation but until now he had not discussed it with him. He knew August well enough to be sure that he would not dare question his decisions, any more than he would dare quarrel with his superiors in Washington. He took the pipe from his mouth and continued: "I want it to be understood that any deviation from the plan presented to you will be undertaken only by agreement and joint consultation."

"Joint consultation?" Leonard stopped scratching his chin. "What are you talking about, Henry?"

"In surpervising the operation you will cooperate with the Israelis."

"Jesus Christ!" moaned Leonard, shaking his head in disbelief. "What's happening to America?"

"This is a joint operation," Portilio tried to explain, throwing away the butt of his cigar. "Everything will work out for the best," he said solemnly. "I'm sure of that."

"Really?" Leonard turned to Portilio. "Would you go out under such conditions, August?"

"August will do as he is told!" said Schreiber firmly.

"Okay. . ."

Schreiber smiled, stepped forward and patted Leonard's shoulder, then he took him by the elbow and led him toward the busy group at the end of the hall. His voice once more took on a relaxed and playful tone as he exchanged light-hearted greetings with the others. He paused alongside the man who was checking the weapons. "Have you tested the equipment?" he asked.

"Yeah," the man nodded. "Everything's checked, sir, to the last detail. The gear's in great condition, graduated sights, the works. Everything's fine."

"And the revolvers?"

"All types, just the way we ordered them."

Schreiber glanced at the weapons arranged on the table and picked up a brand-new pistol with a thick butt. "Crystal," he said, "is this a good weapon? Have you fired it?"

"Yeah, it's good. It's heavy and it won't take a silencer but it's got a big magazine—fourteen rounds."

"Fine." Schreiber looked around him and suddenly turned to Portilio and Leonard who were following him. "Know what?" he said, "I'm beginning to wish I could go with them . . . I'd give anything to go up in that Hercules!"


Arik sat at a corner table in the hotel restaurant staring apathetically at the other diners. He had eaten a square meal of Russian borsht, steak and roast potatoes and now he sipped his Turkish coffee, smoked and waited. He had learned nothing more about the operation since the perfunctory briefings in Haifa and Tel Aviv, and now he could only await the call to action.

Passing through the lobby on his way to the restaurant, he had seen her in the little glass cubicle behind the reception desk. She had not responded to his gesture, and now he wondered if she had noticed him at all. Thinking of her only increased his restlessness. It was as if he could still smell the fragrance of her body. For a moment he thought of confronting her at the reception desk, but he stayed where he was, scrutinizing the restaurant with no real interest.

He signaled the waiter for his check, which he did not bother to read. Signing it quickly, he made his way to the cloakroom, took his overcoat and went out into the cold street. For an instant he thought of going back, then he shrugged and set off down the busy sidewalk. Soldiers and armed policemen seemed to be everywhere and across the street, behind the brightly lit windows of a long single-story building, he saw immaculately dressed officers entertaining their guests. As he was about to cross the street he felt a light touch on his shoulder. He turned and came face-to-face with the reception clerk from the hotel. She was wearing a black raincoat and was clearly out of breath.

"Are you sure you want to do this?" she said.

"It was the only way I could get to talk to you," he replied.

"You're crazy."

"Maybe . . ."

She looked round uneasily. "Let's go back," she suggested. "I can't chase you all over Ankara."

He smiled. "You have no choice."

Her gray eyes flashed behind the lenses of her glasses. "What is it you want?" she asked.

"To talk to you, that's all."

"All right," she said after a moment's pause. "I know a little cafe."

"Who are you?"

"My name is Salima, and if you carry on flirting with me in the middle of the road you'll cause an accident. Look, everyone's staring at us. Don't forget, this is Turkey!"

He followed her down a side street which rejoined the main thoroughfare some distance from the hotel. A tall narrow building seemed to dominate the hill rising in front of them.

"That looks like a mosque," he said, sounding surprised.

"Yes, that's what it is."

"I heard clericalism was out of fashion," he said.

45

"You know nothing about it," she said, "and anyway, why should you care?"

"Are you offended?"

"Why should I be? I'm not even Turkish . . ."

He looked at her in astonishment.

"I'm Armenian. I'm actually an American citizen. I was born in Turkey, that's all."

"I see." He lit himself a cigarette. "And you're part of our group?"

"I didn't say that."

"But you knew—"

"Let's say I know what I need to know, and I know what I want."

"I'm glad you came after me just now."

"It was a shock to see you leave the hotel."

"I've got to find out about you."

"You could have called Reception," she said drily.

It was a little modern cafe with plastic furniture and soft piped music, and they sat and drank coffee served in heavy white mugs. Aside from a few bored-looking customers propped up against the bar, the place was deserted.

"What about your husband?" Arik was the first to break the silence.

"You don't give up, do you?"

"I need to know. At any moment somebody might walk in and recognize you. Are you married or not?"

"It really doesn't concern you," she said, then added with a smile, "I don't even know your real name and you're interrogating me about my husband . . ."

"My name is Arik," he said.

"Arik?"

"Yes, short for Ariel . . . like the angel."

She laughed. "A good name for a man like you." She leaned forward and laid her pale hand on his. "You don't need to worry, my husband isn't around. He doesn't exist."

46

"Dead?"

"In a way. He went off two years ago and didn't come back. It seems he never will . . . he was a man like you. Your profession."

"An American?"

"Yes, red-blooded American." She smiled but he saw her eyes. "May I have a cigarette?" she asked. He offered her his pack of Panamanian cigarettes. She smoked clumsily, like most non-smokers who lapse occasionally.

"He was sent on a mission two years ago," she said.

"I understand."

"Do you? A few months ago they agreed to take me on. I wanted to do something. I'm fluent in Armenian, Turkish and Russian . . . they accepted me for training."

"Do you enjoy the work?"

She stubbed out her cigarette and smiled at him. "Did you think otherwise, Arik?"

"No."

"Of course I enjoy it. I've gotten used to the fact that he isn't here, maybe he'll come back and in the meantime . . . I'm young and just as interested in sex as you men."

"You're very frank," he said.

"Is that good or bad?" She took off her glasses and wiped her eyes with the back of her hand.

"That's interesting."

"And now tell me about yourself. Isn't there a little woman somewhere?"

"No."

"Has there ever been?"

"No."

"Interesting. You're hardly a child . . ."

"That's right." It was not a subject that he cared to discuss. He looked down and hurriedly drank up the remains of his coffee, then looked at his watch. "We'd better go back," he said. "They'll miss us." He looked at her again. As she put on her glasses her expression was serious and he noticed that her cheeks had turned pale.

"I've been talking nonsense," she said. "That isn't something that I do often."

"It wasn't nonsense." He put out his hand and gripped her elbow tightly. Their legs touched under the table and he noticed with satisfaction that she pressed her knee against his.

"Listen to me," he said, "Sally or whatever your name is. I like being with you." He released his grip and looked at her hard. "Do you believe me?"

"Yes," she said, "yes, really."

As they approached the hotel he let her go ahead. At the reception desk he asked, "Any news for me?" and she did not smile at him, just took the key to room 32 and handed it over. For a moment their fingers made contact. "Any newspapers?" he asked.

"Only what you'll find on the rack over there," she said, "but if you like, sir, I'll send someone out to buy you some European papers. I'll have them delivered to your room."

He looked at her closely and saw a mischievous twinkle in her gray eyes. "Yes," he said, "that's not a bad idea."

He took the elevator to the third floor, walked down the empty corridor and unlocked the door of his room to find Eldad waiting for him. "Hey, isn't there any privacy in this fucking place?"

"Relax, you sound like a goddam tourist." Eldad ran his hand through his graying hair and sighed. "I've been waiting for you a long time . . ."

"I went for a walk."

"Yes, that figures . . . Danny and I saw you go out, we thought you'd gone to your room."

Arik took off his overcoat and threw himself down on the bed. "What's so important that you have to break into my room?"

Eldad shrugged, then opened his eyes. "In an hour they'll be coming to collect us from here."

Arik sat up, suddenly alert. "Is this it?" he asked.

"I don't know . . . there's going to be a meeting with . . . our friends."

"Fuck it!" Arik moaned.

"What's the matter?" asked Eldad, surprised and a little concerned. "I thought you couldn't wait to get started."

"I had plans," said Arik, then shook his head and stood up. "When are we going?" he asked.

"An hour, maybe two. I suggest you dress warmly."

"Do I take all my gear?" he asked, pointing to his leather travel bag.

"Yes, I don't know if we'll be coming back here."

"Okay." He went to the window and pulled back the curtain, looking out at the street and the dark sky. Only a few buildings were visible in the mist. In the street below people hurried along in heavy winter coats and he saw women opening umbrellas and cars flashing past, their wipers moving rhythmically.

"It's raining," he said.

"That's no problem," replied Eldad. He stood up and looked at his watch. "I'm going to rest awhile. This could be the last chance we get for a long time."

Arik heard the door close, paused for a moment at the window and then picked up the telephone. "Reception, please." He heard a rustle and a few clicks and then her voice.

"Yes?"

"Room 32," he said. "I asked for newspapers."

"Not now." She sounded impatient.

"I'm leaving soon."

"I know."

"What are we going to do?"

She slammed the receiver down without replying.

# 4

Dariush parked his Hillman Hunter near a guarded, sandbagged emplacement at the local police headquarters and climbed out. At the main entrance and down the corridor he was asked to show his identity papers, but most of the sentries and policemen recognized him and some even saluted him formally. As he walked along the bright green corridor he could not help but reflect on the bad news.

His mood was ugly. The night before, on the midnight news broadcast, the situation in Iran had been painted in the darkest colors. Accusations and counteraccusations had been thrown about, and there had been a prominent account of the Kermanshah demonstration and the part played by General Khorasad in suppressing it. Dariush was worried that Khorasad's name had been mentioned. Dariush himself had always been careful to steer clear of direct confrontation with demonstrators in Tabriz, but his close relationship with Khorasad was well known. It was no secret that he admired the general and owed to him his rapid promotion in

50

the ranks of Savak. He belonged to a small group of young officers of Azarbaijani origin who had been sent to Tabriz six years before. Khorasad, then a colonel and divisional commander, had chosen him as his personal aide and since then they had seldom been apart, except when Dariush was sent to attend courses and training sessions designed to accelerate his progress to the higher echelons of the secret service.

The general had taken a personal interest in his career, and Dariush was a willing pupil. He showed no surprise when the general let him into the secret of his connections with the Americans and he accepted as a matter of course the cash payments and bank transfers that regularly came his way. He had amassed a considerable personal fortune over the past few years and once he had even spent a marvelous week in Rome and Paris, all expenses paid. His general duties involved the collection of information and the researching of secret files and archives on the general's behalf, also the transmission of coded broadcasts and the testing of radio call signs. Until recently these broadcasts had been made on an experimental basis, at regular monthly intervals on varying frequencies, the numbers of which the general gave him. "It's a security precaution," Khorasad told him, "testing a communication system that we may never need."

Now Dariush paused outside the office of the deputy commander of the local detective branch and cleared his throat. He rapped on the door with clenched fist, then without waiting for a reply he opened and entered the cramped little office. A pale young police sergeant rose to attention. On the wall to his right Dariush saw a photograph of the royal family in dress uniform, the Shah, the empress, the young princes. He found himself wondering just when that picture would be torn down.

"Is Anwari here?"

"Yes, sir. Excuse me a moment, I'll see if he's free." The sergeant went through the inner door leading to the deputy commander's office and returned a few seconds later. "Would you like to go through, sir?"

The short, bald, dark-skinned detective welcomed Dariush cordially and offered him a seat. "What have I done to deserve this honor?"

Dariush put down his heavy attaché case and settled himself in the solid armchair. Here too he saw the photograph of the royal family. "I've come to ask a favor," he said.

His host looked at him with a hint of surprise. "To do with the general?" he asked.

"Yes."

The little man leaned forward and laid his hairy hands on the table. "I have no authority in the matter," he said. "I'm sorry. Maybe you should talk to my boss."

"No, that would take too long. I understand he's in Teheran. I phoned in here a short time ago."

"All right, then, what do you want? But before you start you should know that this business is not under the jurisdiction of the Police Department. All arrests have been made on direct orders from Teheran. I'm told that the orders were signed by the prime minister himself."

"I know." Dariush coughed. "I'm asking you to hear me out and then decide. After all, we've been working together for years and anyway . . . who knows how things will turn out?" He looked at the perspiring face of his host and hoped that the last sentence had hit home.

The man in the blue suit leaned back and stared at him thoughtfully. There was a short silence, then he asked: "What is it that you want?"

"To talk to the general."

"Impossible."

"Why?"

"He isn't in our custody. The army is holding him."

"*What?*" Dariush could not restrain his astonishment, but he managed to conceal a sense of relief.

"He's under camp arrest, in his office. He's better off than the others."

"Yes . . . of course. Is there any chance of getting things through to him, food or newspapers?"

"He's being properly looked after."

"Even so . . ."

Anwari paused for a moment, fidgeting nervously with his tie. Then he wiped the sweat from his face with the back of his hand. "I don't know," he said at last, "I wouldn't advise it . . ."

"What?" Dariush leaned forward until his chest touched the edge of the table. "Just to get the general a few newspapers and some proper food? Listen to me, Anwari, you're the boss around here and if the situation improves, by God, the general will remember the favor you did him . . ."

"And if not? You've heard the news. The Ayatollah's coming back."

Dariush sat up, narrowing his eyes. "The general is a brave man," he said, "but if he decides to talk he won't go down alone!"

Anwari turned pale, drumming his hairy fingers on the table with growing anxiety and fiddling with a big silver pen.

"What does the general have against me?" he asked.

"Think, man!"

"I've never overstepped the mark, I've always obeyed my instructions to the letter."

"What about the interrogations, Anwari? Eh?" Dariush's eyes grew narrower still, his face was pale and his fists clenched.

"I never went beyond what was permitted . . ."

"Indeed?"

Anwari rose from his chair. "The most I can do," he said, "is make inquiries for you."

Dariush leaned back in his chair. "All right," he said, "that will do."

Anwari picked up the receiver of the telephone on his desk. "Get me Army Staff Headquarters," he said, "quick!"

As Anwari waited for his connection there was silence in the room, broken only by the ticking of an old wall clock. Dariush watched the deputy commander who stood there pale and perspir-

53

ing, clasping the silent receiver to his head. The man did not look back at him but stared vacantly at the window which had misted over with condensation. Dariush glanced at the fat hairy fingers and shuddered for a split second as he remembered how he had seen this innocent little man beating with his open hand the face of a young Azarbaijani girl suspected of belonging to the underground. His train of thought was broken by Anwari speaking into the receiver.

"This is the deputy commander of the Detective Branch," he said. "Good morning!" He paused for a few moments as he listened to the voice at the other end of the line, then continued: "I want to know how many prisoners you have and if I can be of assistance." He paused again and nodded, while Dariush stared at him intently, then added: "What about General Khorasad?" He nodded vigorously, thanked the other man for his help and slammed the receiver down.

"Well?" asked Dariush.

"As I said, he's at the army camp, detained under guard in his office."

"What else?"

"They're waiting for instructions from Teheran," Anwari replied. "They have about a dozen prisoners."

"What instructions?"

"To transfer them to the capital, of course. They can't deal with them here."

Dariush stood up from his seat and buttoned his coat. Then he picked up his attaché case and smiled at the little man.

"Thanks," he said. "Someday I'll return the favor."

"Yes," Anwari murmured, "someday . . ."

Dariush took his leave of the deputy commander with a damp, soft handshake and left the office, walked down the neon-lit corridor and returned to the parking lot.

He drove north out of the city, past the artisans' quarter and the street market where business went on as usual, past fields and rolling hills. The sky was full of clouds but there was no rain, and the roads were clear of mist. In the distance he could see the foothills of the mountains, their peaks hidden in the clouds. He left the asphalt road and took a narrow dirt track, its thin surface of muddy gravel pitted with frozen puddles. He shifted into low gear and slowed to a crawl, passing peasants leading their flocks and women carrying piles of firewood, and soon came within sight of the refugee village.

He parked outside the first house, which was built of crude mountain stone bound together with straw and mud, its tin roof weighted down with rocks against the strong winds from the fields. The village consisted of about a hundred similar single-story houses. There was no electricity and the only running water was in an open channel winding between the low houses and carrying a weak trickle of water from a nearby spring. Most of the houses were surrounded by low stone walls which separated the backyards and in some places also served as enclosures for sheep or cattle; the air stank of woodsmoke, excrement and urine.

Dariush stood for a moment shivering in the icy cold, then turned up his collar against the wind and made his way cautiously through a flock of ragged chickens and into the nearby yards, where two boys in Kurdish national dress were tending a few hairy black goats and a flyblown mule. They did not so much as glance at Dariush as he walked past and arrived at the door of the house. He hammered on the greasy blue panels until he heard the voice of the householder speaking rapid Kurdish.

"It's me, Dariush!" he shouted.

After a few seconds the door opened wide and before him stood a man of about sixty with a broad dark face, green eyes and a thick moustache, as white as the hair on his head. The man looked at him in astonishment and put on a forced smile which disappeared rapidly from his strong face.

"It's you," he said drily.

"Yes, may I come in?"

The man shrugged. "Why not?"

Inside the windowless little room, they sat among the old

mats, cushions and tattered blankets until the old man spoke:
"I hear the general has been arrested."

"Yes."

"Is there nothing you can do?"

"That's why I came to you."

"I see." The host stood up with a swift agile movement and disappeared through the doorway. Dariush heard him speaking in a low voice to an unseen woman. He closed his eyes and let his head fall forward on his chest, enjoying the warmth of the stove beside him. He knew that the rescue of the general was the key to his own safety, and he smiled bitterly when he remembered how, before his last journey to Tabriz, he had asked Khorasad to share with him the details of the escape plan. The general had refused, for "security" reasons.

"Here, your tea!" His host stood over him with a small tray in one hand and a steaming kettle in the other. The man stooped and sat down beside him to pour the tea, setting out the tiny gold-rimmed cups and the dish of sugar cubes. For a few minutes they drank in silence, and again it was the Kurd who spoke first:

"What do you intend to do?" he asked.

"Rescue him . . ."

"How?"

Dariush took a gulp of hot bitter tea, coughed and replied: "With your help, Hasan."

Hasan wiped his eyes. "You must be out of your mind, my friend! Asking me to help you, and take on all the crazy Iranians of Kermanshah?" He began to laugh.

"I don't need anything special. I just want you to drive a truck."

"Really?" Hasan stopped laughing and looked him squarely in the eyes. "Listen to me. The revolt ended three years ago, remember? It's over, and I'm a refugee . . . my days of action are long past . . ."

"You owe it to Khorasad."

*"Owe it?"* Hasan rose to his bare feet and paced up and down

the little room, his shoulders drooping forward and his large head bobbing from side to side in a dismissive gesture.

"That is a joke," he said at last. "First you sell us out and then you come asking me to get Khorasad out of trouble!"

"Khorasad didn't sell you out—he made it possible for you to escape from Iraq, Hasan, don't forget that!"

"A Kurd never forgets, as God is my witness a Kurd does not forget! But . . ." Hasan spat on the floor. "Your Shah forgot. Why should I help him?"

"I'm not asking you to help the Shah . . ."

"It's a crazy business, all the same. They tell me that in Kermanshah feelings are high, there's talk of demonstrations and riots. Maybe we'll be out on the streets soon . . ."

"You must help Khorasad," Dariush repeated softly.

Dariush slipped through the pine grove near the northern fence of the Savak camp with swift, quiet footsteps. He wore a beige overall smeared with stripes and patches of black ink which provided a crude camouflage as he crept against a background of snow-covered fields and clumps of frost-laden trees. A woolen mask covered his face. In the knapsack on his back were a pistol holster and a long knife, and in his hands he clasped a pair of heavy metal shears.

At the edge of the grove he went down on his knees, paused, then began crawling toward the tall wire fence which reared up some twenty meters from him. He crossed the open ground rapidly and when he reached the fence he crouched there motionless. The sentry passed him with heavy tread, whistling softly to himself and coughing as his footsteps receded on the path. Dariush raised himself slightly, stretched out the shears and pinched the lowest strand of the wire. He pressed; there was a soft click and the wire parted. He cut an aperture about two feet square, then moved slowly forward, turned on his back and carefully, sliding on his knapsack, passed through the gap. Standing up, he tucked the wire shears in his belt, drew his revolver with the fitted silencer and crossed the open ground between the fence and the row of buildings, slipping through the shadows and avoiding the patches of yellow light cast by a few floodlights. Once he had to hide in a dark doorway when a pair of soldiers approached, chattering noisily.

Most of the buildings in the Savak sector were dark and silent, aside from the main office block which now loomed up before him. He saw a light in the window of the general's room, paused in the shade of a snow-covered pine tree, crouched and inspected the surrounding area. He saw a black sedan parked at the front of the building and behind it, at the top of the steps, two armed sentries in heavy trench coats and white helmets. One of the sentries leaned against the wall, his rifle lying on the steps beside him; the other sat on the step above, by the big glass door which led to the main corridor. Lights were visible in the windows of several of the rooms, as well as the general's office, and behind the opaque glass of one of the bathrooms he saw the silhouette of a man urinating.

Dariush rolled up his left sleeve and glanced at the phosphorescent green figures of his digital watch. It was 2:00 A.M. Most of the occupants of the building should be asleep. For a few minutes he stayed where he was, then carefully cocked his revolver, left the shadow of the tree and joined the asphalt road that led to the building. He walked quickly, his boots softly crunching the thin carpet of snow. As he rounded the corner of the office building he saw the sentries. One was asleep, his helmet tilted over his forehead; the other, on the step, looked up for an instant and saw him. Just as quickly the 9-mm. bullet hit him between the eyes. He fell back with arms outstretched. The other soldier awoke with a start and was trying to raise his rifle when the silenced revolver popped again. The man clutched at his shattered windpipe, dropped his rifle and slid along the wall.

Dariush rushed up the steps, flung open the glass door and ran down the dimly lit corridor. Outside the door of the general's office he saw a sergeant curled up asleep on a padded bench. Dariush shot him as he ran past. The man jerked up in a brief flicker of life, then rolled to the floor with a sickening thud. Dariush went on to the door, kicked at the lock with all his strength and burst in as the door flew open. A young officer in lieutenant's uniform stood up in alarm beside the door of the general's room and a soldier, standing by the window, spun around brandishing a rifle with bayonet fixed.

"What's going on?" yelled the officer.

Dariush bent his knees, gripped the revolver in both hands and fired. His first bullet hit the soldier in the face as he tried to aim his rifle. He was thrown backward, hitting the window and smashing through the glass. The second bullet pierced the chin of the officer who collapsed with a scream. Dariush stepped over the corpse of the officer and tried the heavy steel door of the general's room. It was locked. He bent down and groped in the dead officer's pockets until he found the key. Hastily he fumbled with the lock, and the door swung open.

Khorasad stood there calmly, arms folded on his chest, with his overcoat on. His face was pale and he did not smile when he saw Dariush.

"You took your time," he said.

Dariush rapidly scanned the general's face, the room and the furniture. He saw broken glass piled up beside the table and the shattered portrait of the Shah. He opened his side pack and pulled out a black Beretta pistol. "Here, take this," he said. "Follow me."

They went out into the corridor and were running toward the entrance when they heard rapid footsteps pounding down the stairs from the upper floors. By a glass door where the corridor met the staircase, a half-dressed officer was pointing a heavy Webley revolver at them; Dariush fired one of his remaining rounds. The officer fell, dropping his gun, which fired as it hit the floor.

The shot roused the whole building and they could hear doors opening, running feet and the clicking of rifle bolts. Dariush fitted a fresh magazine to his pistol, then grabbed Khorasad's sleeve roughly and the two men ran down the steps at the front of the building and made for the western fence of the camp. On the road beyond the fence they saw the flickering lights of fast-moving vehicles and from behind came shouting and a few bursts of automatic fire. As he ran, Dariush took the metal shears from his belt. "Here," he yelled to Khorasad, "cut the wire!"

As Khorasad took the shears Dariush turned and aimed his revolver into the darkness, firing off all the rounds in his magazine, the muted shots popping softly. The general reached the wire fence and began hacking at it wildly. Parked opposite on the road beyond the field he saw a pickup truck with dimmed lights. Dariush shouted: "Look out! Grenade!" Khorasad threw himself flat and heard the loud, dry explosion. He stood up and attacked the fence again.

"Hurry!" yelled Dariush, "hurry!" The voices of the shouting soldiers grew louder, and in the distance they heard the roar of engines turning over. At last Khorasad separated the last wires from the gap that he had made, threw down the shears and joined Dariush who was pulling the pin from a hand grenade. The general slapped Dariush's shoulder. "Let's go." Dariush nodded and hurled the grenade at a squad of soldiers emerging from the darkness. As they slid through the gap in the wire they heard the grenade explode.

The short distance between the fence and the road, some fifty meters, was carpeted with snow and thinly frozen puddles. They ran, stumbling, sinking into puddles as the ice cracked noisily, the crisp snow crunching beneath their boots. A few shots passed above them and then a cluster of machine-gun bullets slammed into the snow at their feet. They made it to the road as the truck engine sprang to life. Two men jumped down to meet them from the driver's cab, armed with automatic rifles. "Hurry! Get in!" one of them shouted. Dariush and Khorasad climbed into the warm cab beside Hasan and the two youths jumped onto the back. As the pickup moved off, tires spinning on the ice, the first of the pursuers reached the road. More shots, and the rifles of the young Kurds rang out in reply.

Khorasad glanced at the impassive, white-haired driver who

sat tensed over the wheel, gripping it with both hands. Dariush took off the woolen mask and tossed it on the floor, leaning back and breathing heavily. "God!" he said, and laughed briefly.

Hasan drove the truck along the road that skirted the western fence of the camp. The adjoining fields were desolate and the headlights of the truck flickered over dark clumps of trees, stone walls and long empty expanses of frozen ground.

Khorasad smiled broadly in the darkness of the cab. He put his arm round Dariush's shoulder but did not speak to his exhausted aide. His eyes were fixed on the twisting road before them as they left Kermanshah behind and headed north toward the refugee village. Eventually, as they approached the village, swaying on the dirt track, Dariush started fumbling with the knapsack at his feet. "Here," he said finally. "Something to chew."

The general took two pieces of chocolate, handed one to Hasan and kept the other for himself, smacking his lips as he chewed it.

"You think of everything," he said to Dariush.

"Yes."

"This is good." The general swallowed his chocolate, coughed and went on in a low voice, staring ahead at the road flickering in the beams of the headlamps. "I don't know what would have happened if you hadn't shown up."

"You'd have been all right." Dariush's voice was hoarse and he shivered as his hands played nervously with the buckles of the knapsack, his eyes tightly closed.

"I'm not so sure . . . I was beginning to lose hope in there."

"I know."

"How?"

"I saw the broken glass, the picture . . ."

Khorasad smiled and leaned back in his seat, stretching his legs which ached from the running and the bruises he had received when he stumbled and fell in the snow or slipped on the ice. "Yes," he said, "I broke it."

"I can't believe all this is happening," said Dariush. "It's just incredible."

"Shah-in-Shah . . ." murmured Khorasad.

Hasan shifted to low and the whine of the engine grew louder as he threaded his way between the potholes in the road, expertly avoiding the obstacles, his green eyes sparkling in the lights from the dash and his lips tightly clenched. He did not speak but occasionally glanced briefly at the two men who sat beside him or at the mirror, searching for a movement or a silhouette in the canvas-covered rear section. As they entered the village he slowed down, dimming the lights and coasting to a halt, pulling up outside a stone house surrounded by a low wall at the edge of the village. He switched off the lights and cut the engine. "That's it," he said.

He left the cab without waiting for Khorasad and Dariush and went into the house. Khorasad stood in the road helping Dariush to unload his equipment, then turned and followed Hasan. He stooped in the doorway and went inside, blinking in the bright light of a storm lantern, and sat down beside the rusty iron stove as Hasan attended to the firewood.

Dariush and the two young men joined them. Dariush laid down his packs, the two Kurdish youths put down their rifles by the door and went to help Hasan who was busy lighting the stove. Khorasad watched them for a few moments and then when a little flame began to dance among the kindling wood in the stove, he took off his coat and threw it down on one of the mattresses.

Hasan, speaking for the first time, said, "This isn't a fancy hotel, but welcome, Khorasad . . ."

The general stepped forward, opened his arms and embraced the old Kurd. For a few seconds they stood locked together and then Khorasad kissed the old man's stubbly cheek.

"It's good to see you, Hasan. I'm grateful . . ."

"Nonsense!" The smile faded from Hasan's face and he glanced toward Dariush who was sitting on the mattress taking off his shoes. "You should thank that young man of yours, General, he planned everything."

Khorasad nodded. "Yes, I know, but without your help it would have been difficult."

Hasan shrugged and gestured around him. "I'm sorry I couldn't arrange a better place than this . . . the john is outside, but otherwise try not to leave the building. My boys will fetch water, then we'll fix some food for you."

"Fine." Khorasad looked at his watch. "When shall we meet again?" he asked.

"Get some sleep. I'm going to turn in. I'll sniff around and come back to report."

"Yes." Khorasad suddenly repeated his gesture of affection, embracing the old Kurd with an almost theatrical flourish. "Yes, my friend, thank you!"

Hasan again inspected the fire, which had taken hold and was giving out a pleasant warmth. Then without another word he went out of the house, signaling to the two young men to follow him.

Khorasad sat down on one of the mattresses, watching Dariush who had taken off his wet socks and was now unbuttoning his shirt. "It's cold," he said.

"You'll find dry clothes and underwear in the knapsack," said Dariush. "How long are we staying here?"

Khorasad took off his shirt, folded it carefully for use as a pillow, bent down and started unlacing his boots. "We'll discuss it tomorrow."

"What do you intend to do?"

"We'll have to get Nero and Redwood here."

"And then?"

"Call in Swordfish."

Dariush stood up on his bare feet and began to unzip his ink-stained overall, his small expressionless eyes fixed on the general. "I thought everything was worked out," he said, "the calls I made from Tabriz and the reply . . ."

"Yes, that was vital," replied Khorasad. "That told them they needed to set the process in motion." He breathed hard, lay down on the mattress, pulled the blankets up to his chin and looked at Dariush who was undressing slowly.

"As I see it, my friend, Swordfish and the others are ready to go. They know everything, the route we're supposed to use out of Kermanshah, the rendezvous . . ."

"So what's the problem, General?"

"They must be told that we're on the move."

"How?"

"I have a plan."

"General!" Dariush stood there with the upper half of his overall hanging down. "I want to know," he said.

"The original plan was to make it to the border and send a message from a police station."

"And now?"

"The deck has been shuffled . . . I think Swordfish will have to come sooner, closer . . ."

"How are we going to contact him?"

"Have you got a map?"

"Yes, of course."

"Excellent!" The general stirred under the woolen blankets. "In the morning we shall locate the nearest police station. Understood?"

Dariush went back to grappling with his overall. "Are we going to take the station over?" he asked.

"Yes."

"What about the guys in the hotel?"

Khorasad laughed. "Tomorrow we'll go and get him and Nero and the American girl. They're going to set off on the most interesting journey of their lives."

"General?"

"Yes?" Khorasad looked at Dariush who was getting under his blankets. "What is it, kid?"

"I would have come to get you out no matter what."

"I know."

"Even if I'd known the escape route, General . . ."

"Yes." Khorasad frowned. "You're a reliable bastard."

Dariush turned over on his back and smiled. "Are you going to tell me?" he asked.

"Tomorrow. Let's get some rest now."

Dariush closed his eyes. "Just remember, I'd have come for you no matter what."

Khorasad smiled. "When we were in the corridor I saw a man lying beside a bench outside the door, right?"

"Yes," Dariush replied, "a sergeant, he was asleep when I shot him."

"You bastard!"

Dariush smiled again. "By God, General, you were as white as a sheet when I opened the door."

Khorasad paused for a few seconds before replying. "Perhaps I was afraid," he said at last. "Yes, perhaps I was."

A few hours later Hasan and the two young Kurds woke them. This time they were carrying a shining aluminum tray laden with fried eggs, salted cheese, sliced cucumbers and tomatoes, oatmeal bread, cups and a steaming blue kettle. Hasan attended to the stove, adding wood to the previous night's embers, and as he worked Khorasad and Dariush got up and dressed in silence.

"You can wash outside," said Hasan. "You'll find a bucket of warm water at the door."

The two men went out into the cold and muddy backyard. The whole village was swathed in dense white mist and only in a few places, close to the house and the yard, was it possible to pick out the trunk of a tree or a moving shape. They heard voices, some close and some distant, the bleating of sheep, the lowing of a cow and the sound of a car engine. One of the young men came out carrying a rough army towel. He stood beside them as they washed their faces.

They returned to the house, where Hasan and the young men were already sitting around the stove eating in silence. Hasan poured the tea and handed around a saucer of sugar cubes. Khorasad squatted down and began drinking in short, measured sips. He did not look at anyone present, instead fixing his gaze on some point in space, and asked: "Everything all right, Hasan?"

"No . . ."

"What's been happening?"

"In Kermanshah there's total chaos, General. There are demonstrators everywhere, everything's closed up and tense . . ."

"Supporters of Khomeini?"

"There are new slogans"—Hasan smiled—"and some that haven't been seen for years . . ."

"Nationalists?"

"Patriots," Hasan insisted, "patriots!"

"For example?"

" 'Democracy for Iran, autonomy for the Kurds,' I saw that slogan on every other wall. It's new."

"That's good."

Hasan looked at him in surprise. "Aren't you opposed to that, General?"

"In the present circumstances?" Khorasad put down his empty cup on the aluminum tray. "What could be better than that, Hasan?"

"There were Communist posters too."

"Those are the ones I can't stand."

"Nor me . . . not yet."

"Anything else?"

"They're hunting for you."

"Really?"

"Yes. They think you escaped to Tabriz."

"Excellent!"

"There are roadblocks."

"How the hell are they managing to organize things like that in the present situation?"

"Committees," said Hasan, "and anyway they're still receiving orders from Teheran . . . the prime minister is issuing all kinds of directives . . . they say he's delivered a strong warning over the Kurdish and Azarbaijani question."

"That won't help him."

"I know . . ." Hasan paused. "They tell me that some of the

leaders of the Kurdish Democratic Party are supposed to be coming back to Iran, maybe Barzani himself." The old man's voice shook slightly but his face showed no sign of emotion. "Who knows," he said, "maybe this collapse will save us . . ."

"That's the irony of fate," said Khorasad. "If you know how to exploit it you may end up on top."

"Will you help the Kurds?"

"Me?" Khorasad laughed. "I'm a refugee, can't you see that, Hasan?"

"You could say things in the right places, if you get the chance."

"All right."

"What do you need?"

Khorasad sat down on the nearest mattress. "Clothes first of all," he said, "and a car."

"You'll get them."

"And then some men."

Hasan was silent for a moment, then asked: "For a long time?"

"No, just for a day or two, no more."

"That can be arranged."

Khorasad scratched his stubbly chin. "I need shaving gear," he added, "and a toothbrush."

Now it was Hasan's turn to laugh. "Are you so concerned about your appearance when all this is going on, General?"

Khorasad smiled. "I'm a Savak general, not some Kurdish refugee. A general of the Shah-in-Shah. Understood?"

"Oh God," moaned Dariush, who up till now had sat drinking his tea in silence, listening to the conversation between the general and the Kurd. He coughed and looked at Hasan. "You see, my friend," he said, "nothing has changed . . ."

"Yes." The Kurd rose to his feet. "I'll go and see what I can arrange in the village and then you can tell me what we must do to help you. I want you out of this area as quickly as possible."

Hasan signaled to his two companions who picked up the tray and the dishes and followed him outside.

"Good people," said Dariush.

"Yes," agreed Khorasad. "I hope this rebellion doesn't destroy them."

"They're always searching for some kind of national identity . . ."

"It's hopeless," the general declared firmly. He shrugged and smiled, shaking his head dubiously. "Democracy for Iran, autonomy for the Kurds . . ." he repeated the words of the slogan. "It won't work, Dariush, but right now it's working in our favor."

"I don't understand."

"The rioting, man! The rioting and disorder. The more chaos there is, the better for us. And now, get out that map and let's chose ourselves a police station. There isn't much time."

# 5

It was Portilio who set up and organized the briefing, in a large hall on the second floor of the sugar refinery. There were no windows and the vents and chinks had been sealed with panels of wood. Against one wall stood a small table, three chairs, a bulletin board pinned with photographs, maps and diagrams, also two large recording machines.

Portilio himself stood at the top of the stairs leading up from the factory hall, greeting the arrivals with handshakes, smiles and the occasional light-hearted joke. Behind him, Schreiber watched with amusement. "You look like the host at a garden party," he said.

Portilio smiled and nodded. "It is a bit like that, Henry." Leonard, looking sullen, was followed by Mike, Tom and Glenn and a few members of the technical team. These were all Schreiber's men and it was to their boss that they paid most of their attention, addressing him as sir. The arrivals took their seats behind folding tables arranged in a semicircle, with name cards. The echoing voices gave the impression of a huge gathering.

Portilio waited until the Hercules pilots arrived, two young men in their late twenties sporting identical flying jackets with fur-lined collars. The captain, George Obis, was a blond, bronzed Texan who wore dark glasses, a solemn expression and a flamboyant little moustache which did not match his reticent nature. His copilot, Jack Schneider, was a powerful, broad-shouldered Floridian with big hands and with a long scar running across his chin.

"Good morning," said Schreiber, once the men were seated, leaving six empty seats at the farthest table. "This meeting is the last occasion at which . . . only Americans will be present . . ." He took the pipe from his mouth and his voice became clearer. "The operation involves the rescue of agents, that is, agents operating in Iran . . ." He coughed and studied the faces of the assembled company. All watched attentively. "The objective is somewhere between Kermanshah and the Iraqi border, here." He turned to Portilio who took from his pocket a folding pointer about the size of a fountain pen, opened it and pointed to the region of Kermanshah on a large map resting against a blackboard easel. He repeated this process, indicating other locations, as Schreiber's briefing continued.

"The method of approach will be by air . . . a Hercules flown by Obis and Schneider and their assistants will fly from Ankara to Tatvan near the Iranian border on an apparently routine mission, using an international civilian flight path. From Tatvan they will continue on a course which will enter Iranian airspace over Kermanshah, en route for Kuwait, but on the way they will drop . . . the operatives who will rendezvous with the agents and arrange their evacuation." Schreiber paused to relight his pipe and continued: "Soon we shall be going into the details of the operation . . . you will see that it's a complicated business, but first I must touch on a point which according to our normal methods is quite unconventional . . . agents from Israel will participate in the operation and at the objective itself, that is, on the ground in Iran, the operation will *not* be controlled by our boys. The Israelis will be here soon and I want this to be clear right from the start. My explicit orders, and those of my superiors, are that you act on their instructions and obey without argument. Take it from me, the Israelis who are being sent here are top quality. A-one."

He took a deep breath, hoping that his words had been sufficiently decisive. There was nothing in the faces of his audience to indicate indignation; only Leonard looked worried.

"The question has been examined from every angle and perspective. I don't want to go into the details of the motives for our decision, but I will emphasize just one thing . . . out there in those mountains the leader must be a man who knows the terrain and its problems . . . the commander who has been chosen to lead the operation is well qualified in this respect. He's spent years there and he is well known to those whom you are to rescue."

Portilio signaled to him urgently and pointed to the stairs. Schreiber looked round and saw Trenshaw eyeing him. Behind him stood a group of grim-looking strangers.

Trenshaw shook Schreiber's hand firmly and said: "Allow me to introduce my gang, Henry."

"Why don't we introduce ourselves first," said Schreiber, "since we're hosts?" He indicated that the Israelis should spread out beside him. "I'm Henry Schreiber, and this is August Portilio. I guess you could call us the desk hands of this operation. As for the real field workers . . ." he pointed to Leonard, who rose, hands tucked firmly in his pockets, frowning.

"Leonard Dixon," he said, "leader of the American team." Leonard looked straight at Schreiber, who was fiddling nervously with his pipe, and sat down. "Leonard is an expert in the operational sphere," said Schreiber, turning to the Israelis. "He's the leader of our team with all the responsibilities that that involves. I'm sure there will be no problem of coordination," he added, unconvincingly. "Leonard is a professional, just like you guys." He went back to sucking on his pipe.

The next man stood up. "Walter Gabriel," he said, "deputy team leader. General operations." Schreiber made no comment. Other members of the team stood up in turn.

"Michael Mackintosh." The tall young man spoke slowly but firmly. "General operations, specialty radio, electronics, weapons."

"Thomas Barrett, general operations, mountain combat." Barrett paused for a moment, then smiled broadly and added: "Paramedic and midwife." A light ripple of laughter swept the room, and Schreiber felt relieved when he saw Leonard's broad shoulders heaving slightly.

"Glenn Dyer." The young black man took off his woolen cap and turned to the Israelis. "General operations, explosives, mechanical equipment, the works!" There was more laughter, and then the pilots introduced themselves, followed by the rest of the team, each identifying his particular role in the context of the operation—weapons, parachuting, emergency equipment. When the Americans had finished, Schreiber pointed with an almost theatrical gesture at Danny, who sat beside him looking serious and nervously adjusting his green knitted tie.

"Danny," he said loudly, "Danny, from Israel. I am in charge of the Israeli side of the operation." He paused and smiled at Schreiber who looked back at him with amusement.

"Danny from Israel, eh?"

"Yes, and these are my men," he replied, pointing to Eldad, Arik and the others, "They are all from Israel." Again the hall echoed to the sound of soft laughter. Then Eldad stood up and introduced himself briefly, followed by Arik who stood leaning forward, his hands thrust deep in the pockets of his windbreaker, his eyes half closed and his strong face turned toward Leonard.

"My name is Arik Hod, I'm an expert on Iranian and Kurdish affairs and . . . what do you call it? Oh yes, general operations . . ." He paused, a smile flickered briefly over his face, then he swallowed a lump of spittle and added, looking this time at Schreiber, "I understand that I am to lead the operation."

"Yes." Schreiber stood up, leaning forward over the table. "This is the boss, boys. Arik Hod . . . his second-in-command will be Leonard. Is that clear?"

"I haven't introduced my men," said Arik softly, and without waiting for Schreiber's go-ahead he turned and pointed. "This is Yosi Kimchi, an expert on Iranian affairs, fluent in all the languages and dialects . . ." Yosi stood up and sat down again at once.

"This is Shraga, general operations, specialist in weapons and sabotage . . ." Shraga stood up, winked at Arik and sat down. Arik also returned to his seat and pulled a pack of Panamanian cigarettes out of the pocket of his windbreaker. Schreiber coughed, wrinkling his brows, then rose to his feet to continue the briefing.

"Okay, then, now that everybody knows everybody else—or at least a few names—let's get down to business . . . later you will receive files containing all the relevant material. We shall discuss all the issues in detail, every problem will be examined thoroughly until we have the right answer and then . . . it will be your responsibility to read and learn by heart the entire contents of the files." He paused to fill his pipe and then went on.

"The agenda will be as follows: Portilio—background and command structure. Schreiber"—he smiled—"technique and method of approach to the objective in Iran. Trenshaw—supervision and coordination of command. Obis—flight and rescue details. Time allotted—four hours. Then there will be a break, followed by study of the material. Tomorrow there will be another session, and final instructions will be distributed to all participants. In the afternoon you will have the opportunity to train according to your individual roles . . ." He took a deep breath and added, "I reckon that the operation will be under way the day after tomorrow . . ."

Leonard was holding his hand aloft. Schreiber was not pleased. "Yes, Leonard?"

"Everything that's marked on the maps and diagrams, the information in the files that we shall receive, is that the final plan?"

"Yes, more or less . . ." Schreiber made an effort to smile, unsuccessfully. He was annoyed. "In our profession there *is* no final plan, Leonard, there are only firm guidelines. Our special skill is . . . dealing with the unexpected."

"And how firm are the guidelines in this case?"

Schreiber turned to Portilio who stood at the blackboard holding the pointer. "I'm handing over to you, August," he said. "I don't want to get drawn into a time-wasting discussion. Let's get started, that way the fellows will get the answers that they need." Schreiber glanced around the room and then sat down, nodding to Portilio.

Portilio removed the map from the board and pulled away a sheet of black paper, revealing three sets of portraits, faces and profiles of Khorasad, Amiri and Yasarian. "Here they are, gentlemen, our objectives," he said.

The hours passed quickly. Twice it was necessary to change the ribbons of the tape recorders and to send for flasks of strong coffee and fresh sandwiches, prepared downstairs on the factory floor where some of Portilio's men were still working on the equipment. When the last stage was concluded and Trenshaw had given details of the structure of command and supervision, two men in dark suits came into the room carrying red cardboard files which they laid down in a pile on the table beside Schreiber.

"These are the files of the operation," he said. "We will collect them from you before you leave . . . you will find all the details in them." He smiled. "Everything from the flight path and the altitude of the drop to . . . the sexual habits of Penicillin." He paused and looked at his watch. "It's late," he said, "we'd better declare the meeting closed."

"You're staying where you are, gentlemen," said Portilio. "No more comfortable hotel rooms for you. Downstairs you'll find mattresses and sleeping bags . . . from this moment on, nobody leaves the building except by order."

Schreiber stood up and stretched, the pipe clamped, as usual, in the corner of his mouth. "I want a quiet word with Leonard and Swordfish," he told Portilio.

Schreiber led Arik and Leonard to a corner of the room. "Listen to me, I don't want you to get the wrong impression . . . in spite of everything that's just been said, this is a complicated mission and nobody knows exactly what's going on out there, or how the situation may develop. If you fail, it may be even a cover story won't help."

Both Arik and Leonard were silent.

"I'm saying this because it's vital for me to know that from now on you really will work together as a team. When you're out there, on your own, I won't be able to help . . ."

"As far as I'm concerned there'll be no problems," said Arik.

"That goes for me too." Leonard took a deep breath and the two men shook hands, but as they turned to join the others, Arik hesitated slightly, deliberately. Schreiber glanced at him.

"Something on your mind, Swordfish?"

"Call me Arik."

"Okay, Arik, what's your problem?"

"There's something I want to ask you."

"Yes?"

Arik paused, lit a cigarette and smoked in silence for a few seconds before speaking.

"In the hotel, in Ankara . . ."

"Yes?"

"There's a woman named Sally."

Schreiber shrugged. "I wouldn't know," he said simply.

"I know."

"Well?"

"Listen to me," Arik said, "Tomorrow morning, before we leave here, I want to talk to Sally."

Arik could not sleep. He was lying fully clothed on his mattress covered with a simple army blanket. He gazed into the darkness.

Some of the men who slept beside him on the floor of the large hall snored or tossed from side to side in their sleep.

Arik felt tired but as always on the eve of an operation he could not doze off. He forced himself to lie still, in his mind going over the details of the operation for the hundredth time. He could hear the muffled steps of the Turkish guards who walked monotonously back and forth in the corridor outside the hall, sometimes talking to each other in quiet voices. Suddenly he heard English, then the beam of a pencil light was jumping from one sleeping face to another. The man stood close to him, the yellow light came to a halt upon his face. "Don't say anything and follow me."

He identified the voice immediately as Trenshaw's. He threw the blanket aside and followed the American quietly out into the corridor, where they stopped under a small lamp. "Listen, Arik, Schreiber told me about you and Sally." Trenshaw spoke to him in a low voice.

"I didn't know gossip traveled so fast. What of it?"

"I took the liberty of arranging something . . ."

"What do you mean?" Arik's heartbeat quickened.

"Sally's here and would like to see you."

"What?" Arik stammered, astounded.

"A little private enterprise never hurt anyone!" Trenshaw chuckled and hit him lightly on the back. "I have a weak spot for everything romantic. Besides, I've known Sally a long time. If she likes you then it's okay with me."

Arik cleared his throat in embarrassment. "Where is she?"

"Outside in the car."

They walked quickly through the corridor, passing two Turkish guards in heavy winter coats, and stepped into the night. White frost blanketed the large yard, glistening in the light thrown by the security lights on the walls. The black limousine was parked near the gate. Arik could see the glow of a cigarette inside.

"I'll take you someplace you can talk . . ." Trenshaw said. He opened the rear door of the car and Arik, slightly shivering from the cold, slipped in.

"Well, well." Sally smiled at him.

"I couldn't have dreamed up a better surprise."

Trenshaw drove cautiously out of the factory compound and onto a dark road. In a while they reached what looked to Arik like a small military camp. If he'd figured right, it should be just on the other side of the factory.

"This is where the guards stay," Trenshaw explained. "I've got the keys to the commandant's place. You can stay here awhile. I've got some things to take care of."

He stopped the car in front of a small white hut, turned around and offered Arik a key. "That's it," he said.

Arik hesitated for a moment, then looked at Sally who had not spoken during the short ride. Finally he took the key and stepped out of the car. Sally followed him quietly.

Arik turned back to Trenshaw. "How long do we have?"

"Enough." Trenshaw answered and drove quickly away.

"Funny man," murmured Arik.

"He's a good friend. I've known him for years," Sally explained. "Open the door. I'm freezing."

Arik quickly turned the key and opened the door which led into a dimly lit room with a small table, chair, a locker and an army bed covered with blankets. An electric heater spread warmth. A huge picture of Kemal Ataturk hung over the bed.

Sally turned around slowly, taking in the room, then threw off her black raincoat and sat on the bed. "I'm not sure I'm doing the right thing," she said. "But when Trenshaw came to see me I knew I had to come. Please don't think I would do this kind of thing for anyone else . . ."

"I'm glad you're here." Arik opened his windbreaker and sat down beside her. "I feel like a schoolboy."

"Not in the hotel you weren't!" she laughed.

Arik chuckled. "You have beautiful eyes," he said and took off her glasses slowly.

"Kiss me," she murmured.

He pulled her toward him and kissed her, slowly lowering her onto the bed. He could feel her heart beat against his chest. Sally edged him back. "Let me undress," she whispered. His eyes followed while she slowly pulled her sweater over her head and he watched and remembered the firm white flesh, the firm breasts. He tore off his clothes and lay back on the bed watching her.

"I feel as if I've known you all my life, Sally."

She moved slowly toward him, her skin glowing in the red light of the heater.

"Move." She smiled and lay down beside him.

With the touch of her body, Arik could feel his member throbbing. "I love you," he said. His hands caressed her breasts and he felt her nipples harden under his palms.

"Come!" she whispered urgently. He felt the fiery touch of her fingers traveling over his body. He looked at her face, her eyes shut tight. Straddling her, he slowly moved himself into her welcoming warmth. She moaned softly and he quickened his thrusts; her hips rolled back upon him as he moved. The moaning grew, her body pressed up hard at him. Desperately Arik searched, thrust, searched, reaching for the place of places, together. She reared up under him, huffing, yelling in loud sharp sobs. With one last thrust he was with her.

He bathed her face in kisses, holding her body tightly against his.

Moments later, Sally spoke. "Will you come back?" she asked quietly.

"I don't know."

"I want you to come back," she whispered.

Suddenly he felt very tired. "Damn! I'm falling asleep!"

Sally laughed. "Close your eyes. I'll wake you in time."

It was still dark when Trenshaw finally returned. They entered the car like strangers and did not touch until they were at the gate of the factory and he leaned toward her and kissed her neck lightly. She shivered, silently.

"You should not mention tonight to anybody," Trenshaw warned quietly. "Schreiber'd tear my head off . . ."

Arik did not answer. He left the car and closed the door. Behind the car window he could see the reflection of Sally's glasses. He turned quickly and entered the building.

# 6

"That's where you need to get to? Exactly there?" asked Hasan. His clean-shaven cheeks shone with enthusiasm from under the white moustache. He wore a black kaffiyeh on his head, a coat of thick felt trimmed with canvas and a pair of bandoliers which crossed on his chest. A revolver and a curved dagger hung from the broad leather gun belt at his waist. He looked thoughtfully at the map which Khorasad had spread out on the floor beside the stove.

"That's the place," said the general, stabbing with his finger at the black spot. "No one there besides a few air force men and gendarmes, three at the most. And what's more, it's got a long-range transmitter."

"All right." Hasan nodded. "I see there's a good road leading to it."

"Yes." The general stood up. He was wearing his uniform and beneath it, a clean white vest that Dariush had lent him. Dariush still crouched over the map, his red polo-neck sweater giving him a somewhat dandified appearance.

"What do we do then, I mean after we've sent our message, general?"

"We pick up Nero and Redwood."

"Will they be coming back here?" asked Hasan.

"No . . ." Khorasad pointed to the map. "As I told you, from Kermanshah, we go north toward Wadi Shirwan . . ."

"Rendezvous 34," murmured Hasan.

"Yes." The general smiled. "I see you haven't forgotten anything . . ."

They put on their coats and then checked their weapons. Dariush picked up his side pack, heavy with hand grenades, and fitted the silencer to the muzzle of his revolver. "I'm ready," he said.

"All right, let's go and may God be with us!" The general turned up the collar of his trench coat and led the way, out into the little yard where the two young Kurds were waiting for them, brandishing their automatic rifles.

Again Hasan took the wheel, driving the pickup truck over muddy dirt roads, through farms and pastures which at this time of the year were almost deserted. Here and there they saw peasants leading donkeys or mules laden with firewood. To the east rose the mountains of Kermanshah, tall and dark, their lower reaches shrouded in gray mist.

After driving for about an hour they came to a steep mountain road covered with a tight layer of gravel. The track wound its way between gigantic black rocks thrown aside when the road was hacked out and now, years later, still looking out of place, towering heaps of rubble piled up at the verges where the bulldozers had left them. In a few places clumps of dark-green pine trees appeared, alongside low stone walls built as shelters for the sheep which came up from the valleys in summer.

They followed the narrow mountain road for about half an hour before arriving on a small plateau, about the size of a football field. In front of them stood a square two-story concrete block-house, surrounded by a high wire fence and a forest of tall radio antennas. A Russian Gaz jeep, and an American Waggoneer were parked outside the building. Thin smoke rose from a tall chimney on the roof, dispersed itself among the revolving radar saucers and high-tension cables. A generator hummed in its small hut beside the main building. Hasan stopped the truck and cut the engine.

"There's no one at the gate," said Dariush. He leaned forward and wiped the condensation from the windshield. "I can't see any movement . . ."

Khorasad bit his lip, his face tense and alert. He unbuttoned his coat and reached for his revolver. "Remember, everything according to plan."

Hasan turned and glanced at the little window that overlooked the dim rear section where the two young Kurds sat, clutching their rifles.

"Get ready," he shouted, "we're going in!"

He started the engine and drove slowly toward the gate, a tangle of wire mesh on a framework of steel tubes. At the gate he stopped, sounded the horn and waited, his foot on the clutch. Khorasad and Dariush cocked their revolvers.

"You go first," said Khorasad, nodding to Dariush, who was studying the signs on the gate: MICROWAVE STATION, KERMANSHAH 6, and AIR FORCE RADIO STATION 2005. Above the signs hung the Shah's symbol, the golden lion and the sun. They waited a few minutes and then the door of the building opened. An elderly gendarme stood at the top of the steps and stared at them blankly.

Hasan pressed the horn again. The gendarme left his post and walked slowly toward them, his rifle slung over his shoulder. He stopped behind the gate.

"What do you want?" he asked.

"We've got a problem, we need to use the radio-telephone, it's urgent," said Hasan, winding down the side window.

"This isn't a post office!" shouted the gendarme.

"Now," whispered Khorasad, "hit the bastard!"

Dariush opened the door with his left hand, pushed it with his right shoulder, and in the same swift movement jumped down. With one foot on the road and the other inside the cab, he took aim and fired, hitting the gendarme in the chest before he had time to unsling his rifle. The man collapsed, his tin helmet clattering on concrete.

"Go!" shouted Khorasad as Dariush clambered back into the cab.

Hasan released the clutch and rammed his foot on the gas. The truck lurched forward, hit the gate and flung it aside, crushing the tubes and wire. Within seconds they were at the foot of the steps. Hasan cut the engine and the three leaped out of the cab and ran up the steps as the two young Kurds jumped down from the tailboard to bring up the rear, their rifles trained on the shuttered windows.

Khorasad, the first to reach the door, flung it open and raced inside. In the narrow corridor he almost collided with a fat, panic-stricken old man who was running toward him. Khorasad punched him in the face, then downward till he fell. Hurriedly Khorasad scanned the blue arrows on the walls, then he crossed the corridor and bounded up the iron staircase toward the transmission room. Behind him he heard cries and shots but he went on without stopping until he reached the upper floor. Dariush was close behind him. For a moment Khorasad paused and studied the signs again. "Over there!" he shouted, pointing to a door marked TRANSMISSION ROOM—ENTRY PROHIBITED.

Suddenly three shots rang out in rapid succession, three bullets whistled between them and slammed into the wall. Khorasad threw himself flat. At the end of the corridor a young officer in air force uniform sheltered in a doorway, firing. Khorasad's shot missed and he saw the officer aiming again. Pain stabbed through his left shoulder; he fired again and heard the muffled thump of Dariush's gun. The officer cried out for a second, then crumpled.

Khorasad, standing, panting, probed the wound in his shoulder.

"Are you all right?" asked Dariush.

"Nothing . . . a scratch." He went to the door of the transmis-

sion room and opened it, coming face to face with a pale, bespecta-
cled young man in civilian clothes.

"Don't shoot!" the man pleaded, "I'm the station director."

Khorasad pushed the man aside and strode into the small
windowless room, making his way among the jumbled receivers,
transmitters and electronic gadgets toward the main console. He
glanced hurriedly at the equipment, then turned and shouted:
"Over here!"

Dariush rammed the silencer of his revolver into the civilian's
back and pushed him roughly toward the console. There were
sounds of sporadic shooting from the lower floor.

"Hurry, damn you!" he shouted.

"Don't shoot!" the civilian pleaded. "In God's name, don't
shoot!"

Khorasad took a sheet of paper from his shirt pocket, un-
folded it and handed it to the man. "Get me this wavelength,
hurry!"

The man took the note and read it with trembling hands, then
chose one of the instruments and began pressing buttons and
twisting tuning knobs. "Ready," he said at last, and pointed to the
console microphone. The loudspeakers came to life with a loud
hiss, and a metallic voice emerged from the crackle of the static:
"This is Alpha Delta 99 . . . this is Alpha Delta 99." The call sign
repeated ten times, then there was a pause of about a minute and
the sequence began again. Dariush grinned. "It's all right," he said,
"the system's working." Khorasad nodded, sat down at the console and picked up the microphone. He waited for the end of
another sequence of call signs, then slowly pressed the transmission switch.

"Penicillin calling Wild Bird. Message for Swordfish. Moving
to Rendezvous 34. E.T.A. 48 hours." They heard the call sign
again, then came a loud cackle and the words: "Alpha Delta 99.
Understood. Over and out."

Khorasad stood up, glanced at the trembling civilian, then at
Dariush. "You know what to do," he said, and walked out of the

transmission room. As he passed through the door he heard the thump of the silencer, a loud groan and a thud. At the top of the stairs, he saw Hasan coming toward him with a big ledger.

The Kurd was unharmed and seemed relaxed, though under his headcloth little beads of sweat gleamed on his forehead. "Everything all right?" he asked.

"Yes, Dariush is wiping up. What's that there?"

"The radio log. Here, look at this." Hasan held out the book. Khorasad leaned against the wall and glanced at the most recent entries, skipping over the general information until he reached the final paragraph—the Kermanshah police reporting a loss of control, riots in the town near the City Hall and the hotel, requests for reinforcements.

"When was this received?" he asked.

"There," growled Hasan, "can't you see? This morning!"

Khorasad frowned, thought for a moment, then said: "In that case there's even less time than I thought. Follow me."

He returned to the transmission room with Hasan close behind. Dariush stood above the corpse of the civilian, ripping out plugs and cables. "Not like that!" yelled Khorasad. He pointed to a rack of fire-fighting equipment, began tearing pickaxes and twin-headed hatchets from their stands and handing them to Dariush and Hasan. The smashing commenced and soon the room filled with smoke rising from the broken equipment. "I think that's enough," said Dariush, putting down his hatchet. Khorasad nodded. "Let's get out of here!"

They went out into the corridor, checking the other rooms for any soldiers or gendarmes who might have escaped. "We must finish them all off," said Khorasad as they came down the steel stairs and returned to the main entrance. Hasan said nothing and Dariush, who was the last to descend the stairs, coughed and said quietly, "I think they're all accounted for, General."

Outside the door they met the Kurdish youths. "Everything clean!" said one of them to Hasan. Dariush took the magazine from his pistol and replaced it with a fresh one. He looked at the two young men who were whispering to Hasan and he suddenly realized that he had not yet exchanged a single word with them, not even during his stay in the refugee village. He looked around and saw Khorasad in the parking lot, opening the door of the Russian jeep and glancing inside, then leaving it and examining the Waggoneer. The general completed his inspection and as he came back to join the others, Dariush noticed a large red stain on his left shoulder. "You're hurt," he said. "Take off your coat and I'll see what I can do."

"Forget it!" Khorasad smiled. He turned to Hasan and said, "Grab anything that may be useful to you, Hasan. Load it all on the truck. Dariush and I will take care of the two vehicles in the parking lot."

"Are you taking them?"

"Yes." He looked round and then pointed to a little hut beside the generator building. "There's fuel in there. Load up all the gas you can find."

"You'd better let me look at that shoulder," Dariush insisted.

The general shook his head. "I tell you, it's nothing."

He walked past Dariush and returned to the main building, stepping over the body of a soldier in air force uniform who lay spreadeagled on the floor. He glanced at the corpse, then looked up and saw the sign COMMANDANT'S OFFICE on the open door of one of the rooms. He went inside. A color photograph of the Shah hung on the wall. A small desk had been overturned, the contents of its drawers scattered in a pool of blood and behind it, under the table, lay a body dressed in blood-soaked underwear. Khorasad spat, took down the portrait of the Shah and glanced briefly at the calm gray face that stared back at him, then threw it down on the floor. He inspected the contents of the room, picked up a pair of binoculars and went out. In the corridor he saw Dariush carrying a crate of tinned food and behind him Hasan with four rifles and a box of ammunition. Outside the two youths were carrying cans of gasoline to the parking lot.

Khorasad led the way briskly to the parking lot. "I'll drive the

Waggoneer," he said to Dariush, "you take the jeep. We'll hide the jeep near the village and carry on to the town . . ."

"The hotel?"

"Yes, we don't have much time."

Hasan joined them in the parking lot. He helped Dariush load the fuel cans into the back of the jeep, then turned to Khorasad. "What's the plan?" he asked.

"We're driving to the hotel to pick up my people."

"Who's that?"

"Two Iranians and one American chick."

"Anyone I know?"

Khorasad opened the door of the Waggoneer and took his seat behind the wheel. "I don't think so," he said, "that is, unless you're interested in atomic research . . ."

Hasan adjusted his headgear and wiped the sweat from his face with a handkerchief. He shook his head, then repeated his question:

"What's the plan?"

"We'll go back to the village and make our preparations."

"I read those reports in the log, about the riots in Kerman-shah . . ."

"Yes," replied Khorasad, "so there's no time to waste. We may be too late already."

When Dariush was through loading the jeep, he returned at a run to the main building, hurled himself inside and dashed up the iron stairs to the second floor. The acrid smell of smoke choked him. He glanced through the open door into the transmission room, which was in flames. Coughing violently, he pulled a phosphorus grenade from his side pack, jerked out the pin and tossed it to the end of the corridor where documents, papers and torn ledgers lay scattered beside the body of the air force officer. He turned back down the stairs and huddled next to the banister as the explosion came. On the ground floor he threw another grenade into the commandant's office before racing out of the building.

"I'm ready!" he panted, climbing into the cab of the Russian jeep and starting the engine. The green pickup was already through the gate, followed by the Waggoneer with Khorasad at the wheel. As they glanced back, they could see smoke billowing up from the gutted building.

The little convoy returned at high speed to the refugee village. They met nobody on the road; the weather was grey and menacing, with lightning flashes rending the sky. Soon there was thunder, then a heavy shower that rapidly became snow, falling and melting on the wet ground. At the village, Hasan led them to a deserted sheepfold hidden in a grove of pine trees, where they abandoned the Russian jeep.

Inside, Khorasad hurriedly stripped to his underwear and let Dariush examine his wound. "It's a very deep graze," said Dariush. "I don't think the bone is damaged." He took a first-aid kit from his knapsack and started treating the wound. "How do you intend to get them out of the hotel?" he asked. "How do we get into Kermanshah?"

The general winced as Dariush cleaned the wound. "When I'm dressed as a Kurd, even you won't see through the disguise."

Dariush smiled as he wrapped a broad bandage around Khorasad's shoulder. "I remember," he said. "Three years ago I saw you dressed like that, a place near Mehabad . . . there was someone else with you, a guy I didn't know . . . wearing the same kind of gear."

"Yes." Khorasad smiled. "You'll be seeing him again in a few days."

Dariush did not seem impressed. "You know," he said as he put away the kit, "I never thought I'd have to trust a Kurd to save my life."

Khorasad chuckled. "That's fate for you. Personally I've always admired them . . . the mountain creatures."

"Who are the two young men with Hasan?" asked Dariush suddenly.

"His nephews."

"I see."

"No! I don't think you do," said Khorasad. "Hasan is their master, those boys owe him absolute loyalty . . ." He smiled at Dariush, patting his shoulder affectionately. "What you don't see is that you're just the same as them . . ."

"Maybe." Dariush scratched his tousled head and yawned. "Up to now I haven't said a word to them . . ."

"No need to." The General laughed. "With things like loyalty it's actions that count, sacrifice . . ."

Hasan came into the room carrying a bundle of Kurdish garments which he handed to Khorasad. "I see you've got a scratch," he said when he saw the general's bandaged shoulder.

Doctor Yasarian stood by the window that overlooked the street. Behind him, like a shadow, stood Janet Simpson. He moved the curtain aside and looked down. Yasarian's face turned white and he felt a choking sensation in his throat. Janet Simpson was hyperventilating, her bosom rising and falling hysterically, though she clamped her arms about herself and tried to calm down, all the while staring over Yasarian's shoulder into the street. The horror grew in her eyes.

Down in the street the crowd was on a rampage, hundreds of men and women, most of them young, some waving placards and huge portraits of the Ayatollah, others brandishing sticks, wooden posts and chains. The mob had broken into the nearby shops and vented its fury on them. The sidewalks were littered with broken glass and vandalized cash registers. Here and there lay men bleeding on the ground, most of them policemen or officials seized by the demonstrators. At street corners and the entrances of public buildings soldiers and armed policemen stood huddled together like frightened sheep. A few members of the security forces had apparently joined the rioters, their uniforms clearly visible amid the seething crowd.

Directly opposite the hotel a large and noisy group had gathered around a huge statue of the Shah, who stood leaning on his right leg in a walking posture, his eyes raised to the gray sky and his left hand outstretched in greeting. The bronze arms of the statue had been bound with ropes and chains and on one of the broad shoulders sat an excited boy, tying a thick rope around the monarch's neck. The boy finished his work and jumped down into the arms of the crowd. Immediately, to the sound of rhythmic groans, hundreds of people started pulling on the ropes and chains. "Death to the Shah!" they shouted in unison, "long live the Islamic Republic!" The giant statue budged slightly and the yelling grew louder. Men, women, even children swelled the tumultuous crowd, shouting and waving clenched fists.

Suddenly the statue split from its pedestal, tilting sideways, then toppled forward. The great bronze figure crashed to the ground amid screams of excitement and fear. People fled in all directions and many were hit by flying debris. One man lay motionless, trapped beneath the statue.

Yasarian watched with horror as the bronze head broke from the body and rolled slowly down the street. The collapse of the statue drove the crowd even more frantic. Hundreds of chanting rioters attacked the recumbent figure, lashing it with clubs and chains. "Death to the Shah! Long live the Republic!"

At the other end of the square looters rampaged through the gutted shops, some staggering under bales of colored fabric pillaged from a clothing store. A car burned at the corner of the street and a Golden Lion ambulance tried to thread its way through the mob, but the wailing siren and flashing light only added fuel to the general hysteria.

Janet moved closer to the window and gripped Yasarian's arm tightly. He turned to her. "Better keep clear of the window," he said, "they may start throwing stones." Someone knocked at the door and before they had time to respond Doctor Amiri walked in wearing a pinstripe suit and bow tie. His hands trembled wildy.

"The crowd is breaking in. We don't have a chance!"

Yasarian ran to the open door and locked it. From the corridor came hysterical screams. "Where is Khorasad? Where the fuckin' hell is Khorasad?" he shouted desperately.

A few seconds later the shouting intensified, this time not only from the streets but from inside the hotel as well. They heard marching feet in the corridor outside, loud voices, and then somebody tried the locked door.

"Keep quiet!" whispered Yasarian in a croaking voice. He held Janet's trembling shoulders and felt his legs grow numb. His stomach hurt and his mouth was dry. "Oh God," he murmured, "oh God . . ."

The door shuddered, then burst from its hinges, crashing inward with a loud racket. Janet screamed as a dozen excited young men burst into the room waving iron bars and daggers. One of the youths smashed his fist into the startled face of Doctor Amiri. The dapper little man tottered and fled whimpering to the corner of the room. "We are Iranians!" cried Yasarian. "What in God's name are you doing? I'm a scientist."

"Death to the enemies of the Revolution!" shouted the leader as his comrades swooped upon the closets and the bathroom cabinets, throwing things in the air, upending the broad bed, ripping suitcases open, smashing everything in their way. Yasarian dropped to his knees, his eyes staring wildly. "I beg you!" he screamed, "I beg you in God's name!" A violent kick sent him sprawling on the carpet. "Damn you, imperialist dog!"

Behind him he heard the desperate cries of Janet. On the ground, he rolled over on his back to see four youths dragging her to the sofa. There were tearing off her clothes. She kicked and scratched and screamed at them, but her resistance only inflamed them more. "Hurry!" yelled on of the attackers. "Get that blouse off, let's see her tits, the American bitch!"

"Amin!" entreated Janet in terror. "Amin!" Yasarian could not, would not move. Pain, fear and horror paralyzed him where he lay. He watched as the men stripped her writhing body. One of the youths unbuttoned his trousers. "Hold her legs," he yelled excitedly, "hold her legs apart!" Yasarian closed his eyes and when he opened them he saw the man thrusting himself into Janet, shuddering and groaning as the others stood by laughing and leering. For a second Yasarian's eyes met Janet's; she stared at him like a startled, wounded animal. Her mouth was open and a trickle of blood oozed from the corner. "Amin! Amin! Help me!" He stayed rooted to the spot, motionless, panting, watching the naked ass of the man pumping away between Janet's thighs. Around him the orgy of destruction continued.

Khorasad drove the Waggoneer. He wore a red-and-black speckled headdress like a turban and a Kurdish caftan under his army trench coat. He gripped the wheel with both hands, his bronzed face tense and expectant. Beside him sat Dariush, his little dark eyes expressionless, his lips pursed. The side pack loaded with hand grenades lay on the broad seat between his knees. Hasan sat behind them, his face wrapped in a kaffiyeh which revealed only his intense green eyes. Behind him crouched the two young Kurds, rifles in position.

The surburban streets were deserted with shops boarded up and windows of houses shuttered, but as they approached the center of the town they began to encounter groups of people, men, boys, even young children, running or walking briskly toward the main street. Here and there they saw youths waving banners or placards. The crowd grew steadily more dense as they approached the center. They passed the main police station, where policemen cowered behind iron gates and bullet-proof windows, some armed with submachine guns or carbines, others unarmed, watching the chaos and destruction that they were powerless to prevent.

Nobody tried to stop them and in some places they were even greeted with jubilant cries of "Long live Kurdistan! The Kurds are with us!" Near the hotel demonstrators had jammed the streets, looters roamed shops and burned cars and thousand of pages of documents and files rained down like confetti from the windows of government buildings.

Khorasad stopped about a hundred yards from the hotel. They saw demonstrators swarming up the steps of the building, overturning the giant flower urns and tearing down the lobby curtains. The crowd pressed forward while behind them, on the roof of a wrecked car, stood a mullah in traditional clothing, a black turban and a long gray robe, waving a black walking stick. "Forward!" he yelled. "Forward! Slaughter the infidels! Tear down the building, throw out the liquor and slay the whoring women!"

"Any ideas, General?" asked Hasan.

"Let's move it!" said Khorasad. He drove into a side street that bypassed the hotel and led to a municipal park, passing quickly through an avenue of trees and crossing a frost-covered lawn to join the narrow road leading to the service entrance of the hotel. He pulled up beside the spiral steps of the emergency stairs.

"There!" he said, pointing to the fire escape. "First floor. Dariush, Hasan, you come with me!" He turned to the Kurdish youths. "You guard the car. Open fire the moment you're attacked. Don't hesitate!"

He jumped out of the car and ran to the steps, closely followed by Dariush and Hasan with drawn pistols. Khorasad clattered up the iron stairs to the emergency door, which he pulled. The door was locked from the inside. He kicked at it fiercely and cursed. Dariush pointed out a frosted window above the door. "The window!" he cried.

Khorasad, making a support of his hands, said, "Get up there, quick!" Khorasad pushed Dariush up hard until he was level with the window. He smashed the glass with the butt of his revolver and looked inside. Excited youths packed the corridor, some loaded up with loot, others yelling as they wrecked furniture and equipment. He leaned forward and squeezed his head and shoulders through the window. Splinters of glass grazed his cheek. The general pushed him farther. Now his shoulders were clear. Gingerly, holding his breath, he stretched out his arm and reached down for the bolt on the inside of the door. "A bit more," he shouted, "another four inches!"

"I can't do any more." Khorasad heaved desperately at Dariush's feet, helped by Hasan who put his dagger between his teeth and gripped the young man's heels.

"Go on, I'm nearly there!"

Dariush touched the end of the bolt, but could not move it. "The bolt won't move!"

"Shoot the fucker!"

"Hold on, I think I've got it." With a last, desperate effort he managed to catch the bolt and pull it back. The door swung open and for a moment he was left hanging, trapped in the narrow window. Khorasad helped him down. Blood streamed from the cuts on his face and his clothes were torn. The dark little eyes flashed fiercely.

"I'm all right!" he cried, "Let's go."

"This way, follow me!" Khorasad pushed aside an excited young man, his arms full of plundered bed linen and crockery, slammed his fist into the face of another who ran toward them shouting "Khomeini! Khomeini!" and reached the door of Yasarian's room. The door lay on the floor, and in the doorway stood a powerful-looking man brandishing a iron bar; it fell, missing Khorasad's head by inches as Hasan stepped forward and rammed his dagger into the man's heart.

"Come on," shouted Khorasad. "Inside!"

Inside the room were a dozen young rioters, and in the corner sat Doctor Amiri, curled up and whimpering like a frightened puppy. Beside him knelt Yasarian, sobbing, petrified, a look of insanity in his eyes. One of the youths hurled an iron bar at Khorasad, and at that moment he saw the four men bending over Janet Simpson's naked body and a dark hand squeezing her pale white breasts.

"Yasarian!" the woman shrieked.

Khorasad paused, took careful aim and put a bullet in the back of the man who crouched, bare-assed, between Janet's legs. The other three, shocked, turned their heads, only to receive the same; their bodies fell sprawling onto the carpet, except for the one who collapsed backward onto Janet's naked body. She yelled hysterically: "Amin! Amin!"

Dariush killed a young man who came at him from the bathroom with a dagger, and Hasan shot another who sprang from the wardrobe with Janet's furs. "God!" he exclaimed. "Let's get out of here!"

"Yasarian," shouted Khorasad, "get some clothes on the woman!" Yasarian stirred but did not move, instead staring at him blankly. Khorasad crossed the distance between them with two quick strides, bent down and slapped the doctor's face with all his strength, crushing the bulbous nose. Yasarian recoiled, stood up and limped toward the sofa. Janet lay there shaking, still weighted down under the youth's trouserless body. Dariush got to her first, dragged off the corpse and helped the naked woman to her feet. Blood, hers and the attackers's, dripped down onto the floor.

"Here," he said, pushing her toward Yasarian, "cover her up somehow, quick!" Janet recoiled from Yasarian's touch but was powerless to resist. He put a blood-stained blanket around her shoulders and stood beside her, frozen, his eyes fixed on Khorasad who was supporting Doctor Amiri. Hasan appeared in the doorway. "Hurry!" he cried. "Hurry!" Dariush shoved Yasarian and the woman out into the corridor and led the way back to the emergency stairs while Hasan covered them, planting himself in the center of the corridor and keeping at bay a party of looters. Khorasad and Dariush helped the three fugitives down the iron steps, shouting and pushing them on. Hasan was the last to climb into the Waggoneer, squeezing in beside a trembling Doctor Amiri. Yasarian sat in the middle, his arms around Janet. He recovered some of his composure as he embraced the weeping woman. "My dear," he murmured, "my dear!"

Khorasad started the engine and reversed out of the service bay of the hotel. They headed back the way they had come. Angry demonstrators blockaded the main street and the sidewalks were a solid mass of frenzied humans waving placards, clenched fists, chains and iron bars. "Look, there they are!" somebody shouted. "Savak!"

The crowd surged, howling for revenge. Khorasad glanced behind and to the side, ducked and rammed the gear lever into forward drive. "Now," he shouted, "now!" He pressed the horn and released the clutch. "Shoot! Shoot for God's sake!"

Dariush and Hasan leaned out of the side windows and opened fire on the mob. Those in front tried desperately to disperse, too late. With a sickening crunch the car shot forward and collided headlong with the human barrier. Screams of pain and terror mingled with the crash of shattered glass and the crackle of breaking bones. Khorasad pressed hard on the gas pedal and felt the car climbing on a heap of struggling bodies. The windshield was cracked and covered with blood, the wipers torn off. He leaned forward, gripping the wheel with both hands, deafened by the shouting and the gunfire and the high-pitched whine of the engine.

Suddenly the car broke loose from the fleeing crowd, gathered speed and roared away down the street. The front bumper hung on one screw, dragging on the tarmac with a loud clatter. Khorasad heard terrified screams and his eyes scanned the now deserted sidewalks. But the screams came from Janet Simpson. Khorasad turned to Doctor Yasarian. "Shut that fucking woman up!"

At the edge of the suburbs, as they approached the refugee village, he stopped the Waggoneer to examine it. The others joined him. "A nightmare," he shuddered. "Great God!"

"A slaughterhouse!" exclaimed Hasan.

Dariush pulled off the broken bumper and threw it to the side of the road. Yasarian stood beside Doctor Amiri, embracing the whimpering Janet, who was still wrapped in the blood-stained blanket. One of the young Kurds was violently sick. Khorasad swallowed a thick lump of phlegm and grimaced, surprised at the depth of his own nausea.

# 7

A convoy of trucks approached the commercial sector of Esenboga airfield, their cargo three mammoth blue containers bearing the words TRANS-ASIA AIR TRANSPORT SERVICE. They stopped for a few minutes at customs, then the gates opened and they drove on into the freight terminal, following a course parallel to the perimeter fence.

At this hour of the morning there was not much activity around the airfield. Flights of the Turkish National Airline had already taken off for Istanbul and Izmir, and a Condor jumbo jet that had flown in several hundred Turkish migrant workers from Frankfurt stood parked on the runway opposite the control tower. Visibility was clear, the air bitterly cold. Airfield workers, truck and tractor drivers and the soldiers who patrolled the runways had all bundled up against the chill.

The convoy drove on to the eastern end of the airfield, past a blue and silver KLM 707, until they reached their destination: a bright-blue four-engined Hercules. Beside the Hercules stood a few men in flying suits, a group of airport workers and a pair of Turkish customs men. The convoy halted close to the tail of the plane. The rear ramp of the Hercules dropped for loading. A giant forklift maneuvered into position and after a few minutes of hectic activity the containers were lashed to the floor of the dark, cavernous cargo hold. At once the ramp closed and the engines started up, hissing loudly and then settling into a regular throbbing beat that shook the aircraft. In a few minutes the revolutions increased. The brakes were released and the Hercules taxied forth.

"Esenboga control from Asia Air 77. Standing by. Request clearance for takeoff, destination Tatvan, Turkey."

Seconds later the blue Hercules was racing down the runway, lurching upward, its black nose rearing east toward the Iranian border. At about the same time a small U.S. Air Force executive jet carried the supervisory staff to the east.

Inside one of the containers in the belly of the Hercules, the flying team set to work in a frenzy, unlocking the bolts and letting themselves out into the cargo hold. Arik was the first to emerge. He stretched and looked around cheerfully as the other six followed. Leonard shouted above the engine roar, "Not a bad idea, eh?"

"Fine!" He looked back at the equipment crammed into the container and asked: "What's in the others?"

"General freight . . . *something* has to be delivered to Kuwait . . ."

"Yes." Arik and Leonard drifted toward Yosi and Shraga. The two men were engaged in an animated conversation with a member of the American team. He heard the name of Idi Amin.

"What's going on?" he asked.

Shraga chuckled. "I'm telling our pal about the Hercules, about Entebbe . . ."

"I think you should be preparing yourselves. We don't have much time."

"Don't worry."

Arik's expression turned severe. "Study the maps!" he said

and walked off toward the front of the quivering aircraft with Leonard following him. At the foot of the steps to the cockpit he and Leonard stopped for a minute to look back into the hollow space of the vast hold. The operational team were dutifully at work.

In the cockpit the pilots, Obis and Schneider, sat at the controls, while another crew member inspected the radar screen. Arik and Leonard settled down in the rest area at the rear of the cockpit, taking seats on the lower level of a bunk bed. Leonard offered a cigarette.

"Got any Panama?"

"Tobacco or gold?"

"Cigarettes, cigarettes from Panama."

"No such luck," answered Leonard, unbuttoning his breast pocket and pulling out a pack of Lucky Strikes. "Have one of these," he said, "they're unfiltered."

"Suits me." Arik took a cigarette and Leonard lit it for him. He took a deep drag of pungent smoke and exhaled it slowly and thoughtfully. "This reminds me of my childhood," he said.

*"What?"*

"Lucky Strikes," said Arik. "When I was about thirteen I went out one day and bought myself a pack of these." He smiled and closed his eyes, engrossed in memories of the distant past, but Leonard was in a talkative mood.

"I switched from Camels when they changed packs," he said. "What do they smoke in Iran?"

"Everything. Local brands and a lot of American types."

"Really?"

"Yes." Arik was tired of the small talk, but knew he ought to try. It was just that Leonard reminded him so much of the army, the pain of his whole army career. It had nothing to do with Leonard himself, really . . .

The American smoked in silence for a while, then said: "I understand you were a military man."

"Yes." Arik smiled. "I hoped I'd make general."

99

"Don't we all, the first day we put on the uniform."

"To hell with it, I couldn't . . . I left."

"Any special reason?"

Arik hadn't talked about it in a long time. It made him uneasy. But he answered, "You can say I was sacked. They threw me out."

"You don't have to talk about it."

Arik laughed. "I guess I don't take it so hard anymore. There's no real reason why you shouldn't know. They said I was too much of a loner—that I can't work by the book."

Leonard said thoughtfully, "A good army finds out about those things pretty quick . . ."

"I spent years in Iran. That's when I met Khorasad. There was no discipline there at all then and I liked it. I liked working solo. When I came back, I couldn't get along with the system. Finally, the army got rid of me, that's all."

"Still angry?"

"Oh, I used to hate them."

Leonard smiled. Arik thought for a moment about his meeting with Trenshaw back in Haifa. "I really wanted those stripes . . ."

George Obis took a last look at the instrument panel in front of him and released his safety harness, then rose from the captain's seat and crossed the cockpit to join them. He smelled of aftershave. "How d'you feel in this bird of ours?" he asked.

Arik smiled. "This isn't the first time."

"Yeah, I guess not . . ." Obis scratched his chin. "This bird's a combination military and civilian model." He pointed to the radar operator. "Look over there, it's a regular radar station."

"So?"

"So?"

"So what difference does that make to our flight?"

*"Does it make any difference?* I'll say it does!" Obis declared in his Texan drawl. "Look, you guys want to drop from minimal height. That means I have to hold course between different-height mountains, say nine to eleven thousand feet. Smallest mistake and we're all dead. Without this gear we couldn't do it."

"Will those instruments work in any conditions?"

"I hope so."

"You *hope* so?" exclaimed Leonard.

Obis laughed. "Don't worry, boys, I'll get you there safely."

Leonard yawned and looked around for an ashtray, then tossed the stub of his cigarette into a big empty tin fixed to the bottom of the bed.

Obis scowled. "Hey, that's for peels and nut shells only!"

"Come off it!" cried Leonard.

"No, I mean it."

Arik looked at the strong, tanned face of the pilot. "You know," he said, "if you don't get back to us at the right time and place we'll really be in the shit."

"Don't worry."

"I'm not sure we'll be able to use a regular airstrip."

"You know the requirements of a Hercules. Stick to them and we'll have no problem."

"I hope you're right. Those mountains are scary."

Obis laughed again. "Nothing's so bad as the Himalayas, believe me!"

Arik look at Obis curiously. "Have you been there?"

Obis shot a glance at Leonard, who shook his head. The pilot shrugged. "I guess not," he said simply.

Arik smiled. "I see." He stubbed out his cigarette. "What difference does it make anyway? What matters is that you get us safely into Iran and are there in time to lift us out . . ."

"I've told you not to worry, pal." Obis took a deep breath and looked straight at Arik. "Do all Israelis worry as much as you?"

"That isn't the point."

"What's the point?"

"Everyone agrees that you people are good, in fact the best," said Arik after a short silence. He looked at Leonard as he went on, "I have to accept that, believe that it's true, but really . . ." He took a deep breath and tried to smile. "I'd prefer it if things were different . . . I'd rather be in a different airplane with a different team, with my own people . . ." He paused for a moment and then added hurriedly, "I hope you're not offended."

"Nope." Leonard stood up. "I'm going down to check on the boys." Before going he bent over Arik: "Just for the record, I feel exactly the same."

"I guess so," replied Arik. He sighed. "There's nothing we can do about it."

"Right."

Leonard put his foot on the first step, then stopped and turned back to Arik. "You'll probably never know *my* story," he said. "I wish I could tell you. But I want you to know at least one thing: I'm also a military man originally, but I didn't spend much time in it and I never wanted to be a general. My life is special, this kind of work. I like it that way." He looked straight at Arik. "I never experienced the problem of disobedience or change of orders. With me it's perfectionism, not ego-tripping."

"It's a shitty business," said Obis, looking ahead at the grey sky and the big wipers moving slowly on the forward window. "Still, I'll do whatever I can to make it work. You guys do the same, okay?"

"No problem," said Arik. "Just give us a safe flight. Leave the rest to us."

Obis returned to the captain's seat and strapped himself in. "Any problems, Jack?"

"Everything's okay," replied Jack Schneider. "Radio contact with Alazig, nothing special."

"Any other flights on VG 8?"

"Turkish Airways a few minutes ago. DC-9 on a routine flight."

Obis nodded and spread out on his knees an American aerial map of the Middle East, and ran his finger along route VG 8. "The highest obstacle is ten five," he said.

Schneider stared straight ahead. "I can read a map too," he said drily.

"Okay."

"How do you rate this mission?"

Obis looked at Schneider. "From their angle or ours?"

"Both."

"Nothing we can't handle . . ."

"I'm not so sure."

"The exercises went off all right."

"Yes."

Obis tightened his grip on the controls and glanced at the radio compass. "When we land at Tatvan, check all this electronic gear again," he said. "If the climate over Iran isn't friendly we'll have to rely on instruments."

Arik was now leaning on the back of Obis's seat, staring at the dials and instruments. "How do you guys know what you're doing with all this gear around you?" he asked.

Jack Schneider laughed. "That's the difference between us and the rest of the human race, pal! Do you know anything about flying?"

"I know how to jump out of planes, that's all."

"That's something."

Suddenly the plane began to rock from side to side as it hit a series of air pockets. The pilots crouched over their instruments intently and Arik's view was blocked. He turned and went down into the cargo hold.

Most of the men now sat on benches beside the containers. Leonard stood talking to Walter Gabriel, his deputy, who punctuated his remarks with excited gestures, bracing himself against one of the containers whenever the plane rocked or shuddered. Arik watched the two men, considered joining them but thought better of it. He sat down on the nearest seat, leaned back and closed his eyes, systematically going over in his mind the operation in all its details. He felt confident now as he considered the plan, the personnel and the equipment, assured of the quality of all three.

Schreiber was waiting at the airport in Tatvan. As soon as the plane halted he came over with his entourage, rounding the Hercules in a wide circle and taking care to avoid the danger zone of the propellers. They stood behind the tall plane and waited as the ramp was lowered, then climbed up into the hold, where they were met by Leonard and Arik.

"Everything all right?" asked Schreiber.

"No problems," replied Arik.

"I hope we won't be boxed up too long," Leonard said.

Schreiber smiled. "You'll be off in a couple of hours."

"Is that final?" asked Leonard eagerly.

"Yes, we've received a final message from Penicillin. He's gotten the agents out of Kermanshah. But there are new problems. We've heard from another source that Khorasad's in trouble. He was arrested by the government but managed to escape. Messy business . . ." He breathed hard and frowned. "We've also heard that in Kermanshah, Mehabad and all along the Iran-Iraq frontier there have been riots. We've got to move fast."

Schreiber led the group down the ramp and across the runway, toward a small hut painted with red and white squares, a Turkish army jeep parked beside it. A pair of military policemen wearing white plastic helmets sat in the jeep.

At the door of the hut stood Portilio and Danny, who talked in low voices. Portilio smiled at the newcomers, slapped Leonard's shoulder, shook hands with Arik and then opened the door and ushered them inside. The hut contained a few benches, a folding camp table and a huge radio set on a low metal stand. When the men crowded inside there was barely room to move.

"Okay, boys, this is it," Schreiber said finally. He coughed and sucked on his pipe. "They're waiting for you now."

"Any change in the drop zone?" asked Leonard.

"Rendezvous 34," replied Portilio. "We reckon Khorasad, Penicillin that is, is already on his way there."

"So we'll be dropping as planned," said Arik,

"Yes."

"The weather?"

"Cloud, low sky."

"Shit."

"Nothing we can do."

"I hope Obis knows his job."

"Don't worry."

Arik shrugged. "Why should I worry?" he asked drily. "All I have to do is hope I don't land on some mountain."

"What's the overall situation?" asked Leonard.

"The Ayatollah's coming back. He's expected to arrive at any moment. The riots are likely to intensify. And there's serious fighting in Tabriz, a real civil war."

"And in Kermanshah?" asked Arik.

"Trouble," said Schreiber. "The leaders of the Kurdish Democratic Party are plotting an uprising. There are reports that Mullah Mustafa Barzani plans to return to Iran."

"He's sick," said Arik. "Very sick."

"Yes, but he's planning a comeback. He hopes he'll get there in time to set something alight."

"In about an hour we'll get everyone together," said Portilio. "We'll hold a final briefing in the plane and then it's all up to you."

Danny, who had been silent, coughed drily and said, "All communication lines are open. There shouldn't be any problems on that side. As far as we're concerned, the operation can go ahead." He paused for a moment and then added, addressing Arik in Hebrew, "There are some final instructions for your ears only."

As they were returning to the plane Schreiber signaled to Arik to slow down and the two of them hung back. They walked in silence for a while and then Schreiber spoke.

"I talked to Sally this morning," he said. There was a slightly mocking tone to his voice.

Arik felt anger flare up inside him, but he controlled it. "That wasn't necessary."

"You know it is," Schreiber hissed softly.

"It's personal."

Schreiber tugged at Arik's elbow and stopped him. "Listen to me," he said. "I know the score. I've been in this business a hell of a lot longer than you have . . ."

"So?"

"In Ankara I saw a familiar look in your eyes."

"Bullshit!"

"You're hung up on that woman, Sally . . . I don't want it to get in the way."

"It was just a passing friendship."

"You screwed her."

Arik stared at him. He clenched his fists.

"Did she tell you *that* too?" he asked furiously.

"Yes . . . it's her duty. She works for me. You know that."

"Yes . . ."

"She told me about you leaving the hotel." Schreiber smiled. "And the coffeehouse, and . . ."

Arik bored into him with his eyes.

"You know what happens when personal feelings become more important than our work."

Arik stood motionless.

"You know what the penalties are when you disobey orders."

Again Arik was silent.

"You've traveled that route before."

"I am not in the army anymore."

Suddenly Schreiber broke into a smile, and the severity in his expression dissipated. "No, you're not . . . and we're very lucky to have you on this operation. Really. And also, about Sally—well, in some ways I guess I should be pleased."

"I don't understand . . ."

Schreiber released Arik's elbow. "Come on," he said, "let's get back to the plane." As they approached the Hercules he went on, "Our psychologists recommend that any agent who's going into action should be allowed an intense sexual experience . . ." He

106

smiled. "Unfortunately our conservative superiors don't always agree."

Now Arik grinned. "You make us sound like gladiators."

"A fair analogy, don't you think?"

"What else did Sally tell you?"

"I shouldn't tell you this."

Arik, relaxed now, chided him gently. "Come on. After what you just put me through?"

"Well it's hard for me. You see, her husband . . . worked under me too. And he was a friend, a dear friend. I feel like I already lost her one mate . . ."

"I guess I understand."

"But since you insist . . ."

"Yes?"

"She wants to see you when you get back."

"She said that?"

"Yes." Schreiber bent down and knocked out his pipe on the concrete. As he straightened up he said, "I hope you're not angry."

"Well, it is an intimate matter . . ."

"I guess so, but it was you who approached me yesterday in Ankara, remember? It was unconventional. I had to check out exactly what happened."

Arik shrugged. His spirits rose as they approached the aircraft and he recalled with a thrill her grey eyes and long neck. "She's Armenian," he said suddenly.

"Yes." Schreiber chuckled. "She was born somewhere around here." He waved his right arm in a broad, circular gesture. "Tatvan," he said. "Know anything about the place?"

"Not much."

"Armenian territory, this was their kingdom . . ." He laughed. "This Sally of yours would have been a princess or something. She's beautiful."

"Yes," Arik agreed. He lengthened his stride, drawing away from Schreiber, past the fuel truck which was still filling the tanks of the Hercules. He climbed the ramp into the cargo hold. He saw Leonard, Danny and Walter Gabriel standing in the forward section and went over to join them as Schreiber followed.

"What's up?" he asked.

"Nothing," said Walter. "We're waiting for the fueling to finish and then we'll get the boys out of the container and the cockpit and have ourselves a final briefing." He smiled at Arik and grimaced. "Looks like it's go, boss!"

# 8

Janet stood naked and trembling in an old iron tub. The level of gray soapy water sloshing around her bare feet rose as the two Kurdish women emptied their buckets over her shoulders. The women were old and fat and wore voluminous black robes and yellow shawls which shielded everything except for their faces. They chuckled softly every time Janet's tall body shook, which was often. The sobbing was no longer continuous, but in brief, sporadic seizures. Lacerations and livid gray bruises marked her breasts, thighs and stomach. The gashes from the teeth of one of her attackers on her right shoulder had left the whole area a ghastly purple. Her entire body ached.

In the next room men talked in low voices. She heard the voice of Khorasad, Hasan chuckling, the plaintive whispering of Doctor Amiri and the thick voice of Doctor Yasarian, who seemed to have recovered. *Bastard,* she thought. He would never be the same to her.

She signaled the women to finish the bath. They nodded and

drenched her with a fresh supply of lukewarm water, raising the water level so that the suds overflowed onto the concrete floor. As they handed her a big coarse towel she heard Yasarian's voice again. She remembered him crouching in the corner of the hotel room, watching, paralyzed with fear yet almost fascinated, spellbound as the youths pinned her to the sofa. He had been staring at her from behind the back of the man who mounted her. Her head spun. She couldn't bear to think about it. The Kurdish women supported her and helped her dry, then dressed her in a long black robe, bound a kerchief around her head and put a shawl about her shoulders. Still trembling, she left the little kitchen and walked into the living quarters where the men sat around the warm stove. Silently, they made room for her between Khorasad and Yasarian. She paused, shook her head and motioned Khorasad over, so that she could sit between him and Hasan.

"How do you feel?" asked Khorasad sympathetically.

She did not reply. Yasarian reached across Khorasad and clumsily laid his heavy arm on her sore shoulder. Janet screamed in pain and recoiled, jerking away as if a snake had bitten her.

"Don't you dare touch me!"

"Janet!" Yasarian protested, looking at her in amazement. He reached for her again. "My dear!"

"Take your hands off me!" She sprang to her feet, trembling. Yasarian tried to rise but Khorasad pushed him back roughly. He lost his balance and sprawled heavily on the pile of mattresses. "What was that for?" he cried, staring indignantly at Khorasad and at the others who now sat there in silence. Only the two Kurdish women whispered softly to each other as they took the bathtub and the bundle of towels through the room.

"Don't move!" Khorasad shouted. "Understand?"

"What the hell's going on?"

"Relax," said Khorasad to Janet. "Come back and sit by the stove or you'll catch cold."

"I'm not going anywhere near that pig," she said loudly, her face pale.

There was silence for a few seconds and then Khorasad smiled, leaning back and looking in turn at Janet and at Doctor Amiri. "Go to the kitchen, Yasarian," he ordered. Yasarian balked, but Hasan's nephews stood him up and marched him out. "Now Janet," he said calmly, "why don't you sit next to Amiri, he needs cheering up."

Amiri crouched by the stove, his white hair awry and eyes quivering fitfully in their sockets. He fiddled nervously with the buttons on his suit. "Here, come over here," he said at last.

Yasarian tried to reenter the room but was pushed back again. Khorasad shook his head in disbelief, then he stood up and gently caressed Janet's shoulders as he led her to the stove. "Sit down," he said. "You'd better pull yourself together. We haven't much time, we've got to move on."

"I don't want him to touch me," she said in a broken voice, "I won't let him lay a finger on me!"

"That's all right," said Khorasad. "He won't get near you if that's what you want." He hugged her lightly and she pressed against him. He led her toward Doctor Amiri and when she had sat down beside the stove he went back to his place. Yasarian stood in the doorway, staring at the floor.

Khorasad sat down, cleared his throat and began. "Soon we'll be moving on. I want you all to put on warm clothes. We'll be using light transport—the Russian jeep—and on the way we'll pass through some cold and difficult terrain. Hasan's men will bring us the clothes we need." He pushed up his sleeve and glanced at his watch. "Yes, it's time to get organized."

Doctor Amiri knotted his fingers anxiously. "Do you really believe we're going to make it out, General?"

Khorsad looked at the frightened little man, and after a moment's silence replied, "If I thought we had no chance, dear Doctor, I'd never have got myself involved in this business. Understood?"

"But if we turned ourselves in, General . . ."

Khorasad laughed. "If I didn't believe we were going to make it I wouldn't have bothered to get you out of the hotel. I'd have left you there to rot, and I'm beginning to wish I had . . ."

"All the same," Amiri murmured, and he clicked his false teeth in his mouth, "I would like to know what the prospects are."

"Prospects! This isn't theoretical science, we're not in one of your seminars! When we succeed is when we'll know."

"We are entitled to know," said Doctor Yasarian from across the room.

"You're not entitled to anything," replied Khorasad. He looked at Hasan who sat beside him, his wrinkled face expressionless, then at Dariush. He thought he saw a flash of animation in his aide's drooping, lifeless eyes, but he did not stop there, looking at each one of the group in turn until he came to Janet's pale face. The red eyes stared back at him with a look of keen interest, and he smiled at her.

"You have no rights," he told them firmly. "As long as I'm in charge, you have no rights."

"That's not reasonable!" exclaimed Yasarian. "By God, General, that's not reasonable!"

Khorasad tensed and stood to face Yasarian. "Here there is no reason, Doctor! Do you think it was reasonable to get you out of the hotel, to shoot people, run them down? No! You know it wasn't, but you let me and Dariush and Hasan get on with the job. You're prepared to stand aside and watch us killing and slaughtering . . ." He went and stood beside Yasarian, slapping his shoulder derisively. "Do you hear me, Doctor? Here only *men* have rights."

Yasarian did not reply. He shuddered, his eyes still fixed on the floor. Khorasad straightened up and looked again at his watch. "We'd better finish the plans," he said to Hasan. "We've wasted too much time already."

"Yes." Hasan stood up and stretched. He looked across at Yasarian. "Doctor!" he called. When Yasarian did not respond he called again.

"Yes, what is it?" Yasarian asked feebly.

"The woman, Doctor!" Hasan pointed to Janet. "Is the woman yours?"

Yasarian hesitated. He glanced at Janet, their eyes met briefly and then parted. "Yes," he murmured in a barely audible voice. "She's mine."

"That's all I wanted to know," said Hasan. He shrugged, buttoned his coat and opened the door, letting a blast of cold air into the room. Khorasad looked out, noting the gray skies with satisfaction.

"No snow," he said. "The sooner we get out of here, the better for all of us."

Dariush drove the jeep. Beside him sat Khorasad and behind them Yasarian, Amiri and Janet. The canvas-covered rear section was crammed with canned food, blankets and folded sleeping bags. Cans of fuel were lashed to the front and back bumpers; a spare wheel and a long wooden box containing ammunition, hand grenades and first-aid equipment had been fixed to the mudguards. Khorasad turned up the heat, but still it was bitterly cold inside the vehicle. They all wore thick clothing, mostly Kurdish winter garments and thick woolen caps supplied by Hasan. Janet wore a padded overcoat over her masculine Kurdish clothes, and a fur-lined hood which Hasan had presented to her with a courtly bow before they set out.

A short distance behind on the narrow road came Hasan's pickup truck. The convoy traveled north, past quiet little villages, a few flocks of sheep which at this hour were already being led back to their shelters, and here and there a farm tractor or a brightly painted small bus carrying villagers returning from the markets of Kermanshah. They also met a light truck crammed full of excited youths waving placards, but this too passed at speed. Nobody tried to stop them.

Khorasad held the map open on his knees. At intervals he passed on information to Dariush or told him to reduce speed when he thought that the heavily laden jeep was going to skid on the narrow gravel road. He was satisfied. So far everything had worked according to plan. He had forgotten his imprisonment in the camp in Kermanshah. Or at least the fear no longer oppressed him. He looked in the mirror and saw the large head of Yasarian who looked absurd under the red woolen cap. Beside him was Amiri and next to him he could see a part of Janet's hood. *A good-looking woman,* he thought, and winced when he remembered the sight of the youth shuddering between her legs.

"How do you feel, Miss Simpson?" he asked.

"All right."

"Are you cold?"

"No, this coat is fine."

He smiled to himself and then looked again at the map spread out on his knees. Daylight was fading fast. Dariush switched on the headlights and at hairpin curves their beams sometimes met those of Hasan's truck which drove behind. For a long time they were the only vehicles on the narrow road. Now they were forced to slow down, as the bends became sharper and the road surface deteriorated. In the jeep there was total darkness and only the speedometer gave off a pale flickering light.

"We'll have to stop soon," said Dariush.

"Why?"

"We may take a wrong turn, there are too many side roads to negotiate in the dark. Besides, we're all dead tired."

"Yes . . ." Khorasad saw thin patches of mist swirling on the road ahead of them and he knew that visibility would soon be down to a minimum. "I think you're right."

"Anything on the map?"

"Nothing. We'll go on a bit farther and see."

"Maybe we can stop at that wood."

Dariush pulled up beside a group of tall pine trees. He left the engine running, jumped down with a big flashlight and scoured the woods. The beam flickered over the tall trees, a few rocks and a deserted sheep enclosure built of stone. A cold wind was blowing

114

from the north. There would soon be snow or hail. "It's all right," he shouted. "We can camp here. Let's get the cars up into the trees."

"Fine!" Khorasad moved into the driver's seat while Dariush went over to Hasan's truck.

"We're spending the night here," he said, pointing to the trees. "Drive the truck over there."

They parked the vehicles side by side. Hasan and the young Kurds set to work gathering wood which they heaped up against the stone wall of the deserted sheep pen and with the help of a few drops of gasoline they soon had a fire burning briskly. The others warmed themselves around the flames and watched in silence as Hasan and his boys prepared thick sweet tea. They ate cold meat from the tins collected from the radio station. The wind had freshened and now it blew strongly, whining among the rocks and pine trees, as the sky darkened and the mist grew thicker.

Khorasad looked at the group sitting around the fire. It was difficult to pick out features amid all the clothing. He tried to distinguish Janet's face but she was almost shapeless in the heavy overcoat and hood.

"Janet, Amiri and Yasarian will sleep in the back of the truck," he said. "That's the best place. Spread out your sleeping bags and you won't feel the cold."

"I'm sleeping outside," said the woman.

Khorasad smiled in the darkness. "As you wish," he said. "Or you can sleep in the jeep or the cab of the truck . . ."

"Janet?" Yasarian made one last attempt. The woman did not respond. Khorasad chuckled softly, picked up a small stone and threw it in the direction of Yasarian. "Shut up!" he hissed. "I don't want to hear another word from you!"

He saw Janet stand up and walk toward the jeep. *A good-looking woman,* he thought. *Hell, in a different time and place . . .* He took a last gulp of lukewarm tea and turned to Hasan. "Two hours watch apiece," he said. "All right?"

The Kurd did not reply but nodded his head.

"I'll take the final watch," said Dariush. "You take the first, General."

·Khorasad agreed. He walked over to the jeep where Janet was unrolling her sleeping bag. For a moment he watched her in silence.

"Getting yourself sorted out?" he asked.

"Yes," she replied. "And I don't need a man," she added.

"Don't worry," he said. "I just came to see how you're doing. No need to get excited."

She put the sleeping bag down for a moment. "I don't know what to say, General."

"I think you're being a bit hard on Doctor Yasarian," he said in a voice that lacked conviction. He tried unsuccessfully to make out the lines of her face under the hood.

"You're not showing him much sympathy yourself."

He shrugged. "I don't like the guy . . . never did . . . not him or his kind . . . but you, he worked hard at persuading me to get you out as well . . ."

She went back to fumbling with her sleeping bag. "You saw what happened there, in the hotel," she said in a low voice. "How . . ."

"Yes," he said, "of course."

"He didn't do anything to prevent it," she said. "You understand? He just stood there and let them do what they wanted with me."

"They'd have killed him," said Khorasad. "No doubt about it, they'd have smashed in his skull."

She glanced toward the fading light of the fire. "You know," she said, "I'd like to have seen that . . ."

Khorasad shrugged. He turned and walked away without another word.

When dawn came the ground was covered with bright frost. The sky was gray but the strong wind that had blown in the night had died down and now the tall pine trees stood almost motionless.

Dariush gathered leaves and twigs and added them to the remains of the fire, along with a pile of droppings from the sheep pen. He waited until he saw white smoke curling up from under the twigs, then he went over to the truck and roused the rest of the party. He helped Hasan make the tea and warmed some frozen pieces of flat Berberi bread over the little fire.

The men moved slowly, yawning as they folded their blankets. Khorasad stood erect by the jeep, stripped to the waist, his face covered with stubble. Behind him in the jeep he saw movement: Janet was awake and folding her sleeping bag. Khorasad began flinging out his arms energetically, ignoring the pain in his shoulder from the bullet wound. Janet sat staring at the hirsute, half-naked general pumping and stretching in the icy cold. Dariush, who was watching the two of them, smiled to himself. "Bastard," he murmured, "the fucking bastard . . ."

When they sat down around the fire Khorasad was in high spirits, sipping noisily from the tin cup that Hasan gave him, leaning forward wrapped in his heavy army coat. "Let's move," he said, finishing his tea. "We've got a long way to go."

"I can't eat this bread," complained Doctor Amiri with an expression of agony. "My teeth," he explained.

"That's all there is," snapped Khorasad.

"Dip the bread in your tea," Dariush suggested. These words seemed to amuse the general. He laid his cup on the ground and roared with laughter. "God Almighty, never in my life have I led such a bunch of cripples! What a way to end my career!"

Amiri shuddered, bent his bald little head and whimpered. Khorasad stood up and clapped his hands. "I don't care what you do with your bread. Let's go."

As they hurried back to the vehicles a light rain began to fall. Again Dariush took the wheel. He let the engine run for a few minutes to warm up. "Ready?" he asked.

"Yes." The general spread the map on his knees. "Let's go!"

Dariush drove the jeep across a newly plowed field toward the road. Visibility was good. They could see the foothills on the other side of the valley, and behind, the mountains covered with a thin layer of frost over the first green of spring. Here and there were large flocks of sheep, led by black-robed shepherds on mules and herded this way and that by huge brown Karabash sheepdogs. The isolated villages looked like heaps of gravel scattered across the landscape. They showed little signs of activity at this hour, other than plumes of smoke curling up from cottage chimneys.

Khorasad identified on the map the village closest to them.

"There's a police station there," he said.

"Where?"

"Ahead of us, in the next village."

"I see . . ."

"I hope there'll be no problems."

"A gendarme or two," said Dariush with thin smile. "No more."

The general unbuttoned his coat and took his pistol from its heavy holster. "Just in case," he said. "You never can tell . . ."

"All right." Dariush also drew his pistol and laid it on the seat beside him. He looked in the mirror and saw the three passengers sitting sleepily in the back. Ahead of them, around a bend in the narrow road, stood a child with a few mangy dogs. A tethered mule grazed at the roadside. The first houses of the village came into view, low mud-colored cottages flanked by short stubby trees. A few scrawny chickens scuttled through the mud and here and there a heavily veiled woman peered cautiously from a doorway. Otherwise the place seemed deserted. He had driven past the outlying houses and was about to tell the general that he thought the road was clear when he saw the white concrete blockhouse of the local gendarmerie station, a single-story building flying the green, white and red imperial flag. Beside it he saw a steel roadblock made of spiked rails, guarded by three gendarmes armed with Uzi submachine guns. One of them, a sergeant, stood in the middle of the road, in the gap between the serrated strips of the roadblock, and held up his hand.

"You know what to do!" said Khorasad in a low voice.

118

Dariush nodded and slowed down, driving with his left hand and holding the pistol in his right. Beside the gendarme sergeant he stopped. The tall swarthy man looked at them suspiciously. "That's an army jeep," he said. "Who are you?"

"It's all right!" shouted Dariush. The man came closer and glanced inside the car. "Your papers, please," he said, and suddenly his eyes opened wide in amazement.

"It's them!" he shouted. "General Khorasad!"

The two gendarmes who stood behind him hastily unslung their weapons. The sergeant tried to escape but a well-aimed bullet from Dariush hit him as he ran. He fell backward with a howl of pain. Khorasad opened the door beside him and jumped out. Behind him he heard the squealing brakes of Hasan's truck and the screams of frightened women. He gripped the butt of his pistol in both hands, aimed at the first gendarme and fired twice, hitting the man in the chest and stomach. The other managed to fire off one short burst. He heard the rattle and the crash of bullets slamming into the jeep. The gendarme turned and ran but Dariush fired again, hitting him in the waist. He raised his submachine gun in a last desperate attempt to aim and shoot, but Khorasad's bullet caught him between the eyes. He sank to his knees and was dead before he hit the ground.

Dariush swore softly. One of the bullets from the gendarme's gun had shattered the windshield, missing his head by inches. Unintentionally he took his foot off the clutch. The jeep sprang forward and the front wheels mounted the toothed roadblock. The tires burst with a loud pop, followed by the hiss of escaping air. He cut the engine and jumped out. "Shit!" he cried angrily. He looked around and saw the gendarme raise his left arm in a dying spasm.

Yasarian and Amiri climbed out of the back seat. Janet followed and stood beside the vehicle shivering, the winter coat held tightly around her. Behind them stood Hasan and his nephews, their weapons trained on the concrete blockhouse. A few peasant women ran to take refuge in their cottages. One of them, screaming at the top of her voice, clasped a baby to her breast. The general stood beside the roadblock, his pistol in his hand, thoughtfully massaging his injured shoulder.

"The jeep," said Dariush, pointing to the front wheels which lay impaled on the sharp teeth.

"Yes." The general grimaced. "Fuck it, that's all we needed!" He went over to the corpses of the gendarmes and roughly kicked the submachine guns away from them, then climbed the broad steps of the blockhouse, passing the sentry box where a big kerosene stove was burning, then went on to the commandant's office. He opened the door carefully, taking cover behind the angle of the wall, and then, satisfied that the room was empty, went inside, sitting down at the desk and opening the station ledger. He turned the big pages until he found the latest entry. Dariush stood close behind him. "Anything special?" he asked.

Khorasad smiled faintly. "Read it yourself," he said, handing him the ledger. "There, the one that came in last night."

Dariush leaned forward and read aloud: "Savak General Said Khorasad is wanted in connection with the murder of demonstrators and the supervision of brutal Savak operations in the region of Tabriz, Mehabad and Kermanshah. If he resists arrest, he is to be shot. General Khorasad is armed and believed to be accompanied by dangerous accomplices." Dariush straightened up and shrugged. "Not much we can do about that . . ."

"Read all of it!" snapped Khorasad.

Dariush looked at the page again and read the last sentence aloud: "This directive issued by order of the Revolutionary Council of the Islamic Republic." He looked up and stared at Khorasad. For a moment he was silent, then he murmured, *"Islamic Republic?"*

"We must get our hands on a radio," said Khorasad. "From this moment on we must listen to every news broadcast."

He was interrupted by a burst of gunfire from outside, and once again they heard women screaming. They left the room and ran out to the muddy street. One of Hasan's boys stood firing his automatic weapon into a nearby alley. Janet crouched beside the jeep, her hands over her ears, and farther back, beside the green truck, the other Kurd knelt beside Hasan, who lay spreadeagled on the cold ground.

"Oh God!" exclaimed Dariush. "It's Hasan!" He was running toward the old Kurd when Khorasad stopped him with a shout. "Dariush! Over there, in the alley!"

He turned to the youth who stood firing round after round in the direction of the alley. "What happened?" he yelled. "Quick, tell me what happened!"

The Kurd lowered his rifle. "There," he said, pointing to a mud hut with a low stone wall. "A gendarme, he came out into the street and fired on us . . ."

Dariush made a quick estimate of the distance between himself and the wooden gate in the stone wall of the cottage, looked around and saw Khorasad bending over Hasan, then checked his revolver. "Cover me," he said to the youth. "I'll try and get to the hut from behind!"

He stooped and set off at a run, crossed the street and jumped into a grimy backyard where a woman and two runny-nosed children cowered behind a brick-built baking oven, scaled a wall and landed in another yard. He passed quickly between a pair of scrawny cows and vaulted a fence, scattering a noisy flock of chickens. For a moment he knelt down, his chest pounding, then he jumped across a low gate and arrived at the back of the hut where the gendarme was hiding. He peered around the corner of the building and waved his gun as a signal to the young Kurd who had changed his stance and was now firing from a kneeling position.

The youth stopped firing. Dariush advanced into the alley and came to a small window, its green shutter hanging loose on a rusty hinge. He glanced inside and saw the gendarme, who was armed with a submachine gun, running to the door and out into the yard. He drew back and aimed his revolver in line with the top of the wall. When he saw the peaked cap of the gendarme he fired two quick shots. The man swayed sideways, then fell back inside the hut. Dariush heard the soft thud as the body hit the floor. He did not hesitate but ran back to the road where the rest of the group were gathered around Hasan.

He pushed Amiri aside and stared into the face of the old Kurd. His fine features looked serene, his green eyes were open and his white moustache bristled, a thin trickle of blood oozed from the corner of his mouth and ran down over his chin. Hasan's head rested in Khorasad's lap. The general looked up at Dariush and shook his head almost imperceptibly from side to side.

Dariush watched as Khorasad took the dead man's eyelids between finger and thumb and gently closed his eyes. Khorasad's face was frozen. One of the young Kurds sobbed quietly while his cousin stood behind the general fiddling nervously with his rifle strap.

Khorasad laid the dead man's head on the ground. "He must be taken back to the village," he said to one of the Kurds. "Put him on the truck and go home." He turned to Amiri and Yasarian. "You two help carry the body . . ." He took a deep breath and sighed. "Handle him carefully," he said. "With respect. This is a *man,* do you understand?"

He turned and walked quickly to the jeep, ignoring the frightened villagers who peered out at them from their doorways. Dariush joined him. "I'm sorry about the tires," he said. "There's no way we can carry on in this jeep."

"Yes." Khorasad kicked the deflated tire. "One spare wheel's no good . . ." He looked around. "We've got to find other transport."

"The truck?"

"No!"

"There's nothing else here, General . . ."

Khorasad turned and took the map from the jeep, spread it out on the hood and moved his finger to the black spot that marked their position. "We have about two hundred and fifty kilometers to cover," he said grimly.

They were silent a few seconds, then Dariush exclaimed. "The gendarmes' transmitter!"

The general stared at him, then a smile spread over his face. "Yes, you're right. It's possible."

Soon afterward they said their farewell to the two young nephews. Hasan's body now lay under a wool blanket in the back of the truck. Khorasad said little. He had no more promises to make, and the youths seemed to understand. They climbed into the cab silently and drove away. Khorasad watched the truck until it disappeared around the bend in the road. He was silent for a moment, then said, "Now it's up to us."

Janet came and stood beside him. "I'm sorry," she said.

He turned to face her. "We went through a lot together." Then his face stiffened. *We must carry on with Hasan or without him,* he thought. He looked down the street and saw a few villagers, mostly women and children, looking on in silence from windows and doorways. He turned back to Janet. "Come on," he said with a grim smile. "Let's go."

They joined Dariush, Amiri and Yasarian who stood by the steps of the blockhouse. Dariush had gathered up the weapons of the dead gendarmes and dragged the bodies to a nearby sewage culvert. Khorasad noticed the shoulder of one of the corpses protruding above the water.

"Hide the weapons," he said. "Then get the jeep off the roadblock and take it around the back of the station . . ." He looked at Amiri and Yasarian. Amiri's cheeks were deathly white and he ground his teeth nervously, a movement accentuated by his prominent Adam's apple. The wound on Yasarian's big nose had healed over to a tiny brown scab. "Help Dariush," he ordered.

"All right . . ." Yasarian glanced quickly at Janet, then pointed at Doctor Amiri. "He doesn't feel well," he said cautiously. "Let him be."

"He must help like everyone else," replied Khorasad.

Yasarian sighed and bent down over the heap of submachine

guns and magazines. "You too," said Khorasad, turning to Amiri, "Help him!" The little old man stared at him with eyes full of terror. "I . . . I . . ." he stammered.

"Help him!" shouted Khorasad, the veins knotting on his thick neck. He seized the old man by the lapels of his coat and shook him violently.

"That's enough." Janet laid her hand on Khorasad's shoulder.

Khorasad stared at her, then released his hold of Amiri, who sank to the ground and crouched there, sobbing. He turned away and walked into the gendarmerie station, kicked open the door of the commandant's office and went over to the small Motorola transmitter that stood in the corner of the room.

# 9

"Ten more minutes!" shouted the dispatcher as he stood by the open door bracing himself against the icy blast of wind. The men who were about to jump stood facing him, looking bulky and grotesque in heavy camouflage suits and boots, with their chutes hanging mid-chest and big sacks of equipment strapped to their legs. The chute-release cords were connected to a cable which ran parallel to the network of tubes, wires and hydraulic gear that framed the whole interior of the fuselage like the ribs of a skeleton.

Arik stood first in the line of jumpers. He stared through the open door at the leaden sky. Gaps in the cloud bank revealed the menacing profile of the Kurdish mountains. He shuddered slightly and bit his lips. Lucky he was wearing a mask, he thought; he didn't like for the others to see his dread. He looked apprehensively at the rosy cheeks of the dispatcher, then turned and glanced at Leonard. The American winked at him and Arik hurriedly turned back to the open door. He knew the drop zone well, but the tall, sheer mountains reared up at him disquietingly. Some peaks jutted from the clouds like islands in a white sea of wool.

He shifted his weight from one leg to the other and cleared his throat. "How much longer?" he shouted, but the dispatcher did not hear him. He tried again, his voice was drowned again. The plane juddered and the dispatcher adjusted his grip on the big handle beside the door. Their eyes met and the man made a questioning gesture with his gloved hand. Arik stretched out his left arm, bent his elbow and pointed to his watch. The dispatcher nodded to show he understood and held up five fingers. Arik saw his lips move: "Five minutes!" He nodded and looked around again. The others had seen the signal. They tensed and began slowly shuffling forward. Arik's eyes watered in the bitterly cold stream of air.

The private conversation with Danny back in Tatvan had shaken him. Danny's face had been grim, his jaws clenched. "There isn't much time," he had said earnestly. "I have some final instructions for you."

"I thought everything was settled."

"Wrong." At that moment the propellers begun to rotate and Danny had had to raise his voice to keep up with the swelling roar.

"If the evacuation doesn't work out you're to kill Yasarian and Amiri!" he said brusquely.

*"What?"*

Danny frowned and looked at him impatiently. "They musn't remain there alive, understand? There's no time for explanations. Get them out or kill them. That's an order."

The big bell above the door rang. He looked up. Two minutes, the dispatcher signaled. Arik stepped forward and stood in the doorway, taking a firm grip on both sides of the frame. He hunched his body forward, his head just behind the line of the door, his weight poised on the balls of his feet, tensing himself against the

126

buffeting of the wind. *"Kill them!"* The words floated back into his mind.

"Go!" he heard the dispatcher shout, and as he had done hundreds of times before he leaped out of the plane. Now he was spiraling in the cold air and the sound of the engines grew fainter. He felt a sharp tug and, looking up, he saw between the straps the canopy of the big American chute as it opened and billowed out. He shivered and fell quickly in a silence broken only by the soft rustling of his harness. When he came out of the cloud he put his legs together, then released the heavy sack strapped to his thigh. It dropped, unraveling its six-meter cable. He held his breath and braced himself to land, praying that the pilots up there in the big Hercules had gotten their calculations right. Contact with the ground came in a painful shock. He rolled over on the hard earth and hurried to release the straps of the chute.

The landing zone was in the center of a broad valley, a flat expanse of brown-gray earth dotted with sparse green bushes. The cloud ceiling was low and visibility down to about two hundred yards. He heard a rustle and a sharp thud as one of the others dropped beside him. Within seconds the whole team had landed and were busy detaching their chutes and gathering up the sacks of equipment.

Arik opened the fastenings of his sack and took out a shortened M-16 carbine, a back pack and a small walkie-talkie set wrapped in canvas and padded with rubber. He removed the cover of the set, pulled out the telescopic antenna, switched on and tapped out the prearranged call sign, the red control light flashing in time to the Morse: *dash dash dot.* He paused, looked around and silently counted the other members of the party, then tapped out another combination: *dash dot dash dot dot.* Arik nodded with satisfaction. "Quick," he shouted, "move the equipment two hundred meters left! George is coming around again!"

They quickly shuttled their own equipment as commanded, leaving the deflated chutes where they lay. The four engines of the

Hercules grew louder, invisibly, in the low clouds. The plane passed, and from the whiteness dropped a large olive-green container swaying under two chutes. As the container landed Yosi and Walter ran toward it. Arik picked up the transmitter and tapped out the signal: *dash dash dot.*

"Everything all right?" Leonard, kneeling beside him, rolled back his snow mask and stared at the control light as the reply flashed from the Hercules: *dash dash dot.* Arik pointed to the sky where the sound of the engines was fading. "We're on our own now . . ."

"Yup," grimaced Leonard, a bright gleam in his honey-colored eyes. He put on his ammunition belt, hoisted a sack of equipment on his back and picked up an Uzi submachine gun fitted with a silencer. He took a deep breath and then shivered. "It's cold," he said.

"Yes, that's the way it is around here."

"We in the right place?"

Arik stared into the mist. "I think so . . . who can tell in this slop?" He opened the breast pocket of his flying suit and pulled out a small altimeter. Thirty-two hundred feet. "Yeah, this is the place all right. Welcome to the Nidawad valley. And thank you, George and Jack." Arik made a feint to the heavens.

"Sure?" Leonard untied the knot of the kerchief around his neck and spread it out on the cold ground. Arik ran his finger over the map printed on the cloth. "There," he said, pointing. "That's where we are. On a proper map I could show you the exact spot."

Leonard looked around suspiciously, straining his eyes in an effort to pierce the mist and the cloud cover. "I wish there was some landmark."

"No problem," said Arik. "Come on, let's get the boys together and make a start."

"What about the chutes?"

"Nobody's going to find them here. The grazing season doesn't start for another month, and by then . . ."

"Okay. Let's go!"

They picked up their gear and hurried across to their comrades, who were fitting themselves out with equipment from the open container. Arik took an FN pistol in a black leather holster, a small Motorola transmitter-receiver, a compass and a sack of grenades. The distribution had been worked out beforehand, and within a few minutes they were ready to move.

Arik inspected the team. "Everything all right?" he asked. "Everyone ready?"

Each man raised his thumb in turn or nodded. Arik looked around, opened the compass, turned it and chose a bearing. "Let's go," he said. "If I'm not mistaken, about two thousand meters from here we should find a low stone wall and a deserted sheep pen." He smiled and his spirits rose. All traces of his pre-fall nervousness had vanished. "Okay. Quick march!" Arik shouldered his rifle and set off at a quick pace into the mist.

Arik remembered the valley as if he had been there only yesterday. A high plateau surrounded on three sides by mountains and open to the north; the solid bedrock at the base of the valley was overlaid by loose soil and fragments of stone, washed down from the heights over the centuries. In the spring it sprouted lush grazing vegetation that stayed green even over the summer. Now the ground was frozen, and under bushes and at the base of large rocks spread snowdrifts and huge sheets of ice that shone like glass panels. At this season there was not a single sign of life in the valley: no sheep dung, no hoofprints, no vegetation.

Arik walked quickly, sure of his sense of direction. The mist was lighter now, and at a range of two hundred yards he saw the stone wall. He smiled with satisfaction and quickened his pace. The cold and wind were intense but the layers of clothing insulated all but the patch around his eyes and his ears. As he walked he took from his side pack a tube of protective oil and smeared it on the exposed places. "The cold in these mountains is your worst enemy," Khorasad had taught him. He smiled. Here in this valley, where he now marched at the head of a combat squad, he had once trailed in Khorasad's footsteps on an expedition to contact a group of Kurdish leaders who had crossed the border from Iraq. He remembered the rendezvous beside the stone wall, their solemn picnic on the soft spring grass, of sheep's cheese and fresh bread, washed down with tea sweet as honey.

The mist broke here and there and through gaps he saw the rocky slopes of a nearby hill. They walked on in a silence broken only by the sound of ice cracking under the ridged soles of their boots and the rolling of displaced stones.

Arik led his men to the deserted sheep pen, a ramshackle stone structure with a clay-and-straw roof supported by big old beams. There were no windows, only a wide doorway. Farmers from the nearby valleys who came up every autumn to collect the sheep droppings for manure had left the earth floor dry and clean except for a few rusty tins, a broken knife and an empty wooden box.

The men unfastened their loads and stacked equipment against the wall, keeping only their personal weapons slung from their shoulders. Arik had Yosi and Shraga take up watch by the door, then he took the transmitter from its case and repeated the broadcast procedure, confirming the message that had reported their initial landing.

Thomas Barrett, the medic, moved briskly among the men. Like the others the freckled, middle-aged American had taken off his snow mask, exposing a head of reddish, silver-streaked hair. He checked the pulse and temperature of each man in turn, peered into their eyes with his small flashlight and noted his findings in a little black book. "Okay, number 1," he said to Arik as he bent over him. "Let's see how your chemistry's working." Arik submitted patiently. Glenn Dyer joined them, his black bearded face glistening under a film of protective cream. "I've come to check your radio, boss," he said, pulling the little instrument with the finger antenna from Arik's belt. He flipped the switches on and off, then turned to Mackintosh who was doing a similar job with Leonard's equipment. "Hey, Mac, the chief's okay too!"

When Barrett had finished he reported to Arik: "All systems go on everyone," he said. "They're as healthy as horses."

But then the red-haired American scratched his chin. "One thing I don't understand," he said. "Maybe you can explain it, boss. We've been talking among ourselves and we just can't quite figure out why those three guys are so damn important."

Arik shrugged. "They're agents," he said.

"Do we owe them anything? Is their survival that necessary?"

Arik shook his head. "I don't think that's the problem . . ."

Danny's last order rang in his ears.

Barrett still had a questioning look on his face when Leonard and Walter came over carrying little cups of steaming soup. A pungent aroma filled the hut. Arik took a cautious sip. "Hey, this is good," he told Leonard. "My compliments to the chef!"

The tall, long-haired American chuckled. "Thank the space program, pal. You should visit NASA some time, they can feed you a whole meal out of tubes. This soup contains the caloric value of a steak-and-potatoes dinner."

Arik took another sip. Pointing to Barrett he said, "Maybe *you* can tell us, Leonard. What do you think's so important about those guys we've come to rescue?"

"Hey man, I thought Khorasad was *your* friend . . ."

"Friend's not exactly what I'd call him. More like . . . teacher. He taught me some things about survival."

"So they're going to bring him to the States to teach Outward Bound classes," cracked Leonard.

"It's not Khorasad I'm talking about," broke in Arik. "It's those two old professors. What can an Iranian scientist know anyway?"

"They're agents," said Leonard, and even in the gloom of the sheep pen they could see the mischievous twinkle in his amber eyes. Barrett gave him a dig in the side. "Besides that, we have, or our governments have, certain common interests, if that's the right expression." Leonard chuckled and took a mouthful of soup.

131

He was proving he knew more background about this operation than Arik did, and Arik resented it. Not so much that Leonard knew, but that Danny had not told *him*. The old wounds had not died—he was still not entirely trusted by the higher-ups.

"Well, go on Leonard, tell us."

"Redwood and Nero are atomic scientists."

Arik snorted. "There are atomic scientists in Bangladesh and Uganda, too. All over. That isn't the reason."

Leonard looked at him now, plainly. "That *is* the reason. Or part of it. That's all I know."

"Maybe we should have gotten an answer out of Henry or your friend Danny, back there in Ankara," sighed Barrett.

"I tried," replied Arik simply, "in Tatvan . . ."

"Anything?"

"Nope."

"We'll just have to be patient," said Barrett, putting down his soup cup and smoothing down his red hair. He smiled broadly. "When we meet the three musketeers we'll find out the truth, I bet."

"I hope so," said Arik. *Kill them . . .* he could not get Danny's final instruction out of his mind.

"Anyway, I can help them out if they're reluctant," Barrett added mischievously.

"Yeah?"

Barrett pointed to his medical kit. "Voromthalin," he said. "I've got some 300 cc's of it right in here."

"What's that?"

"It's a truth drug. Something like pentathol, boss. One intravenous or intramuscular shot and you pour out everything you've got."

Arik was impressed. "You carry that stuff around with you?"

"Technical equipment," said Leonard. "All our paramedics are issued it. It can be useful . . ."

"Yes . . ." Arik nodded and looked thoughtfully at his tall deputy. Now Mackintosh's intellectual face was wavering above them: "Everything okay from my angle," he said. "All the equipment's in working order."

"Fine!" Arik glanced at his watch. "Two hours till dark," he said. He opened his map case, picked the map he wanted and spread it out in the beam of a powerful flashlight held by Mackintosh. "This is where we are," said Arik, pointing. He ran his finger along the line of a road. "I'll go down there as planned, and take Yosi and Walter with me. I should make it about an hour after dark. If everything's all right we'll call you and we can go on from there."

"It's foggier than hell out there," said Leonard anxiously. "Are you sure you can find your way?"

Arik smiled. "Want to come hold my hand?"

They left the sheep pen and turned down a narrow path beaten out over thousands of years by the feet of shepherds and their flocks. The air was bitterly cold: minus ten degrees Celsius on Walter Gabriel's wrist gauge. The wind had died, but a thin mist drifted slowly from south to north in thick patches and it was impossible to see more than a hundred yards ahead. Arik guided his little party carefully, studying the path ahead and checking at intervals with the compass and map. His snow mask and hood concealed small earpieces connected by a long coil to the radio set strapped to his waist. He carried a rifle fitted with telescopic sights and silencer and moved briskly under a heavy load of equipment —map case, hand grenades, a backpack crammed with rations, flashlight, clothing, Iranian and U.S. currency, a first-aid kit complete with splints, tourniquets, and morphine syringe. Walter and Yosi followed about five paces behind with even heavier loads; Yosi carried a large aerosol can, which he used to spray every large rock, bush or pile of stones they passed: the high-concentration splurge of phosphorescent red paint would mark the route for their comrades to follow.

They walked in silence toward the tiny shepherds' village, which was shown on the map as a single building but in fact

133

comprised six stone cottages and a few sheep pens. The settlement was surrounded by a low wall of loose rock. Arik remembered how the place looked in spring, a tiny picture-postcard enclave perched on the edge of the canyon. It was the canyon that worried him most—two hundred feet of sheer cliff and at the base, in a narrow valley shown on the map as a crescent, a shallow but fast-flowing river, surging down a zigzag course of whirlpools and cataracts and throwing up high plumes of foam against rock walls. When he first saw the valley he had been astonished by its beauty, but now, in the mist and with the rapid approach of evening, it was hard even to follow the winding shepherds' path. At intervals he stopped and checked their altitude and direction. He did not speak to his two comrades, nor communicate with the rest of the team back in the pen.

As darkness fell they slowed their pace, and huddled closer together. The little reflectors Walter Gabriel handed out to hang on their shoulders glinted in the half light like cats' eyes.

In the distance now came the barking of dogs. Arik stopped. "If I'm not mistaken," he said in a low voice, "we have another two hundred and fifty meters to cover."

"I hope you're not mistaken," murmured Walter, his eyes glimmering under the snow mask.

"Don't worry," said Yosi, "we're doing fine."

"Be careful not to turn right," Arik warned. "There's a deep canyon. When you fall down it, there's no way up." He broke off, cocking his ears to the sound of the dogs barking in the village. He strained his eyes in an effort to pierce the foggy darkness, but could see nothing. He checked the altitude again. "Okay, let's go. If anyone asks questions, Yosi'll do the the talking."

"I thought you spoke the lingo," said Walter.

"Not enough for this. Come on, let's move it."

Again Arik led the way, slightly stooped, his rifle pointed forward on the left of the track. Suddenly he saw big dark shapes ahead of him and something that looked like a light source. He knelt down; Walter and Yosi did likewise. Suddenly a pack of huge dogs loomed up out of the mist, barking loudly. They were surrounded. Teeth snapped as the dogs bayed at them from all sides. Some wore heavy metal collars fitted with rusty spikes that hung loosely from their necks. "What the hell's going on here?" exclaimed Walter.

"Shepherds' dogs," replied Yosi. "Don't let them get too close, they're killers!" He squirted his aerosol can toward the dogs and the beasts retreated a few yards where they scurried about, barking incessantly.

"Christ!" murmured Walter. "If one of those monsters attacks . . ."

"Those collars are for protection against wolves," said Yosi.

"They've got wolves here too?"

Suddenly they heard voices, first a soft murmur and whispers, then a man's deep voice. "Who's there?"

Arik stiffened. "Jalal?"

"Who the hell's that?"

"A friend," Arik replied, taking off his snow mask. He felt his face burning in the intense cold.

"Who are you?"

*"Sarabaste!"* shouted Yosi. "Remember our Revolution?"

"What?"

"Remember the weapons training in Sanandaj?" Yosi repeated the questions Arik had told him to ask.

"My God!"

"Jalal!" cried Arik. He coughed and burst into loud laughter. "Call off those goddam monsters of yours!"

"Allah be blessed!" The barking grew louder and out of the darkness, pushing through the pack of excited dogs, appeared a tall figure in a gray-and-white speckled kaffiyeh and a thick leather tunic. A coal-black Stalin moustache highlighted a clear, shining expression. He approached briskly, the dogs at his heels.

"I don't believe my eyes!" he cried. He embraced Arik powerfully, kissing his cheeks and hugging him repeatedly. "A sign from

135

heaven!" Then he turned to Yosi and Walter. "Whoever you may be," he said, "God be with you!"

Yosi raised the flap of his snow mask and the man roared with laughter. "You here too, you son of a bitch! I don't believe it!"

Arik hugged the man, who towered a clear six inches over him. "Come on," he said, "it's cold out here and we've got a lot to talk about. You'll be amazed when you hear why we've come."

"*Amazed?* How do you think I feel right now? Here on this godforsaken mountain, at this time of year, at this hour . . . I still can't believe it!"

"Call off your dogs!" pleaded Walter.

The giant looked at him in surprise. "An American?" he asked in English.

"Yes, call off those goddam animals!"

"I thought you deserted us in seventy-five."

"You speak English?"

"English, Arabic, Russian . . ." Jalal replied. "But what are we doing standing out here in the cold?"

They followed him across a pasture, then over a stone wall and soon entered a warm, low-ceilinged cottage. A woman, a girl and a few young children huddled around a square iron stove in the light of an oil lamp. Most were wrapped in blankets. The fat woman and the girl stood up, a mixture of surprise and delight on their faces. The woman spoke a few words in rapid Kurdish while the girl came over and shook the outstretched hands of Arik and Yosi. Then she turned to Walter.

"Welcome," she said in English with a slight American accent. "My name is Farha."

"Walter took the pack from his shoulder, staring at her in surprise. "You speak American?"

"Yes."

"But you're a Kurdish woman?"

"Your people taught me." She grimaced. "C.I.A. I was trained as a radio operator."

"Well, I'll be . . ."

136

Jalal helped them to pile their equipment in a corner of the room. By the time they had taken off their combat blouses and joined the others around the stove, the fat woman had already prepared tea. From the kitchen next door came smells of baking bread. Arik and Yosi were deep in conversation with Jalal while Walter talked with Farha. The girl wrapped herself again in her colored blanket and warmed herself by the stove. The children gathered around, staring alternately at her and at the big, balding American.

"I thought you women wore veils," he said, fishing for conversation.

She laughed. "What kind of a question is that?"

"Yes," he agreed, "I guess that was dumb thing to say." He smiled. "But the way I see it, any Middle Eastern woman living in a village as prim . . ." He broke off but she finished the sentence for him:

"As primitive as this? We're not like that," she added.

"But in Iran . . ."

She interrupted him emphatically. "We are Kurds, sir! Kurdish women don't wear veils, they work with the men in the field, sometimes they fight alongside them . . ."

"That Ayatollah of yours, I hear he's demanding you people return to the bosom of Islam . . ."

"No!" She shook her head, her long loose hair sweeping across her face. "That old man can kiss my ass," she said softly. "And anyway, we Kurds aren't Shiites, we're Sunnis."

A crumpled cigarette dangled from the corner of Arik's mouth as he, Yosi and Jalal consulted and Jalal rolled cigarettes between his fingers.

The woman, who had been bustling on the other side of the room, called them to the table; it was loaded with food—freshly baked bread, salted cheese and strips of fried meat, pots of sweet tea. Afterward they sat smoking thoughtfully in silence for a few minutes while Jalal, his wife and the girl helped the sleepy children to find their way to the dark bedrooms. When the Kurdish giant returned and sat down, his bare feet folded under his body, Arik picked up the little radio set.

"Wolf to Fox . . ." he said. He paused for a second, then repeated, "Wolf to Fox . . ."

"Fox here." Leonard's voice sounded bright and alert. "Receiving you loud and clear."

"Wolf here . . . in the den . . . are you ready to join us?"

"Wolf from Fox . . . is the trail marked?"

Arik looked at Yosi who nodded. "Fox from Wolf, affirmative."

"Wolf from Fox. Message understood. Reporting to Neptune and moving out. Over and out."

Arik switched off the radio set and turned to Jalal. "Well, my friend," he said, "now that's set. What's new around here?"

"We're rearing sheep . . . as always. What else? That's all that's left, working and hoping . . ."

"Maybe now?"

"Yes," Jalal shrugged. "Maybe, if they give us a chance . . ."

"Do you expect that?"

"No." Now the Kurd's face looked solemn and dejected. He glanced at his daughter who stood in the doorway of the bedroom, wrapped in her blanket, tense and listening to every word. "No," he said. "I heard on the radio that the Shiites are vowing revenge. The Ayatollah talks about eradicating the sins of the Shah . . . the goddam Peacock Throne . . ." Jalal spat on the floor, took a deep breath and pulled out his old tobacco tin from the pocket of his black breeches. As he rolled himself a cigarette he added, "The Ayatollah will never allow us to realize the ancient dream . . ."

"We're going to try!" Farha interrupted, her young eyes flashing.

Jalal looked at his daughter with a mixture of pride and pity. He smiled as he stuck the cigarette between his lips and lit it. "Yes," he said, "we will try . . ."

"I'm sorry I can't help," said Arik, frowning. "Really sorry."

"You could stay with us . . ." Jalal glanced at the corner where the men's equipment was stacked. "We can always find a use for weapons like those . . ." He smiled at Arik, leaned forward and slapped his shoulder. "We had some good times together . . . the Mullah, you, the general . . ."

"He's an Iranian!" Farha objected. "An Iranian!"

Jalal smiled at her. "That's right, an Iranian of the Peacock Throne, the Golden Lion and the Sun. Yes, but by God, my daughter, just like this Israeli, Khorasad bears a Kurdish heart!"

# 10

A few hundred yards south of the village, Khorasad and Dariush sat behind a big gray rock almost overhanging the road. Behind them rose a small hill. They had left Janet, Yasarian and Amiri in the gendarmerie station, and were watching the roadblock they themselves had improvised with the serrated strip from the gendarmes' roadblock. They hunched together, touching shoulders. Dark circles ringed Khorasad's eyes. Dariush shivered and scratched his stubbly chin. The chill was showing its first effects. "Do you think they'll come?" he asked.

The general nodded.

"But only a few?"

Khorasad shrugged. "It's a small garrison, a communications squad. Three, maybe four . . ."

"And they fell for it! Amazing. What did they say exactly?"

"That they were on their way . . ." The shadow of a smile flickered over his weary face. "Everybody wants a slice of the action. It isn't every day a gendarmerie sergeant is invited to arrest a general . . ."

"A Savak general, too," murmured Dariush.

"Yes . . ." Khorasad stiffened. "They nearly jumped for joy when I told them the . . . the great criminal was in custody here."

"Do you think they've told Teheran?"

"I hope not. It's a long ways anyhow. And probably they want the glory to themselves."

Dariush looked up at the low clouds. "Lucky for us the weather's so rotten. They might have come in a chopper."

"That's right," said Khorasad drily.

They watched the narrow road in silence, straining for the rumble of an engine. But everything was quiet. Khorasad leaned back and closed his smarting eyes. Dariush would stay awake. He began to doze, but was the first to hear the vehicle. He sat up with a start and picked up the submachine gun in his lap. "That's it!" he said. "They're coming!"

Dariush listened intently for a moment, then smiled, relieved. "Yes, a car. It's them all right."

"Even if it's a civilian car we'll stop it and commandeer it," said the general. He cocked his Uzi and leaned against the rock. "For God's sake aim at the car, not at the wheels!"

"I'll try." Dariush clutched his submachine gun tightly. The loaded pistol lay at this side.

The gendarmerie Waggoneer came hurtling around a bend in the road, swerving erratically from side to side, headlights blazing and the radio antenna waving crazily from the roof. Behind the wheel sat an elderly lieutenant, beside him a sergeant armed with a submachine gun and in the back a young gendarme in a long tunic, with a German G-3 assault rifle. It was the young soldier who was the first to get down and inspect the roadblock. To Khorasad's relief, the sergeant and the lieutenant also climbed out. "What the hell's this?" the lieutenant demanded in a loud voice.

"It belongs to the local gendarmerie," said the sergeant, kicking it with his foot. "I recognize the color."

The lieutenant looked around suspiciously and reached for his revolver.

"Don't move!" shouted Khorasad. "Drop your weapons!"

The three gendarmes jumped like startled rabbits. The youngest dropped his rifle and slowly raised his hands above his head. The sergeant stood rooted to the spot, while the officer fumbled with the buckle of his holster.

"Drop your weapons!" shouted Khorasad.

Dariush leaped out from behind the rock, machine gun in his right hand and pistol in the left. As he ran toward the vehicle the lieutenant managed to draw and fire one poorly aimed shot. Dariush returned fire instinctively. The officer howled with pain as the bullet ripped through his shoulder. Khorasad jumped down into the road and picked up the gendarmes' weapons. "Good work!" he shouted to Dariush. "Quick, get the car!"

"Khorasad!" exclaimed the lieutenant. A big red stain was spreading on his coat and blood dripped from his sleeve. "My God! Khorasad!"

The general observed the man's pain-wracked face. "Yes," he said. "Take a good look. It's Khorasad!"

"You'll pay dearly for this!"

Khorasad stared at him in amazement. "What did you say?"

"You'll pay dearly!"

"Again?"

"You, Khorasad . . ." the lieutenant panted wildly. "They'll hang you!" He struggled for breath. "The Revolution will hang you!"

"Shut up!"

"You and your kind, your time is up!" The officer spat on Khorasad with all his strength. "I'll see you hang, Khorasad! You and all the Savak murderers! To hell with you all!" The man fought to master his pain, his face deathly pale. "The others will be here soon, you don't stand a chance!"

"What did you say?" Khorasad grabbed the man by the throat. "Say that again!" The lieutenant choked and retched loudly. "What was that you said?" shouted Khorasad. He raised the submachine gun that he held in his free hand and rammed the steel butt into the officer's face, smashing his teeth and jaw. The officer tottered and fell, narrowly missing the spikes of the road-block. Dariush thrust the muzzle of his pistol into the stomach of the trembling sergeant and trained his Uzi on the young soldier, who stood motionless, watching. "Quick!" he said. "Talk or I'll spill your guts! Who's coming here?"

"Don't shoot!" the sergeant pleaded. "For God's sake don't shoot . . ."

"Talk!"

The sergeant swallowed a gob of his own spittle, glanced at his commander on the road, then looked back at Dariush. "The Revolutionary Committee," he said. "We reported to Kerman-shah. The Revolutionary Committee's coming . . . they've an-nounced they're going to try Kh . . . the general and sentence him . . . Oh God, don't shoot! I've got nine children!" he pleaded. "For God's sake don't shoot . . ."

"General!" shouted Dariush. "We've got to get out of here fast!"

Khorasad stared savagely at the wounded officer. "Give me one good reason why I shouldn't kill you!" he yelled. "Just one good reason!" he yelled. The man did not answer. Khorasad stood there as if ready to fire, then suddenly seemed to change his mind and instead ran to the car.

"Get out of here!" Dariush said to the gendarme sergeant. "Quickly! You're lucky to be alive!"

The sergeant glanced hesitantly at his wounded commander and then looked straight at Dariush, moving his head slightly, questioningly. Dariush nodded brusquely and the sergeant went over to the stricken officer and lifted his bleeding head from the road. "Go and help him!" Dariush shouted to the petrified young gendarme, then backed to the car.

Khorasad and Dariush slammed shut the car doors, and Khorasad started up the engine. "Fuel tank's full," he said hoarsely. He revved the engine and before releasing the clutch and hand brake looked back at the three men beside the roadblock. "We're going soft," he said to Dariush bitterly. "I swear we're going soft!" He hunched grimly over the wheel and drove back to the village.

He leaned on the horn as they passed outlying houses to disperse the villagers who now thronged the street, men and women in black robes and dark shawls. The civilians stood back and watched them pass in silence. "Stupid Iranian idiots," groaned Khorasad, "standing around like sheep."

*Not true,* thought Dariush. He did not speak as he looked out at the cottages and the low mud walls, at the bearded men and veiled women. A godforsaken race? He shuddered. Suddenly the violence and slaughter of the last few days came flooding back into his mind. He remembered the sergeant asleep on the bench in the command post at Kermanshah, the gendarme at the gate of the radio station, the crowd trying to escape from the speeding Waggoneer. He glanced at Khorasad, who looked more irritable than he had ever known him. "There's nothing we can do!" he said.

"What?" Khorasad turned his bloodshot eyes towards him.

"These people, General, this race . . . Iran . . ." He leaned back and stared at the roof.

Khorasad pulled up a few yards short of the gendarmerie station. Immediately Janet was hopping down the steps, closely followed by Doctor Amiri, who looked sick and confused. Yasarian stood at the top of the steps, awkwardly holding a submachine gun. Khorasad breathed hard and looked at Dariush. "I think you're sick," he said. "You've got a chill and there's that cut above your eye . . . but we'll be okay, don't worry . . ." He paused to swallow a gob of spit, licked his dry lips and went on, "But for God's sake, kid, you mustn't weaken! Look at this bunch of morons we're stuck with. You musn't weaken, do you understand?"

"Iran," mumbled Dariush. "General, what's happening to Iran?"

Khorasad thumped the wheel angrily with his fist. "You heard what that lieutenant said. The bastards are after our blood, they're out to hang us . . ." He shook his head grimly. "That guy was right, our time's up and there's nothing left for us here. Look

144

at these people, just look at them! Standing there watching us like a bunch of stupid sheep, hoping to see us die!" He opened the door and stepped down into the road. "Get out of here!" he yelled at the lingerers. "Go and hide in your stinking hovels, all of you!"

"Can we come aboard?" asked Janet.

Her question defused his anger. He turned to face her. "Yes," he said, "but first we've got to get the weapons and fuel cans loaded. Quickly now!" Janet and Yasarian joined Dariush who was already unloading equipment from the crippled Russian jeep. "What about you, Amiri?" he asked scornfully.

"I . . . I can't, General, really . . . blood pressure . . . I'm tired, please . . ."

Khorasad looked at him stonily, then pointed to the car. "All right, get in . . ." Amiri mumbled unintelligibly and shuffled toward the car. Khorasad crossed the street and approached one of the cottages. In the doorway stood a tall old man wearing the black turban of a mullah. He stood there motionless, his face pale and his toothless mouth gaping. One of his dim gray eyes was inflamed with trachoma.

"I'm Khorasad!" said the general.

The man nodded.

"They'll be here soon . . . people from Kermanshah and other places. Tell them to go home. Khorasad is not going to be caught! I'll fight. You saw yourself what happened this morning . . ."

The man answered softly: "It was on the radio . . . Ayatollah Ruhollah has ordered your arrest . . . the Ayatollah." The old man's voice shook with emotion, a single tear fell from his inflamed eye and ran down his wrinkled cheek. "The Ayatollah . . ."

"You're all mad!" exclaimed Khorasad. He turned and headed for the car. Janet, Dariush and Yasarian came up laden with weapons and gasoline cans. "What's that for?" he asked Yasarian, pointing to the submachine gun on his shoulder.

"I know how to use it!" the scientist replied grimly.

"Oh you do?" teased Khorasad. He blocked Yasarian's path

145

and looked at him scornfully, hands on his hips. "Yesterday you didn't seem like such a man."

"I know how to use it. I've been trained . . ." The scientist paused. "I'll prove it to you."

*"Prove it?"* Khorasad let out a short, venomous laugh. "You could have proved it yesterday, in the hotel . . . I saw you, cowering on the floor!"

The two men stood motionless for a few seconds, staring at each other. Finally Yasarian dropped his eyes, shrugged and retreated to the Waggoneer. "Dirty Savak bastard," he whispered to himself, his fists clenched around the submachine gun. *There'll be other opportunities,* he thought.

"What was that all about?" asked Janet.

"Nothing," said Khorasad. "A man's argument."

She smiled and shook her head. The bruise on her face had turned a grayish blue and her lips were still swollen but she seemed less fearful than the others. *Strange,* he thought, *this big-breasted American who got beaten up and gang-banged is so cool.*

"I do not understand women," Khorasad muttered to himself.

They drove out of the village. Khorasad glanced in the mirror and for a moment his eyes met the woman's, then he studied the heavy face of Yasarian. The fact that the scientist was armed made him uneasy, and he decided to deal with it at the next stop. He drove the stolen vehicle at a steady speed. It was too loaded with the equipment transferred from the Russian jeep to go faster. The jeep had been left burning outside the gendarmerie station. The Waggoneer's radio set was working, but so far they had heard nothing but a continuous crackle of static. Dariush sat in gloomy silence, wrapped up in himself and coughing at intervals—a deep, throaty cough. His scarred face was deathly white under patches of iodine Janet had smeared on the cuts.

Before the next village, Khorasad consulted the map, then turned off down a dirt track that bypassed the settlement. From now on he was determined to avoid inhabited places. He knew he had acted carelessly in the last village and he hoped that the precious hours wasted there would not prove fatal. He flipped the switches of the radio receiver, and finding no news station, he tuned to the Voice of America. A low-keyed American voice faded in and out. It was a lecture on the history of jazz, illustrated with examples. "Fools . . ." murmured Khorasad. He looked into the mirror and spoke to Janet.

"This music should make you feel at home."

"I only wish I *was* at home!"

"Why, have you got something against Iran?" asked Khorasad facetiously.

She shrugged. "What do you think?"

"You're a good-looking woman is what I think." She blushed, and they both lapsed into silence. He smiled as he remembered the last woman he'd had, a high-class call girl from Beirut who'd somehow found her way to the Officers Club in Tabriz. He thought of the woman's slim body and dyed hair, firm breasts and long legs. He tried to recall the color of her eyes—green or blue? He shivered. "How long ago?" he murmured. "Shit! It was weeks and weeks!"

"What's up?" His aide sat up with a start and glanced anxiously at the front and rear windows.

"Nothing . . . just a question . . . do you remember that call girl from Beirut?" he asked in Farsi.

Dariush stared at him blankly for a moment, then the little eyes lit up with a faint gleam of interest.

"By God, General!" He smiled weakly, for the first time in hours, and scratched his iodine-painted eyebrow.

"Remember her?"

"The stripper?"

"Yes, yes! How long ago was that?"

"General!"

Khorasad roared with laughter. "Hell, kid, I could find a use for her!"

*"Here?"*

"Right here and right now!"

Dariush laughed and then broke into a fresh spate of coughing. "Yes," he said finally. "About two months ago . . ."

"Less than that, surely."

"Maybe . . ."

"She was good," said Khorasad. "She could move like a fish."

Dariush glanced anxiously in the mirror. Janet's face was impassive. She could not have understood much of what they were saying. He smiled and looked back at Khorasad, relieved at least that his boss had regained his humor.

"It's getting dark," complained Khorasad after two hours of uneventful driving. "We'll have to stop soon . . ."

"Can't we go on?"

"On this road?" Khorasad frowned. "Another five kilometers and we'll be in the hills, and if we can't find a hut or a shelter there we'll have to spend the night in the car." Khorasad looked in the mirror. "Yasarian!" he called. "Are you awake?"

"Yes." The scientist roused himself. "What's the matter?"

"You're on guard tonight."

*"Me?"*

"Yes, goddam it! What do you think that Uzi of yours is for?"

"He isn't capable of guarding!" said Janet, pulling up the hood over her head as if trying to hide herself. "I wouldn't trust that bastard to guard anything!"

In the mirror Khorasad glimpsed her white elbow and her long fingers gripping the fringes of the hood.

"He's going to be on guard," he said.

Yasarian coughed. "Janet . . ." he said, then fell silent. He fingered the black submachine gun which lay on the seat beside him and turned his gaze to the window.

Khorasad decided to stop beside what looked in the headlights like a cavern in the rock face. He was slowly maneuvering the Waggoneer off the narrow road when suddenly Janet touched his shoulder.

148

Leaning across Amiri she said softly, "General, look behind us!"

He looked first in the mirror above his head, then glanced at the side mirror. Down the mountain about five kilometers behind them, he could barely make out the lights of approaching vehicles. He counted two, three pairs of headlights. "Good girl!" he said.

Now Dariush had also seen the lights of the advancing convoy. "Any ideas, General?"

Khorasad looked at the dash. "We need to refuel," he said. "Hurry now, jump to it!" He watched the road behind as the others fumbled with the fuel cans tied to the rear bumper. "Military!" he said. "Hurry, or we'll have a battle on our hands!"

Dariush opened the cap of the fuel tank and poured in a thick stream of gasoline, spilling some of the liquid in his haste. He emptied the metal can and asked, "More?"

Khorasad looked back at the road, saw the lights in the distance. Now he could hear the distant roar of the engines. "Yes," he replied. "One more can. Hurry!"

"What's happening?" asked Yasarian. He stood shivering beside the door of the Waggoneer, Uzi in hand, looking exhausted and dejected. "What the hell's going on now?"

"See those lights behind us?" said Dariush. "They're gaining on us . . . get in the car!"

"I can't . . ."

"*What?*" Khorasad confronted the bulky scientist; in the growing darkness his eyes flashed menacingly. "*What* did you say?"

"I can't go on with all this, maybe I'll stay here . . . they aren't going to hurt me . . . I'm a scientist . . . they need me . . ."

"Cut the crap and get into the car!"

"Yasarian!" shouted Janet. "Get in the car, quick!"

Reluctantly the doctor took his place inside the car. Doors slammed and Khorasad released the clutch and started up. The Waggoneer wheeled round, flinging up sand and small stones in all directions. Within seconds they were speeding along the mountain road. Behind, the convoy followed. As the gradient grew steeper the lights drew steadily nearer. "Small trucks or vans," murmured Khorasad, glancing in the mirror and cursing himself for his carelessness, that morning in the village. *I must be getting tired,* he thought . . .

Dariush sat beside him, silent and gloomy. Behind them Yasarian fiddled nervously with the strap of his submachine gun, every now and then glancing briefly at Janet. He felt desperate and afraid, and ravenously hungry. He wasn't used to deprivation. Now the nausea rose in his throat and mouth; he would have asked Khorasad to stop the car, but he knew he would only be abused for it. He too cursed himself for his weakness. His head banged against the fogged-up window beside him as the Waggoneer lurched violently on the pitted gravel road. His shoulder brushed the smooth head of Doctor Amiri. The old man sat with his eyes closed and his thin dry lips moving in silent prayer. Yasarian looked at him with pity and could not help smiling grimly, in spite of his nausea and despair. He remembered the last time he had sat like this, pressed up against Amiri . . . it was in the El Al plane that had flown them to Israel but then, oh God . . . he felt warm tears flowing down his cheeks . . . there was no Revolution, no Janet . . . He stole another quick glance at her; he thought he saw her blue eyes and he knew he would never embrace her again.

"They're gaining on us," said Janet.

"Shit!" Khorasad shot a glance into the rearview mirror. "A kilometer . . ." he murmured. "One fucking kilometer . . ."

"Maybe we should stop," Dariush suggested.

"There's more than one truck, a lot of men . . . no!"

"How do you know they're after us?" asked Yasarian weakly. "Couldn't they just be civilians?"

"Shut up!" growled Khorasad.

They reached an especially narrow stretch of road. To the right soared a sheer wall of rock and on their left the mountain fell away steeply to the valley below. The rough road shook the Waggoneer and Khorasad was forced to slow down, keeping as close as possible to the wall of rock. For the first time that evening thin patches of mist appeared, hovering like little clouds in the head-light beams. At every turn the lights of the convoy behind swept them. A searchlight on the top of the lead vehicle cut a long swathe through the darkness, apparently trying to keep them exposed. Khorasad switched on the Motorola radio-telephone but the channel was dead. He turned up the volume of the radio receiver which all this time, almost unheard, had been tuned to Voice of America. He heard the theatrical tones of the newscaster reciting the closing headlines—currency problems and the hard European winter.

"We'll have to stop," said Dariush, "hold them up, General."

"No!"

"A few hand grenades . . ."

"No!" Khorasad leaned forward over the wheel. "Soon we'll get to a small bridge," he said. "I know this goddam place, I used to hunt around here. A rotten shitty little bridge. When we've crossed it we'll stop!"

"All right . . ." Dariush coughed and opened his side pack. Groping in the darkness he counted the grooved fragmentation grenades and the round, smooth phosphorus grenades. "How much more do we have to cover?" he asked.

"When we're over the bridge I'll look at the map," replied Khorasad. "When we stop . . ."

"They're closing in!" cried Janet. "They're right behind us!" The beam of the searchlight caught them and the car was flooded with blinding white light. Khorasad shielded his eyes with his left hand and crouched over the wheel. The Waggoneer skidded and the near side grazed the rock wall.

"Be careful!" shrieked Janet. "Jesus, be careful!"

Khorasad cursed loudly, gripping the wheel with all his strength and casting quick anxious glances in the mirror. Suddenly he saw the red sparks of tracer bullets flying up in the road in front and behind. "They know about the bridge," said Dariush.

"They're worried about the fog," replied Khorasad. "Better duck . . ." Another burst of tracers passed close to the speeding Waggoneer. "Duck, be careful!" he shouted.

"If the car's hit, ducking won't do us any good . . ." murmured Dariush. "For God's sake, General, pull up and let's try and handle them!"

Khorasad bit his lips and pressed harder on the gas pedal. The Waggoneer lurched from side to side, at times colliding with the rock face, bouncing and juddering with the sickening crunch of metal and the crash of straining springs. The engine whined. The pursuers kept up. The lines of tracer bullets fired in a steady stream stood out clearly in the pitch darkness. *Lucky the bastards can't shoot straight,* thought Khorasad, shielding his eyes from the glare of the searchlight. *God, if only the situation was reversed . . . I'd give them something to think about!*

"The bridge," shouted Dariush. "The bridge!"

Khorasad saw the narrow bridge, two broad metal strips over a deep gulley, flanked by low railings about fifteen meters long and supported by a construction of wood and steel. He slowed down and stopped just a few feet short of the bridge. "Out of the car!" he shouted, "Janet, Amiri, Yasarian! Grab your gear and run to the other side!" The three obeyed, disappearing in the darkness and thickening mist as they scurried across the bridge. Khorasad looked back; the convoy was advancing rapidly. He bit his lips and then glanced at Dariush who had the machine gun in one hand and the bag of grenades in the other. "This is it . . ." he murmured. He joined Dariush at the side of the road. They both knelt and trained their submachine guns down the roadway. "One full magazine," said Khorasad. "Then we carry on . . ."

"All right . . ."

They waited until the lights of the leading vehicle, a light army truck, swung into view around a bend in the road, at a range of about fifty yards. Suddenly the whole scene—the two men, the Waggoneer and bridge—was lit up in the blinding glare of the searchlight. "Now!" A hail of 9-mm. bullets riddled the lead truck, knocking out the searchlight first, then the windshield of the cab. They heard the squeal of tires and the crash of metal and glass. The truck careened across the road and slid over the edge of the crevice. Screams pierced the night, terminated by a deafening thud and the echoing rumble of falling stones. The other trucks ground to a halt. There was shouting and a few shots rang out. "Quick!" yelled Khorasad. They jumped up and ran to the Waggoneer. Dariush fired off two quick volleys at the stationary vehicles while Khorasad drove to the center of the bridge and switched off. He left the car, drew his pistol and fired into the fuel tank and the reserve cans tied to the bumper. Then he called Dariush. They crossed the bridge together and knelt behind a low rock.

"Is the canyon deep enough to hold them?" asked Dariush.

"It's deep . . ."

"Okay . . ." Dariush handed Khorasad a phosphorus grenade while he himself pulled the pin on a fragmentation model. "Now!" he cried. Dariush's grenade hit the Waggoneer with a soft thud, while Khorasad's landed right in the pool of gasoline that had spilled from the punctured tank. The explosion flashed loudly. Huge flames wreathed the Waggoneer, then the fuel tank went up in a deafening roar that echoed around and around the rock walls and valley; then the bridge collapsed, dragging the burning wreckage with it.

The smoldering wreck of the Waggoneer sent up a dim light from the foot of the deep chasm. They heard angry voices shouting on the other side. A few shots split the darkness, then total silence.

"Let's go," said Khorasad. "We'll find a place to spend the night and carry on tomorrow."

"Right . . ." A prolonged fit of coughing shook the young man's shoulders. "I'm cold, General. By God, this cold is a bitch!"

They found Janet, Yasarian and Amiri behind a clump of rocks. Janet stood behind the crouched form of Amiri, her winter coat wrapped tightly about her and the tall hood covering her head. She looked at Khorasad and asked "What now?"

153

"We'll find a place to spend the night . . ."

"What about those guys?" She pointed to the bridge.

"They'll leave us alone tonight . . ." He coughed. "Fog and mist . . . they can't cross the gorge."

"It's cold," she said.

"Yes . . ." he listened anxiously to the hacking cough of Dariush. "Are you all right, kid?"

"I'm fine, General."

"Right, let's move."

"It's cold," complained Yasarian.

"Please, Yasarian, please shut up," answered Khorasad in a low, tired voice. "Let's go!" he said. He strode down the pitted dirt road with the others at his heels. They kept up a bedraggled rear, their small loads weighing them down and Doctor Amiri slowing them all as he laboredly shuffled, the flaps of his blanket trailing in the mud. After ten minutes of slow groping in the dark mist, they came to a group of rocks at the side of the road. Khorasad inspected the rocks until he found a small cleft in the shape of an inverted funnel, the narrow end open to the sky, and close by it a little cave.

"Look, over here!" he said, pointing to the funnel-shaped cleft. "Spread out all the blankets and sleeping bags down there. We'll wait here till morning." He turned to Janet. "There's a cave over there, I suggest you use it. Have you got a sleeping bag?"

"Yes," she replied. He stared at her intently, straining to catch a glimpse of her eyes in the darkness. He stretched out his hand and touched her face. She did not resist. She touched his hand softly and then turned and went to the cave.

Meanwhile Dariush had found a few twigs, a pile of straw and some sheep droppings. He got a fire going with his lighter. By its weak light they spread out the blankets and sleeping bags, then lay down to rest.

"I'll take the first watch," said Khorasad. He cocked his Uzi and sat down at the entrance to the funnel, his back against the cold rock. From the cave nearby he heard the zip of Janet's sleeping bag. "Hell!" he murmured, then stood up and paced back and forth on the road, his collar turned up over his ears. He kicked moodily at a little pile of stones, then turned and went back to the rocks.

He stood and looked down at Dariush, Yasarian and Amiri lying side by side. The little fire was already out. An overpowering silence was broken only by snoring and by Dariush's dry cough. Khorasad licked his lips, hesitated and then, with a set expression on his face, his brows knitted and mouth pursed, he walked over to the cave where Janet lay. He stooped and looked down at her.

"It's me," he said in a low voice. "Khorasad . . ."

"I know," she replied in a whisper, and he knew that she would not resist him. He knelt down beside her. "Were you expecting me?" he asked. His head brushed against the roof of the cave and a smell of damp and mildew filled his nostrils.

"Yes."

He unfastened his coat and heard the zip of her sleeping bag opening. He leaned over and kissed her roughly.

She touched his stubbly cheek lightly with the back of her fingers. "I'm lonely and afraid," she whispered. "Please understand."

"Okay, okay." He kissed her again. Their tongues met and he felt her move beneath him. He rolled off her and fumbled with his belt and fly buttons. "Open your legs," he whispered, "quick!"

Janet bit her lip and tears began to trickle down her cheeks. *Oh, God,* she thought, *what am I doing?* She tried again to touch his face. His strong shoulders seemed to engulf her. She tried to talk but his mouth was pressed hard on hers and hurt her lips. He moved his head and whispered urgently, "Go on, open your legs, quick!" She obeyed. Brutally he thrust into her, his mouth on her neck, one hand pulling her toward him and the other kneading her breast. Within seconds it was all over and he lay there panting heavily.

155

She wanted to say something but by then her whole body was shaken by her sobs. Finally she murmured, "Bastard!"

"Take it easy," he said, a little surprised. "I thought you'd like it this way." He caressed her shoulder and kissed her lightly.

"Stop it, bastard!"

He attempted to take her again, but she shook her head and moved her face away when he tried to catch her lips.

"That's enough!" she whispered firmly, "enough!"

He grinned, his eyes flashing. The blood still pounded in his veins. "Some other time, some other place," he said. Then he stood up, buttoned his trousers and coat, and left the cave. When he was outside, shivering in the cold night air, he heard the zip of her sleeping bag. He smiled. As he went back to the road, submachine gun in his hand, he saw fog rolling toward him like a gray wall.

Suddenly his hunter senses went alert. An unpleasant feeling of danger seized him. Janet was forgotten. He stood without moving a muscle and listened. Finally he called, "Who is there?" but there was no answer. He pointed his submachine gun toward the fog and advanced a few cautious steps. Suddenly a clear and menacing shape stood out against the background of the mist. Khorasad recognized the heavyset silhouette of Yasarian. "I've seen you. Don't be a fool, go back to the others," Khorasad said quietly.

Yasarian bit his lips. He hesitated for a moment, then lowered the muzzle of his Uzi. Warm tears ran down his cheeks. "No," he murmured, "I can't do it, not for Janet, not for Teheran . . ." He turned and disappeared slowly into the fog, leaving Khorasad behind.

Eldad and Trenshaw stood watching the sheet of paper emerge from the terminal of the Telex machine. When the chattering stopped, Trenshaw tore off the sheet and took it through to the next room where Schreiber sat with the other members of the team.

Crowded and smoke-filled as it was, the room in an isolated building at the edge of Tatvan air base gave off an air of calm efficiency. The men sat at a square table laden with maps, sketches and papers, exchanging comments in low voices against the crackle of the radio transmitters and receivers which filled one corner of the room.

"This is it!" declared Trenshaw. "Teheran station has picked up the Hercules."

Schreiber took the pipe from his mouth and put it down carefully on the edge of the table. "Excellent," he said in a low voice that did not match Trenshaw's excitement. "What does it say?"

He took the Telex form and read aloud: "Everything in order. Swordfish confirms merchandise delivered to forwarding agency in excellent condition." Schreiber put the paper down on the table and smiled. "What else do we have?"

Portilio bent over the pile of cables which lay before him on the table. " 'According to latest reports, there have been fierce street battles in Teheran,' " he read aloud. " 'The Imperial Guard is firing on the demonstrators who have erected barricades at the junction of Shimran and Jamshid. We have monitored desperate messages from the air force, most of the technicians have deserted and the planes at Mehrabad air base are grounded.' "

"Kurdistan," said Schreiber emphatically. "Kurdistan. Not generalities." Unintentionally he raised his voice. He paused and coughed, and when he spoke again his voice had returned to its normal pitch. "Our business is in Kurdistan, never mind the rest."

Portilio held up a cable. "Here is the bad news from Kurdistan." He looked up at Schreiber.

"What is it?" Schreiber asked, suddenly concerned. His tone drew the attention of all the men seated round the table. Danny suddenly came to life, pressing the palms of his hands on the table. "What's happened?" he asked.

Portilio coughed and said: "It is the translation of a radio

157

broadcast, something to do with the gendarmerie, Penicillin . . . it doesn't sound good . . ."

"Spell it out for us, August." Schreiber stuck the pipe back between his teeth. The nerve below his right eye started twitching.

"Okay, this is it . . . 'Revolutionary forces acting in conjunction with the revolutionary gendarmerie and loyal Muslims from the Kermanshah sector are in pursuit of Savak General Said Khorasad. The general is traveling in a gendarmerie vehicle of the Waggoneer type with armed accomplices. The pursuers have orders to arrest or liquidate the general according to the circumstances. This directive is authorized by the Islamic Revolutionary Committee of Kermanshah.' "

Schreiber stared thoughtfully into the smoke-filled air, tapping his fingers nervously on the table, then turned toward Danny. "What do you think?" he asked the Israeli.

"If Khorasad lives up to his reputation, I reckon there's a good chance he'll find a way out," said Danny. "Anyway, in the meantime, there's nothing to suggest he's been arrested, is there?"

"That's correct," agreed Schreiber. "The question is, where is he now? Jesus, I hope it's somewhere near Rendezvous 34!"

"Yes, it could be serious if Arik and his boys get there much before him . . . very serious."

"What message shall I send to Kuwait?" asked Trenshaw.

"Tell them to wait for instructions," replied Schreiber after a moment's thought.

"I hope Nero and Redwood are all right," said Danny. He stood up and stretched, then yawned noisily. "I very, very much hope so!"

A ghost of a smile flickered across Trenshaw's face. "You guys certainly take this thing seriously." He lit a cigarette. "Is there something we don't know?"

Danny shrugged. "You don't know? Well, not exactly. I mean, we've kept you abreast of the situation since first contact. Still, we're the ones who had direct contact with Yasar—with Nero and the other. *Not* impressive characters, let me say."

"And therefore?"

"They can be bought—easily. By either side."

Schreiber eyed the Israeli thoughtfully. "Are you saying they will betray us?"

"Not as long as Khorasad has them under his wing. And Khorasad has too much to lose. It's just that sometimes I think we would have been better off if we'd just let the crowds have them all."

"If indeed they finished them off," interrupted Trenshaw. "If not . . ."

"If Teheran realized what they'd captured," remarked Schreiber.

"Unlikely," snorted Danny. "But possible. And on that possibility we have had to act. Those two scientists have had a look at every advanced military installation in Israel. They know nuclear plans and blueprints inside out. They may not look or act like real people, but they've got it upstairs, believe me. And if they fell into the hands of the crazies . . ."

Schreiber looked at Trenshaw. "But that is impossible, correct? You gave Danny the word, didn't you?"

Trenshaw nodded, silently.

Danny looked at the pipe-smoking American. "Oh, yes. Arik has his instructions. I sometimes hope that it does come to that. It would be simpler now, wouldn't it?"

Schreiber scowled at his Israeli counterpart. "But we have *our* instructions, too. From Washington. And there will still be an Iran after this is over, and we may need them . . ."

Danny was chuckling. "Too bad about that. You folks do look at the long term, don't you?"


Doctor Amiri stared at Khorasad with exhausted eyes. He licked his chapped lips with his pale tongue and this, coupled with the sporadic contortions of his face and the frantic gestures of his thin hands, gave him the appearance of a lunatic. Khorasad gazed intently at the scientist, standing there wrapped in the wet dirty blanket and shaking uncontrollably. *God!* he thought, *please don't let him flake out on me now* . . . "Are you all right, Doctor?" he asked.

Amiri glanced at him, then lowered his eyes and began moaning. Khorasad slapped him on the shoulder in an effort to show a little sympathy, but there was no response to his gesture and the touch turned to a punishing grip.

"Listen, Nero," he said. "Our troubles will soon be over."

"My heart . . . the medicine," whispered Amiri. "The medicine . . ."

"What are you talking about?" Khorasad asked impatiently. He did not wait for a reply. There had been no chance to salvage anything from the hotel in Kermanshah. *A heart attack is all we need now,* he thought. *Why wasn't I told earlier?*

Khorasad had turned away and was now walking toward the highway. He could see the mist dispersing, the road ahead of them suddenly clearing and in the distance, under a pall of grey cloud, Mount Nidawad. He looked anxiously at the bend in the road. There at the end, by the gorge, hung the mangled remains of the bridge. He thought he saw movement on the other side and he knew his pursuers would now be making an attempt to outflank him. They might even go west, toward the valley, and block his approach to Rendezvous 34. *The chances are getting slimmer,* he thought. He felt a dull knot tighten in his stomach. *Just a sign of hunger,* he told himself, *not fear. It couldn't be fear* . . .

Back at the camp the rest of the party worked in silence, rolling up blankets and sleeping bags. To a man, they looked tired and unkempt. Yasarian had lost his manly appearance long ago, and now his beard hung in ragged clumps and the bald dome of his forehead was scarred and scratched. Dariush coughed incessantly, and his face was a field of yellow skin with dark patches round his eyes.

*Why is he following me without protest, staying with me right to the end?* Khorasad asked himself. "How do you feel?" he asked his aide.

*A stupid question,* he thought, seeing Dariush bent double, coughing and spitting great gobs of phlegm.

"Not too bad . . ." The voice was hoarse and weak.

"He needs rest," said Janet. "Something hot to drink . . ." Their eyes met and locked together for a fraction of a second. *She looks bad, too,* he thought. Her pale face was still slightly bruised, her eyes red and ringed with black circles, the strands of blond hair peeping out from under her hood knotted and dirty. She clutched the collar of the winter coat close to her throat with both hands.

"Are you all right?" he asked.

She smiled faintly. "I'm hungry."

"Yes, so am I . . ." Khorasad looked up the grey storm clouds gathering in the sky and felt the cold breeze blowing from the north. He glanced impatiently at his watch. "We must move," he said. "We can't wait any longer."

"I've got no strength left," wailed Amiri.

"I'll help you," offered Yasarian. He shouldered his submachine gun, picked up his sleeping bag and put his strong right arm around Amiri's narrow shoulders. "I'm ready," he said. "Where are we going, General?"

Khorasad did not reply but set off down the road. Janet walked beside him, Yasarian and Amiri followed close behind, while Dariush brought up the rear, staggering under the weight of the grenade sack, a submachine gun and a roll of mud-stained army blankets.

After about an hour's walking they came to a section of road that had been left unfinished by highway builders. Assorted tools lay scattered about the road surface, shovels, hoes and pneumatic drills that had apparently been abandoned in a hurry. Khorasad grinned at the sight of a drill coated with frost and ice and dug deep into a pile of gravel. Like a tombstone, he thought. He sighed and turned to Janet, who walked beside him, pale and breathless.

"At any other time I'd be happy to see signs of work here.

When I heard they were paving this road I was glad . . ." He sighed softly.

"What's so good about this road?" she asked without interest. She was tired and hungry and now she felt thirsty as well. *Coffee!* she thought. *How good it would be to have a cup of morning coffee . . .*

"Hunting!" he replied. "This is a wonderful area for the hunt!" He stretched out his hand and pointed to the mountains rising away to their left. "Mountain goats, game birds . . . a good road would mean quicker access."

She stared at the wild landscape which to her seemed grim and threatening, then looked back. She saw Amiri hobbling along painfully, supported by Yasarian, and Dariush wracked by a renewed fit of coughing. "They need to rest," she said. "They can't keep up this pace."

"Soon . . ."

"When?"

"Soon!" He turned to her, frowning. "Soon . . ."

"Aren't you tired?" she asked Khorasad.

"No," then asked, "What's the matter with you?"

"Everything," she murmured.

"It's not over yet," Khorasad said.

*"Where* are we going?"

He gestured forward with a motion of the head. "That way," he said. "A few more kilometers."

"I don't know if I'll make it," she said softly.

Khorasad stopped, turned to her and took her chin in his strong hand. "Listen to me," he said, and his words were directed at them all. "We're going on. Anyone who drops out stays here, understand?"

Doctor Amiri's face showed hardly a sign of life; his head lolled on Yasarian's shoulder and Dariush held his other elbow. *That boy's the only one who believes in me,* thought Khorasad.

"Let's go!" Khorasad started off again briskly, and behind him came the trudge of feet dragging wearily over the gravel. A few minutes later they came to a small windowless hut, a lopsided wooden structure with a rusty corrugated tin roof. He went to the door, kicked it open and glanced cautiously inside. All that was there was an unlit stove, an upturned kettle and a pile of assorted debris. He went in and started probing with the toe of his boot among the old newspapers, empty tin cans and frozen orange peels, then knelt down and gathered up the peel, together with moldering fragments of bread, onion skins and apple cores.

"What are you doing?" asked Janet.

"Preparing a meal," he said.

"You must be crazy."

"You think so?" He pointed to a kettle. "Go and fill that with snow."

"You are crazy."

"Have it your own way!" he snapped. "Those who don't help, don't eat."

Dariush stepped past her without a word, picked up the kettle and went back to the road. Janet hesitated, then came and knelt beside Khorasad. "What do you want me to do?" she asked.

"Check those empty cans, look, over there. You'll find oil in those sardine tins and maybe a fish or two. Maybe the workers weren't very hungry."

"Do you mean to eat this garbage?" she asked.

He looked up at her and breathed hard before replying. "Listen lady, in this weather food doesn't deteriorate. We've got to get something inside us and this . . ." He laughed. "This is the only restaurant round here, okay?"

Yasarian and Amiri struggled inside. Both men collapsed on the floor. Khorasad did not even glance at them. Instead, he piled the remnants of food that he had found and the peel, then gathered up the newspapers, cardboard boxes and a few bits of wood and put them in the stove. Slowly and carefully, as if handling delicate glass, he lit a fire. Within minutes, thin smoke was scorching their eyes and warmth began to spread through the little hut.

Dariush returned with the kettle. Khorasad took it from him without a word, laid it on the stove and tossed in the frozen orange peel and a few cubes of sugar, then put the scraps of bread and the onion skins to fry in a can of sardine oil. "There," he said, "it won't be long now! You wanted something hot to drink, didn't you?"

# 11

By morning the mist had almost cleared and the temperature had risen. Patches of blue sky appeared through gaps in the clouds, and just visible on the horizon were the distant mountains encircling Kermanshah. Plumes of smoke from cooking fires rose above the cottages in the village. On the path leading down the slopes flocks of sheep appeared, most of them led by boys armed with sticks and knives. The young shepherds chattered eagerly, whistling and guiding their animals with the aid of the dogs, throwing stones at the heads of sheep that refused to obey their shouts or the barking animals.

Arik stood with Jalal at the edge of the village, scanning the valley below through his binoculars. Behind them, the others made final adjustments to their equipment. Farha knelt beside Leonard who was busy with the radio transmitter, sending a signal to Neptune, code name for the headquarters in Tatvan. She looked small and fragile in the tattered old combat blouse with the words U.S. ARMY in faded letters above the breast pocket. She wore leather gloves and in her tiny hands she gripped a Russian submachine gun with a drum magazine. Leonard completed his message, fastened the cover of the radio set and smiled at the girl.

"Do you know this kind of equipment?" he asked.

"No, they only taught me simple radio operation." She grinned. "This is all too complicated for me."

"Don't you believe it! A kid could work this stuff."

"Okay." She shrugged. "Leave the set here when you've finished, okay? It's a deal?"

He stood up and slung the transmitter over his shoulder. "Don't count on it. Something else, maybe. This machine gun any use to you?"

She laughed, her white teeth flashing. "It's a deal . . ." Then she looked across at the place where Arik stood with her father, watching the valley. "He's a panther," she said admiringly.

"Your father?" asked Leonard.

"I meant Arik. We've known him a long time . . ."

"Yes, it seems he knows a lot of people. He gets himself into trouble, doesn't he?"

Farha's eyes sparkled. "Why of course. That's why he's a panther."

"I suppose so." Leonard sounded impatient. He turned abruptly and went to join Arik and Jalal. "Well? Everything check out? Are we going down?"

"Yes." Arik pointed to the valley. "Over there, about ten kilometers from here, right at the foot of the mountain. That's Rendezvous 34, a kind of teahouse, a local inn. You'll see."

"Really?"

"Yes, don't you want to have a look?"

"I've done that already."

"Okay." Arik glanced at the men, loaded with heavy equipment.

"Ready?" he asked.

"Ready."

"Right, let's go!" He and Jalal moved toward the broad track

166

leading down to the valley with the men following at regular intervals. The going was not difficult and after an hour they were at the edge of the plain. Here they walked in a long file, weapons at the ready, and from time to time they paused to reconnoiter. Occasionally they met shepherds with their flocks. The dogs were always the first to sniff them out, appearing with heads down, tails in the air and teeth bared. Some had ears cropped close to the skull and docked tails; most were scarred, a sign of the vicious and constant fighting that was second nature to these unruly mountain dogs. The shepherds greeted them in low voices, sometimes with a smile, showing no curiosity or surprise at the sight of seven men in cumbersome gear in their remote pasturelands. Leonard assumed that Jalal and Farha were a sort of pass of safe-conduct. He glanced quickly at the slim girl who was now striding alongside Walter.

After about two hours of steady progress they came to a narrow stream that flowed swiftly at the base of gently sloping crevice. They followed Jalal who led them to a shallow ford, and they crossed over, shivering as the icy water drenched their boots. Once across the stream they kept up with Arik's accelerated pace as they approached their destination.

As they passed through a small forest they saw a group of outbuildings built of light-brown brick and the large two-story building with the triangular tiled roof.

"There!" said Jalal, pointing with his rifle. "The *chai haneh,* the shepherds' inn!"

"Yes," said Arik to himself, "Rendezvous 34." Then he called his men together. "Okay, you guys, now listen carefully. Jalal and Yosi are coming with me. The rest of you wait here, out of sight, and keep your radio sets open." He waited for a few moments while Leonard, the girl and other members of the team took cover among the trees and began checking their walkie-talkie sets. He switched on his own set, pressed the transmit button and listened for a moment to the hum of static. Then he stepped out of the woods.

Parked close to the *chai haneh* were two big yellow trucks, evidently the property of some local construction firm. Beside them stood a short, solid-looking man in Kurdish national costume, armed with a revolver and a curved hunting knife. He stared at them in astonishment and reached for his holster, but when he recognized the hulking shape of Jalal, he smiled and waved a cheery greeting.

"God be with you!" he called loudly.

"God bless you!" replied Yosi. The man came forward and embraced Jalal warmly. *A dwarf hugging a giant,* thought Arik. He smiled.

"Who's this?" he asked.

"A watchman," Jalal replied. "He guards the building equipment."

"Is there anyone inside?" Arik looked at the inn and saw smoke curling from a chimney in the red roof. "Who's there?" he asked.

"The landlord . . ."

"Any of the shepherds about?"

"They're in the fields." The man smiled. "They went out early in the morning."

"Just the landlord?"

"Yes, him and his wife . . . all the laborers have gone. They stopped working on the road, left the steamrollers and bulldozers behind . . . they just beat it." He laughed throatily. "That Ayatollah, he's scared them shitless!"

"Shall we go inside?" asked Jalal.

"Just a moment . . ." Arik turned to the watchman again. "Are there gendarmes round here, soldiers or anything like that?"

The watchman shook his head. "All the Kurdish gendarmes have deserted and gone back to their villages. The officer ran off to Sanandaj . . ." He spat on the ground and smiled at Jalal, baring rows of yellow teeth. "It's only the Shiites still running around here. There's some completely crazy sergeant, a real nutter . . . he's driving round in a jeep looking for a general . . ." The watchman howled with laughter. "Crazy! He's looking for a general. Savak, no less . . ."

Arik and Jalal exchanged quick glances. The giant Kurd leaned over the little man and gripped his shoulder. "Tell us, brother, quick. Who is this general? What's happened?"

"A Savak general . . . the man escaped from Kermanshah, left a pile of corpses behind him, so they say. They call him the Butcher. Yes, that's it, the Butcher."

"And he's supposed to be here?"

*"Here?"* Again the little man shook with laughter. "Why the hell should he come here, where would he escape to from here? Nidawad? Up the mountain and poof?" The man shook his head. "No, not here . . ." Suddenly his expression changed, his smile vanished and he stared intently at Arik. "Hang on a moment . . . who *are* you?"

"My friends," said Jalal threateningly. "Friends, understand?"

"If you say so . . ." The watchman took a rusty tobacco tin and a pack of cigarette papers from his pocket. "Like one of these?"

"Thanks . . ." Arik slapped the man's shoulder. "Let's go inside," he said, pointing to the *chai haneh.*

They went into the main hall of the inn which sprawled across the entire width of the ground floor. A big red-brick stove blazed in the center, surrounded by empty chairs. Long tables and wooden benches lined the walls. The place was dim, with only a bit of light filtering in through the narrow windows. From the far end of the hall the landlord came forward, a plump elderly little man. He wore a peaked cap, horn-rimmed spectacles, rather antiquated European clothes which matched his elegant moustache, and a stained white apron. He shuffled toward them, swaying from side to side like a goose.

"Yes?" he asked in Kurdish. "Can I help you, gentlemen? A little tea or bread?"

He greeted Jalal with a nod and a smile, and went on to peer shortsightedly at Yosi and Arik. Suddenly his expression changed to one of stunned amazement.

"Great God!" he cried. "God the one and only . . . *you?*"

Arik hugged the man. "Mustafa," he said softly, "Mustafa!"

"What in God's name are you doing here?" The landlord took a step backward and stared at the small party, still gaping incredulously. "What *is* this?" He took off his glasses and wiped his eyes with balled-up fists.

"In a moment," said Jalal, "I'll tell you exactly what's happening. Arik and his friends won't be staying here long. It's just a visit . . . a flying visit, you might say."

"Food! You must be hungry!" cried the landlord.

"We haven't much time . . ."

"Nonsense!" The landlord turned and waddled back to the far end of the *chai haneh,* to the wide door which led to the kitchen. "Leila!" he shouted. "Leila! Put the pans on, woman!"

Arik laughed. "He hasn't changed," he said.

"Nothing ever changes here, my friend," said Jalal. "Four years or ten, nothing changes. You'd better call the others. I'm worried by what the watchman said about Khorasad." The Kurd's face darkened. He sat down on a chair and stretched out his long legs. "God," he said, "I'm tired. I must be getting old . . . all this exercise is too much for me."

"Nonsense!" Yosi took the pack from his shoulders and then sat down beside Jalal. "It's time you woke up from your hibernation, got yourself in training . . ."

"Maybe." Jalal shrugged, laying down his Russian assault rifle. "Who knows? This could be just the opportunity we've been waiting for . . . maybe we'll get back to work. It's a long time since the Pesh-merga was in the news. By God, when this business is over I'll get to Sanandaj . . . light a few fires there." The Kurd laughed heartily. "You hear me, Arik? Why don't you come along, over there in Sanandaj we can really get things moving . . . *Sarabaste!"*

*"Sarabaste . . ."* Arik murmured. He switched off the radio set,

went to the nearest window and watched as Leonard, the girl and the rest of the party emerged from the woods and rapidly crossed the short distance to the door of the inn, passing unperceived behind the yellow trucks and the back of the watchman.

A smell of burning oil filtered through from the kitchen. Arik remembered Fishel and the dirty little cafe, his home . . . "I don't believe you, you're getting yourself involved again," the old man had said when they parted at the door of the cafe.

"You're pensive," said Leonard, who was taking off his gear.

Arik took a deep breath and stood up. "It looks like we've got problems," he said. "Khorasad's on the run and there's a posse on his trail." He pointed to the window. "Somewhere out there, that's where Khorasad is . . ."

"A needle in a haystack," said Leonard. "What are we going to do?"

"Wait. He's supposed to be coming here."

"Great," murmured Leonard in exasperation.

Arik stretched. "At the moment waiting is all we can do."

They joined their companions who stood talking with Jalal, Yosi acting as interpreter. The kitchen door opened and Mustafa reappeared, carrying a big tray laden with steaming food and shouting at the corpulent woman who trailed behind him. Arik could sense the loose flesh quivering under her voluminous black garments as she shuffled toward them, bearing freshly baked loaves of bread wrapped in a cloth and a big steaming pot of tea.

"What's all this?" said Leonard.

Arik let out a short laugh. "In these parts hospitality is a duty."

Arik looked around at the members of his party and saw Shraga sitting by the main entrance door, looking through the big glass pane, rifle in his hand. *Good boy,* he thought, *lucky somebody's on the ball . . .* A few minutes before he had let himself get so engrossed in his own thoughts that he had been unaware even of Leonard's presence.

Mustafa and his wife laid one of the tables and invited the

crew to take their places on the bench. He stood and watched them eat with the pleasure of the host who likes to see his guests enjoying every morsel of their meal. As they ate Farha explained the names of the dishes.

"This is *chello kebab,*" she said, pointing to the strips of meat resting on balls of oily rice. "An Iranian national dish . . ." She wrinkled her nose. "But good all the same."

Arik took a small tin plate, piled food on it and then went over to the door and joined Shraga. As he handed the plate to him he said, "Thanks for taking guard."

Shraga smiled and stood up, stretching his long arms. "There's nothing out there," he said. "Just the old Kurd with the revolver, that's all."

"Okay." Arik gazed through the window. The Kurdish watchman paced back and forth beside the pair of big trucks, his hands in the pockets of his tunic and his head hunched slightly forward. He stamped his feet and Arik heard him singing, in a hoarse but powerful voice. He recognized the tune, a wedding song. He remembered Khorasad teaching him the words. When was that? 1974, '75 maybe . . . He smiled, recalling them. "I have a house . . ." He remembered the long line of men, hundreds of them, standing arms linked and shoulder to shoulder, half marching, half dancing to a single rhythm, feet stamping the dusty ground, shoulders swaying, the beat stomper out front, leading the dance and demonstrating steps to the sound of the shrill shepherds' pipes . . . a village near Kasar-a-Shirin on the Iraqi side of the border . . . He sighed, then suddenly stiffened when he saw that the watchman in the parking lot had stopped and was looking to the south, back to the building and then south again. They heard the sound of a car engine. Shraga leapt to his feet.

"What's happening?"

"Vehicle approaching," said Arik. "Stand by."

The men left their food on the table and ran to the windows. Mustafa and his wife hastily returned to the kitchen. The plump woman who only minutes before had been giggling and chattering

172

noisily with the Americans, assisted by Farha, began fearfully whimpering.

Arik saw the watchman start toward the door of the inn, but before he got there a mud-spattered jeep drove into the lot. Behind the wheel sat a large uniformed figure and in the passenger seat a little man in dark civilian clothes. The jeep pulled up beside the watchman and the driver, a tall, thin, swarthy man in gendarmerie uniform and what looked like riding boots, stepped down from his seat. He stood talking to the watchman, pointing to the hill of Nidawad and then looking across at the inn. Finally he gestured toward the building, said something to his companion who stayed behind in the jeep and, accompanied by the watchman, he walked briskly toward the door.

"Son of a bitch!" whispered Farha. Arik looked at her. She stood close behind him, staring out, gripping her submachine gun tightly.

"Do you know him?"

"Yes . . ." Her dark eyes narrowed. "I know him, he's a gendarmerie sergeant . . . a Shiite from Qom . . . an arrogant bastard and a criminal." She raised the submachine gun to her shoulder, pressed her cheek against the butt and closed her left eye, taking aim. "He's mine!"

"Put down that gun," said Arik anxiously. "No shooting!"

She lowered her weapon and stared at him with a mixture of surprise and disappointment. "I . . ." she began.

"Quiet!" Now they heard the sergeant's footsteps and already the tall figure stood outside the door. Through the glass Arik saw the man's gun belt and revolver holster.

"Mustafa!" The sergeant stood in the open doorway. He tried to reach for his revolver but Farha was too quick for him. In an instant she had rammed the muzzle of her submachine gun into the man's stomach. "Not one move!" she hissed.

Arik grabbed the lapels of the thick trench coat and dragged the man inside as Shraga tripped him with the barrel of his rifle.

The man let out a yell of surprise as he thudded to the hard floor, still groping for his revolver.

Arik sidestepped him and ran out the door, knocking down the Kurdish watchman. "The jeep!" But the passenger had already jumped into the driver's seat and started the engine. The jeep spun wildly in the parking lot, then tore away down the broad dirt road.

"Shit!" he cried angrily. "Shit!"

The watchman drew his revolver and fired off two rapid shots at the jeep as it receded. Farha came out and stood beside Arik. Her small bosom rose and fell in time with her rapid breathing. Her face was deathly pale and she bit her lips. "I'm sorry," she said after a short silence. "Really sorry."

Arik looked at her angrily, his cheeks flushed and his eyes gleaming. "You should have waited until he got inside. Look, the fucking jeep is gone."

Behind them they heard the dull sounds of a beating in progress. Arik hurried back inside. Jalal stood over the gendarme, who was crouching on his hands and knees as the Kurd thumped his neck and back with his huge fists. "Dog!" he shouted. "Filthy dog, your hour has come, you Shiite bastard!"

Farha now suddenly slipped past Arik and started kicking the man in the rear. The man howled with pain, which only roused Jalal to greater fury, and he began clubbing him in the chest with his rifle.

"Stop!" yelled Arik. "Stop that!"

The giant Kurd straightened up and stared at him, the rifle in his hand poised for another blow. "He must be killed," he said in a choking voice. "We know this bastard, he's had his way with us and now . . ."

"Leave him alone!" Arik looked down at the tall, thin sergeant who writhed, groaning on the cold floor. He signaled Yosi, who knelt beside the man's head and asked, "Where is Khorasad? Tell me man, quick!"

The wounded man let out a gurgling sound and shook his head.

174

"Where is Khorasad?"

Jalal bent down and slapped the sergeant's face. "Talk!" he yelled. "Talk!" Yosi took off his glasses and waved the Kurd away.

"Talk," he suggested. "Talk and save yourself trouble. Where is Khorasad?"

At intervals Jalal hit the man. Still he didn't talk. By now his features were bathed in blood and one of his eyes had closed under a livid red swelling. He went on stubbornly shaking his head.

Leonard knelt down beside Arik. "This isn't going to work."

Arik looked at him blankly for a moment, then nodded. "Okay, go ahead . . ."

Thomas Barrett had heard the brief exchange between Arik and Leonard. He lifted his pack onto a table, opened it and took out a small medical case. He set to work quietly and efficiently, filling a syringe with white liquid. He pressed the plunger and when he saw drops spurt from the needle, he took a pad of sterile gauze and came over to join the others. "Take off his pants," he said. "The best place is in the butt."

Arik could not resist the impulse to laugh. He shook his head in disbelief as he watched Jalal, Farha and Shraga pounce on the helpless gendarme. Jalal held his shoulders down to the floor, Farha unfastened his belt and fly buttons and as they turned him over on his stomach, Shraga pushed up the flaps of his coat and dragged off his trousers. The man's ass quivered as he tried to rise up. Shraga pulled down his underpants. Barrett smiled, slapped a bare buttock lightly, disinfected it and quickly shot the drug into the muscle. The man tried to resist but Jalal punched him in the back with his huge fist and the sergeant moaned and lay still.

"Let him go," said Barrett. He chuckled, his freckled face bright with amusement. "Jesus!" he said as he stood up. "First time, and what a place to do it!" He inspected the empty syringe and tossed it away into a corner. "Voromthalin," he said. "Let's see how the stuff works . . ."

"What happens now?" Arik looked down at the sergeant who writhed weakly on the floor, his pants around his ankles. After each attempt to lift himself the man sank back to the floor. With a final desperate attempt to rise he rolled over on his back, eyes closed and mouth open. He began to breath regularly and Barrett knelt beside him again. He lifted his eyelids and examined the pupils, then checked his pulse. Finally he opened the man's shirt and pulled up his vest, exposing a bony chest, sparsely covered with clumps of greying black hair. He put his ear to the man's chest, then stood up and nodded.

"It's all right," he said to Arik. "The heart's working normally. He's all yours."

Arik beckoned Yosi. The little man put on his glasses, bent down and spoke to the sergeant in soft Farsi: "What is your name?"

"Daryosh Ka-wa-khan . . ." the words emerged slowly, rhythmically from his swollen lips, in a croaking voice. His eyes were closed and he breathed as if in a deep sleep.

"What is your profession?"

"Gendarme . . . sergeant first class."

"Get to the point," growled Arik impatiently. "Time's running short."

Yosi looked up at Barrett. The American nodded. "It's all right," he said. "He'll answer any question."

"Where is General Khorasad?"

"The Butcher," the man muttered. "The Butcher's on the bridge . . ."

"What bridge?"

"Iron bridge . . . blown up . . . they're crossing it . . ."

"Who?"

"The Committee . . . reinforcements from Sanandaj . . ."

*"Where?"* Arik shouted. *"Where,* for God's sake?"

Yosi translated the question. The comatose man replied at once: "The iron bridge . . . dirt road . . . near the bulldozers."

"Does this make any sense to you?" asked Leonard.

"No."

"I think I know what he means," said Jalal. He stroked his

thick moustache thoughtfully and added: "If I'm not mistaken, a few kilometers from here, down the road where the contractors were working, there's a temporary bridge . . . it's on the route from Kermanshah. Maybe that's the one . . ."

"The map!" cried Arik. "Get me the map case, quick!"

Glenn Dyer ran across to the pile of equipment which lay stacked against the wall and began rummaging in Arik's side pack, but Leonard had already spread out his silk kerchief and was pointing to the map printed on it. "This is where we are," he said.

"Right," said Arik, and suddenly his face lit up. "I've got it!" he cried. "Yes, I remember! That goddam little bridge!"

He turned to Yosi again. "Ask him when Khorasad was last seen."

Yosi bent over the half-conscious gendarme. "When was the general last seen?" he asked. Now the man was having difficulty replying, and his answer came out as an incoherent mumble.

"Slap him, quick!" said Barrett. "I may have overdone the dosage. Normally it has to be weighed."

Before Yosi had time to stretch out his hand, Jalal hit the sergeant in the face with his open palm. The man's head flopped from side to side. He gurgled and for a moment his eyes flickered open.

"Not so hard!" warned Barrett. "You'll kill the man!"

"When was Khorasad last seen?" asked Yosi.

"L-last n-n-night . . . after the b-bridge was b-b-b-blown . . ."

"Is he being pursued?"

"Yes . . . they're coming from all d-d-directions . . . I have to g-get there too . . ." The sergeant was groaning now, grinding his teeth, his eyes closed and his bruised and swollen face turning a livid shade of purple. "I m-must get there . . ."

Arik turned his attention back to the map, then looked at the faces of his men. "Any ideas?" he asked. "It's ten kilometers and we're out of time now."

"We need transport," said Mackintosh.

"Hey, Mustafa!" Jalal stood up. "Come back here." He looked across at the kitchen door where the landlord stood with his wife. "What kind of transportation do you have?"

*"Transportation?* For God's sake, Jalal, get that sergeant out of here!" The landlord shuffled toward them, swaying and nervously fingering the fringe of his apron. "Oh God . . . trouble! Trouble!"

"A car, a truck!" Jalal shouted. "Anything?"

"Only the trucks . . ." said the Kurdish watchman.

*"What* did you say?"

"The trucks, the ones behind the inn . . ."

Arik leaped to his feet. "Are they working?"

"Yes." The Kurd smiled, exposing his yellow teeth. "But I don't have the keys."

"What's going on?" asked Leonard. "For God's sake, man, speak English!"

"The trucks," said Arik. "They're the answer. We'll take one of them and pick up Khorasad!"

"What?"

"It's the only chance we've got."

"Okay. Let's do it. What are you waiting for?"

"We don't know if we can get them going."

"No problem," said Mackintosh quietly. He yawned and flexed his arms. "Something to do at last!" He looked at Glenn Dyer. "Okay, man? Let's move it!"

Dyer was already rifling his pile of equipment. He extracted bundles of tools wrapped in canvas and handed one to Mackintosh. Both men went outside along with the watchman and Yosi.

Leonard stood by the door watching. The two trucks were enormous, with rear tires as high as a man and twice the size of those on the front.

He called back to Arik. "It's going to be a problem . . ." he said.

"What is?" Arik was sitting on a low chair beside the comatose sergeant. He looked up. "What are you talking about?"

"The trucks! They're designed for excavation work, I think. A European or Japanese model, I think."

"Krupp," replied Arik. "German, four cylinders."

Leonard glanced at him, surprised. "How come you know so much about trucks, pal?"

"I drive them," said Arik as if talking to himself.

Leonard stared at him.

"That's my job. I'm a truck driver. What's the matter, don't you believe me?"

"Great." Leonard shrugged. He was watching Mackintosh and Dyer at work on the nearest truck. He switched on his walkie-talkie. "Everything okay out there?"

Mackintosh was the first to answer. "Everything fine, over." And then he heard Dyer's cheerful voice: "Car thief with door open, over."

Leonard smiled. "Good work, boys. Over and out."

Arik looked down at the sergeant who lay stretched out on the floor, his chest rising and falling steadily, almost peacefully. His bruised and bleeding face was grotesque but seemed relaxed all the same. *Poor bastard,* he thought. Farha fidgeted nervously with the bolt of her submachine gun; Jalal stood motionless above the gendarmerie sergeant. It occurred to Arik that if the Kurd were to turn down the corners of his bushy moustache he would be a dead ringer for Stalin. Shraga sat at the table finishing off the meal that had been interrupted, and Barrett stood talking to the landlord in a mixture of sign language, English and broken French. The frightened innkeeper was nervously polishing his glasses on his apron.

"What's the problem, Mustafa?"

*"Problem?* You're asking me what the problem is! What am I supposed to do when this sergeant wakes up?"

Arik did not reply, but Jalal had overheard and he came across to join them, a stern expression on his face. "He must not live . . ." he said simply. He drew two fingers across his throat.

"Then kill him!" said Mustafa. "Kill him, for God's sake."

Arik felt a twitch at the corner of his mouth, a nervous response which, for as long as he could remember, had afflicted him whenever he was confronted by a proposition that his instincts refused to accept. He steeled himself with an effort.

"Relax!" he said to Mustafa. "We won't involve you."

"Now?" asked Jalal.

Arik shrugged and turned to the door where Leonard stood watching the trucks and the men working. Jalal walked back to where the sergeant lay, leaned over the unconscious man and rummaged in the pockets of his coat and trousers, pulling out a few documents in a worn leather wallet and an assortment of banknotes. He folded the bills and tucked them away in his pocket, then called Mustafa.

"Come here, quick!" he said. "Take these papers and burn them in the stove. We mustn't leave any trace."

"What about him?" Mustafa took the papers and pointed to the sergeant. "What are you going to do with him?"

"Don't worry . . ."

"He's mine!" insisted Farha.

"Shut up!" said Jalal, firmly but without anger. He glanced at her briefly.

"He's a pig . . ." she snapped. "An Iranian pig!"

Jalal handed his daughter his weapon and bent over the man again. He took hold of the lapels of his coat and hoisting him up with astonishing ease, slung him over his shoulder and walked out of the inn. Farha followed with the guns.

"She sure does hate that guy," said Barrett softly.

"She hates them all," Arik said.

"What happened to her?"

"Nothing special . . . she was born in the mountains of Kurdistan, on the Iraqi side . . . all her life she's known nothing except war . . . exile in Iran hasn't been a happy experience." Arik shrugged and went on. "And in this country, when people hate they do it with all their hearts."

As they boarded the truck Arik noticed a dark stain on Jalal's left shoulder. "What's that?" he asked.

"I wiped the knife," explained Jalal.

Arik looked straight ahead over the steering wheel; the truck vibrated powerfully to the rhythm of the big diesel engine. A column of black smoke spurted up from the exhaust pipe above the cab, drifting forward with the strong breeze. Arik glanced in the side mirror and saw Shraga tossing up the last of the equipment to the men in the rear section.

Suddenly Leonard looked at Jalal. "What about the sergeant?" he asked.

"In the well," replied Jalal calmly. "Behind the parking lot . . ." He grimaced. "They'll never find him . . ."

Leonard frowned. "You killed him first?"

Arik released the brakes, revved the engine and then pressed down the clutch and shifted into first gear. The big truck moved off slowly, engine roaring. Its massive wheels churned up the dirt road. Arik leaned back and gripped the smooth hydraulic steering lightly. He knew what the Kurd's reply would be.

"Not me . . ." Jalal grinned, stroking his moustache with a delicacy that did not match his ferocious appearance.

Leonard shook his head incredulously, then leaned back in the cab.

Arik looked out at the road. They had left the area around the inn and now were traveling on a wide dusty road which had been torn up for the construction work: little heaps of stones, oil drums, sections of lead piping. The temperature was cold but there was no rain or mist on the fields. Only here and there, far from the road, could one detect signs of life—a flock of sheep, a donkey laden with firewood beside a figure in black, a few clusters of small dark houses built of mud or brick.

The men in the rear sat on a cold metal floor, their backs to the driver's cab. Farha had wrapped her head in a thick, red-speckled kaffiyeh which left only her eyes visible. She heard Arik over the walkie-talkie: "Ten more minutes to the bridge!"

At every bend in the road Arik stopped the truck and peered cautiously ahead through his binoculars before handing them over to Leonard. They saw nothing, so they went on. Arik knew that they would be at the bridge soon, but didn't know what they would do if they got there and Khorasad was nowhere to be found. Arik glanced briefly at Leonard. "That *was* a truth drug you shot into him, wasn't it?"

"Yes."

"No chance he lied?"

"The information was good—as far as the man himself knew, anyway."

"We'll see soon enough." Arik frowned and returned his attention to the wheel.

"There!" cried Jalal suddenly. He leaned forward over the dash. "There," he said, "on the right!"

Arik stopped the truck. "What is it? What do you see?"

"Cars . . ."

"Where?" Arik strained his eyes but could see nothing, just open fields and sparse vegetation. *"Where,* for God's sake?"

"Up there, beside the gorge . . . two, no, three of them . . ."

Arik handed his binoculars to Leonard. "See anything?"

"Yes!" Leonard pressed the lenses to his eyes. "Three vehicles. Two light trucks and a jeep . . ."

"What's happening?" Dyer's voice came crackling through the headphones. Arik banged the truck into gear and drove on as Leonard replied. "Listen boys! We've got company . . ." He paused for a moment, threw away his cigarette and went on. "About six-seven kilometers ahead, near the gorge." He turned to Arik. "What are we going to do?" he asked. "I reckon we should stop, what do you say?"

"No!"

"Why?" He stared at Arik who was hunched forward over the wheel, his foot hard on the gas. "Why not, for Christ's sake?"

"The bridge!" shouted Arik. "We're nearly there!"

"They may cut off our escape route, man!"

"The bridge!" Arik insisted. "Any minute now!"

182

They swung around a tight bend in the road and saw the hut. "There's someone there!" cried Jalal. "Look, smoke!" A large figure in a heavy trench coat, bent double, was running for refuge behind a nearby heap of gravel. Another man, this one thin and emaciated, appeared in the doorway, submachine gun in hand. He seemed to be coughing uncontrollably.

"Christ!" Leonard shouted. "The bastards are going to shoot!"

Arik slammed on the air brakes with all his strength. The wheels locked and the truck skidded to a shuddering halt, tires squealing. In back, Dyer and Mackintosh, who were standing up with weapons trained over the tailgate, tumbled heavily to the floor. "Son of a bitch!" growled Dyer as he rolled over.

"Khorasad!" shouted Arik. "General!" He opened the driver's door and jumped down to the road, lost his balance momentarily as he slipped on the wet gravel, then straightened up again. "Khorasad!" he yelled. "You lousy bastard!"

Khorasad stood up from behind the heap of gravel, his face as pale as death and his eyes staring. Slowly he lowered the muzzle of his submachine gun. "God Almighty!" he murmured. "You've done it . . ." He walked toward Arik. For a moment the two men stood face to face without speaking, then Khorasad stepped forward and seized Arik in a powerful embrace, hugging him tightly and slapping him on the back. For what seemed minutes they stood locked together. Then Khorasad pushed Arik back and stared at him. The color slowly returned to his face. "I don't believe it. By God . . . Arik!" he said at last, "Arik Hod!"

Leonard and Jalal climbed down from the cab and stood beside them without speaking, while the others jumped down from the rear. Farha was the first to enter the hut. She saw Dariush leaning on the doorpost coughing and groaning, Janet huddling by the stove and behind her, crouching in the far corner, Yasarian and Amiri. "You can put that gun down," she said to Yasarian. "Everything's okay."

Barrett followed her, looking anxiously at Dariush, then at Yasarian and Amiri. "Everything all right?" he asked.

Yasarian rose unsteadily to his feet, his whole body shaking, then he moaned and dropped the submachine gun. He felt giddy. The hut was full of smoke and a sickening stench hung in the air, emitted by the steaming kettle. "Oh God!" he said. "I'm going to throw up . . ."

"This is Schreiber's man," explained Arik outside, pointing to Leonard. "Most of the team are his boys."

"Really?" Khorasad laughed loudly. "Hey, I thought that pipe-smoking jerk had forgotten me!"

Leonard smiled and shook the general's hand. "This is a real pleasure, sir . . . I was beginning to think we'd never meet . . ."

"Welcome to Iran!" Khorasad laughed again and turned to Jalal. "And you, you mountain thug! By God, I knew you wouldn't let me down!"

The giant Kurd detached himself from the general's embrace. "Listen," he said, "we'll have time to gossip later, when we're safe . . ."

"What's up?" The smile faded from the general's face. He frowned. "We have a problem, my brother?"

"We have a problem . . ." The Kurd turned and pointed to the fields. "Trucks," he said, "bypassing the gorge."

Arik looked at the door of the hut and saw Doctor Amiri shuffling out, supported by Barrett and Dyer. Dariush, Janet and Yasarian followed close behind, with Farha and Mackintosh bringing up the rear. "Is this all the gang?" he asked.

"Yes," Khorasad chuckled. "Schreiber's chosen few, the finest flower of Iranian manhood . . ."

Barrett gestured toward Amiri with a movement of the head and spoke to Arik. "He needs help," he said. "He's sick . . . I think it's a heart condition. The young guy doesn't look too good either, he's coughing like a regular TB case!"

"Later!" Arik pointed to the truck. "Get them all on board," he said. "Hurry! We're going home!"

Khorasad and Leonard joined him in the cab. He started up and watched in the big side mirror as Jalal lifted Doctor Amiri in his arms and passed him into the outstretched hands of Barrett and Dyer. He switched on the radio set. "Ready?" he asked.

"Give the big guy a chance to get in!" he heard Dyer reply. "And take it easy, for Chrissake, this ain't no Greyhound bus!"

Arik released the hand brake and swung the wheels around in a tight lock. The Krupp turned slowly, its huge tires sliding and screeching as they veered off the road, then came around and took a firm grip on the gravel surface. Arik completed the turn and rammed the gas pedal to the floor.

"You'll kill us!" shouted the general. "All this effort just to die in a road crash!" Arik did not reply, instead he concentrated on the road ahead.

Shraga and Dyer crouched shoulder to shoulder on the top of the trailer, bracing themselves against the steel joists, their weapons trained on the road ahead. In spite of the snow masks their eyes streamed in the icy headwind. Jalal, Farha and Dariush sat in the forward left corner, and nearby Barrett and Mackintosh bent over Doctor Amiri, who lay spreadeagled on a bundle of blankets and sleeping bags. Yasarian crouched at Amiri's feet, staring about him wildly, sprawling painfully with every lurch of the heavy truck. He groaned and looked across at Janet, who was trying to steady herself against the metal wall. His heart thumped madly, his head spun. "Make the bastard slow down," he shouted. "He's driving like a lunatic!" His voice was drowned by the roar of the engine and the rumble of the swaying metal.

Arik instinctively gripped the wheel with all his strength, even though the hydraulic steering obeyed his lightest touch and the massive truck handled easily. Khorasad was the first to see the roadblock. "There!" he shouted. "Look, up at the bend!"

Arik and Leonard had also seen the two flat-nosed panel trucks parked fender to fender across the entire width of the road. Beside the vehicles knelt a few figures in civilian clothes and farther back, at the roadside, stood the green jeep from the inn parking lot. If only they'd stopped him then! "Pay attention, boys!" shouted Leonard. He glanced at Khorasad and Arik. The Iranian wedged the steel butt of the submachine gun hard into his waist and stared straight ahead through the front windshield, which was now splashed with mud and the first drops of a heavy downpour. "Turn on the wipers!" he yelled. "The wipers, man!"

Arik did not reply, he was concentrating too hard on the road. For a fraction of a second he started to brake, then he changed his mind and rammed his foot down hard on the gas. "Hold tight!" he yelled. He saw men fleeing to the side of the road. Two of them stood their ground and fired. He did not hear the shots, or know if the truck had been hit. "Now," he murmured, "now."

The huge front fender of the truck smashed into the two vehicles with full force, wrecking both. The panel trucks crumpled as they were plowed aside like toys. Now Arik heard a burst of automatic fire and two explosions; for an instant he tried to duck, but soon realized it was his own men throwing grenades.

Arik drove on wildly. The truck seemed okay. Aside from a vibration in the steering mechanism and a slight pull toward the right it handled as before; the dash showed no abnormalities. With his gloved hand Arik tried all the knobs and switches until he got the big wipers going. Heavy rain was now falling and the big panes of the windshield were soon awash. They saw the inn and the adjoining buildings and the Kurdish watchman still at his post beside the truck that had been left behind. In the doorway of the inn stood Mustafa, petrified with fright; a thick jet of water streamed down the sloping roof directly onto him. Smoke curled up from the broad chimney. Jalal waved his hand but they apparently did not see. Arik pressed the horn and drove on, rapidly leaving the little cluster of houses behind. Now for the first time he eased off on the gas and steadied the hectic pace of the truck.

"Rendezvous 34 . . ." said Khorasad in a loud voice.

"Where are we going?" shouted Leonard at Arik. "The landing strip is in the other direction!"

Arik turned to Leonard. "Impossible," he said simply.

"Where are we heading?" asked Khorasad. Arik did not hear, so he raised his voice above the roar of the engine: "Where are we going?"

186

"Nidawad!"

"Well," Khorasad said after a moment's thought. "You're the boss!" He turned to Leonard. "I want to thank you."

"Okay!" shouted Leonard. "Okay!" He was trying to get Arik's attention again, but his voice shook with the bucking of the truck. "Whe-e-re are we-e go-o-ing?"

"As close as we can get to the mountain!" Arik shouted back at him.

Leonard scowled at him. "What about the landing strip?"

"I told you, it's impossible."

"Why?" Leonard felt suddenly afraid. "What the hell's going on?"

Arik frowned, then gradually reduced speed and brought the truck to a stop. He cut the engine and immediately turned to Khorasad.

"The chances of getting to the landing strip, quick, friend! What are our chances?"

"What's up?" Khorasad stared at Arik and then at Leonard. "What's the problem?"

"Why don't we carry on according to the plan?" asked Leonard his voice showing the first signs of anger. "This isn't the way north to the border. How the hell are we going to get out of here?"

Arik repeated his question. "What are our chances?"

"Chances are nil," replied Khorasad, leaning back and closing his eyes. "No chance . . . those guys hold all the aces. We'll never make it there . . . not in this state . . ."

"Why?" Leonard persisted. "Give me one good reason why not! This isn't the way we agreed to work," he shouted angrily. "What's this business about Nidawad? Suppose we get up this goddam mountain, how the fuck are we going to get off it?"

Arik paused before replying. He looked at the road stretching out ahead and knew they would soon be forced to abandon the truck. "There's no alternative," he said quietly. "Don't you see? I'm sorry . . ."

Leonard shrugged, his anger subsiding, but the sense of apprehension was as strong as ever. He stared out through the side window. "I hope you know what you're doing," he said at last. He sighed and lit a cigarette, then opened the door beside him. "I'm going to see how things are in back," he said.

"Tell them to gather up their gear," Arik yelled down to him. "We'll be dumping the rig inside of five kilometers."

"I don't know how my young friend is going to stand the effort," said Khorasad in a low voice. He sat beside Arik, leaning against the wall of rock that hung above them, its angle providing refuge from the driving rain. He pointed to Dariush who stumbled toward them up the winding shepherds' path, wincing and coughing incessantly on the broad shoulder of Dyer. A short distance behind them came Yasarian and Mackintosh dragging the frail figure of Doctor Amiri between them while Barrett supported him from behind. Janet and Farha trailed some fifty yards behind with Jalal bringing up the rear. The sky was grim and overcast. Loud peals of thunder echoed around the foothills of the mountain.

"What kind of guy is he?" asked Arik. He looked across at Leonard who stood with Yosi and Shraga, anxiously scanning the surrounding terrain and checking it against his map and compass.

"He's the best," replied Khorasad. "The best I know . . ." He was silent for a moment, then went on. "If it wasn't for him I'd still be back there." He pointed to the dark horizon. "In Kermanshah."

"You'll have to tell me all about it," said Arik. "When this business is over . . ."

"Yes," Khorasad agreed. He was tired. The events of the last few days and the effort of climbing the steep path had sapped all his energy. *I was stronger than him once,* he thought with a sidelong glance at Arik. "It's been a complicated business," he said. "Lots of problems . . ." He stretched his hand and pointed at Yasarian and Amiri. "If it hadn't been for those two . . . scientists, the story would have been different . . ." He felt anger swelling inside him. "Dead wood, that's all they are!"

Arik saw Barrett bending over Doctor Amiri who slumped

weakly against a boulder, his face pale and his eyes shut. "Nero and Redwood . . ." he murmured. "Hey, tell me something," he said. "What's so special about those two?"

*"Special?"*

Arik smiled. "All this effort . . . Schreiber, Israel, why's everyone so interested in them?"

"They're on the C.I.A. payroll." Khorasad smiled sadly. "Like me."

"Okay, but that doesn't explain the Israeli side. I've got nothing to do with that glorious organization anyway. So why me?"

"I thought you came on my account . . ."

"Don't flatter yourself," murmured Arik.

"All right, but I thought you knew."

"No!"

"Those two are involved with the bomb. A few formulas, press a switch and bang, no more world!"

"Yes, but there's plenty more like them . . ."

"America invested heavily in them, very heavily. The Shah-in-Shah . . ." Khorasad cursed softly, wiping his face as a gust of wind carried the rain into their shelter. "The Peacock Throne, he wanted his own nuclear bomb, a nice big mushroom cloud to blow away all his problems . . ."

"I didn't know."

"Of course you didn't." Khorasad smiled. "You're not a Savak general! I guess your people in Jerusalem weren't too pleased when they heard what was going on here. Imagine it, a couple of chefs" —Khorasad chuckled—"cooking up their mushrooms for a gang of crazy priests. No wonder your government was worried, the Americans too."

"Is that all?"

"It's enough, isn't it? Anyway, they'd visited Tel Aviv, the Negev . . . they knew a lot, a lot about you too . . ."

Arik nodded. He glanced at his watch, then opened his pack, took out the altimeter and fastened it to his wrist. "We'd better move," he said. "Come on, let's go!"

"The old man's in a bad way," shouted Barrett. His red hair

189

was wet and his face glistened. "I've given him a shot to help his circulation but he's real sick. I don't think he can take much more of this!"

"Bullshit!" exclaimed Khorasad. "If he's got this far the bastard can go on a bit farther. If necessary Yasarian will carry him."

"He needs rest!" Barrett insisted. "Hot food . . ."

Leonard came up with Yosi and Shraga. "What's the problem?" he asked.

"The old man," replied Khorasad. "Whenever there's a problem, it's always one of those two shitheads. Come on, let's move it."

"Who do you think you are?" demanded Yasarian furiously. He leaped to his feet and stood close by Leonard. His heavy features were creased with anger and exhaustion, but in the company of the American and the others he felt his self-confidence return. "Can't you spare a thought for *us* and *our* feelings? Why all these insults?" The rest of the party gathered around them as Barrett and Dyer helped Doctor Amiri to stand up. The old man opened his blue eyes, shuddered and then looked into Khorasad's face. "General . . ." he began.

"Go to hell!" muttered Khorasad. He shouldered his submachine gun and set off up the steep path. The others followed, Dyer and Barrett in the lead, supporting Amiri. Leonard and Arik walked side by side, while close behind came Janet and Farha, then Shraga, Yosi and Yasarian. Dariush struggled along at the rear of the file, leaning heavily on Jalal's shoulder.

"Khorasad!" Yasarian shouted suddenly. He ran up behind the general on the narrow path alongside the precipice. "Khorasad!"

"What the hell do you want?" growled the general. He went on walking without turning around.

"Stand still while I talk to you!" shouted Yasarian. "I'll make you pay!" he yelled. "I'll make you pay for the way you've abused me!"

Khorasad stopped. He heard Yasarian's voice echoing in the

deep chasm that yawned at their side. The rain was falling heavily now and he shivered in the cold and damp. "What are you talking about; birdbrain?" he shouted in Farsi. "Pay whom? You cripple. You are nothing but a frightened baby . . . a coward! Wimp!" He paused for a moment, then wiped his wet face. "I fucked her too, do you hear? I fucked her in the cave, you eunuch!"

Yasarian stopped dead in his tracks, his face turned pale. Khorasad had turned and was walking up the path. With a bellow of rage Yasarian flipped the safety catch of his submachine gun and raised it to his shoulder. He swung the muzzle around and took aim at the broad back of Khorasad. Suddenly there were rapid footsteps behind and a strangled cry: "General!"

Dariush bounded up the path and flung himself at the burly scientist. A burst of fire rang out, the bullets scudding harmlessly in the frozen mud. Yasarian lost his footing on the wet rock, slipped and fell. He was rolling down the path, then off it toward the abyss. Desperately he clawed at the loose gravel, at Dariush who was still grappling with him. The world was spinning before his eyes. With a final frantic effort he stretched out his hand and caught Dariush's heel. "Help me!" he cried. "Help!" Dariush lost his grip on a rock and together the two men slithered down the steep rock face, gaining momentum until they were falling free of the edge. For a moment there was silence, then a scream of fear. Khorasad was sure it was not Dariush.

# 12

"He's gone mad!" roared Schreiber. He thumped the paper-laden table and threw down his unlit pipe. His normally calm face grew red with anger and disbelief. He thumped the table again. "He's gone mad, I tell you, he's off his head!" He bent his well-groomed head over the cable Portilio had handed him a few seconds before. He took off his spectacles, looked up and stared at Danny who sat beside him in silence, unperturbed by his outburst. The others sat frozen in place, watching Schreiber. For a while nobody spoke. Portilio, his shirt unbuttoned and his tie askew, fiddled with his cigar case. The air buzzed with the monotonous crackle of radio receivers and from the next room came the rattle of the Telex machine.

"We should never have agreed," said Portilio at last. He thrust a cigar between his teeth and lit it hurriedly, avoiding the eyes of Danny and Eldad. "We should never have agreed to put him in command." He took a deep gulp of smoke.

"I see no indication that Leonard is opposed to the idea," said

Trenshaw. He stood behind Schreiber, munching a chicken sandwich. Schreiber turned: "Could it be he *can't* oppose it?" he asked.

"I don't know . . ." Trenshaw walked across to a wall hung with maps, aerial photographs and diagrams. He stretched out his free hand and laid a finger on Mount Nidawad. "We'll have to consult George and Jack," he said. "Only they can decide if the plan is practicable or not. There may be an alternative . . ."

"The general and the agents have been rescued," said Danny. This was the first time he had spoken. "So far we have succeeded, right?"

"*Succeeded?* Is that what you call it?" Schreiber shook his head incredulously. He looked at Trenshaw and then at the map. "At an altitude of three thousand two hundred feet," he said. "In winter conditions and without a landing strip."

"They are on a small plateau up there," said Danny. "The plan isn't that illogical."

"We must ask George," Trenshaw insisted.

"Any pilot will tell you it's impossible," replied Schreiber. He fumbled among the papers on the table until he found his pipe. "Aerial rescue my ass!"

"We have no choice," said Eldad. "We must check everything out and make our decision." He paused for a moment, then added with a chuckle, "If we're not prepared to take the risk, those guys are just going to be stuck there."

"Sweet Jesus!" muttered Schreiber. He pursed his lips, stared at the men around him, then sighed. "Okay," he said. "We'll ask George . . . but even if the pilot agrees, I'll need to consult Washington. This madness may lose us an aircraft."

"I'll get the Hercules," answered Trenshaw. He pulled out a notebook and pencil from his coat pocket and copied down from the map the details of the altitude and contours of the plateau of Nidawad. Then he went through to the next room and switched on one of the Telex machines. He started punching out groups of numbers.

Schreiber read the cable again. "You'll be glad to hear that one of the agents is dead," he murmured to Danny. "Do you think Arik shot him?"

"No. If he'd done that, he'd have reported it."

"Yes . . ." Schreiber filled his pipe. "Hell!" he exclaimed after a pause. "When I saw that Hercules take off I was almost jealous. But now"—he lit his pipe and inhaled noisily—"I sure don't envy those bastards now . . ."

"If George agrees to give it a try, we'll need to obtain precise atmospheric data, wind direction, angle of approach, cloud cover . . ." Portilio looked thoughtful. "I remember, in Nepal I talked to a pilot once." He chuckled. "A crazy Englishman, a Battle of Britain veteran. He was something out of a movie . . . or a museum. He told me of a similar operation."

"Well?"

"I didn't believe it was possible. The Englishman was as drunk as a monkey . . ."

"We could drop them extra equipment," said Danny. "A ground station, or something like that . . ."

"We'd need time to prepare that," replied Schreiber.

"Whatever we decide is going to take time. We've got to know how long they can hang on there." Danny stood up. "Time and preparations, there's no getting away from them." He smiled at Schreiber.

Trenshaw spent half an hour at the Telex machine, then came back into the smoke-clogged room with a closely typed sheet of paper in his hand. "I've got a reply!" he said. "George suggests a way but damned if I understand what he means!"

"Give it here!" said Schreiber impatiently. He took the paper and read it through quickly, frowning. "What the hell?" He read the message aloud:

" 'Rescue possible. Conditions unsuitable for landing. Suggest airborne rescue using Hercules model HC130H if visibility above 500 feet. Plane and crew can arrive inside 10 hours from Adana, Turkey. If plan accepted, returning immediately to Tatvan.' "

"What the hell is the HC130H?" Schreiber asked.

"Something secret, you can bet on that," muttered Trenshaw. "Something so goddam secret only the pilots know what it is?"

"Get me Adana," said Schreiber suddenly, as if his mind was made up. "Let's find out exactly what George is talking about!"

A few minutes later one of his aides handed him a telephone receiver. "Adana, sir . . ."

Schreiber took the receiver. "Schreiber here," he said. "Yes, that's right . . . from the Embassy."

On the line came a metallic voice: "Colonel Howard speaking!"

"What's an HC130H?" he asked.

"A plane, sir, a transport plane."

"Obviously," Schreiber snapped impatiently. "We're not talking about racing cars, Colonel. What's so special about this plane?"

"Rescue . . ."

"Yes?" Schreiber sat up in his chair. "Tell me more."

"It works on the basis of helium, sir . . . it's a coastal patrol aircraft."

*Helium? Helium?* Schreiber did not understand the meaning of the colonel's words, but an idea flashed into his mind. "Do you have such a machine, Colonel?"

"Yes, we're fitting it out to take a part in a big NATO sea exercise next week . . . but like I say it belongs to the Coast Guard, not to us. I'm Air Force, sir."

"Can it pick up personnel? From a *mountain?*"

"Yes sir, given the right conditions, of course."

Schreiber covered the mouthpiece of the receiver with his hand and spoke to Trenshaw. "Send a message to George, tell him to get back there, quick!" Then he turned to Portilio. "August, get me Washington on the hot line!"


Leonard completed his guard duty, hidden in the mouth of the big cave where the party had taken shelter from the wind and rain. Opposite him the houses of the little shepherds' village hunched in patches of swirling mist. He recognized Jalal's house by its tall chimney and green shutters. As he waited for Dyer to come and take his place, he watched the mist thicken to a solid white curtain, blocking his view of the rocky plateau, the canyon and the mountains. He waited a few more seconds until he heard the slow footsteps of Glenn approaching from the inner recesses of the cave. Glenn crouched beside him. "Everything all right, boss?"

"Yes." Leonard glanced at Glenn's dusky face and for the first time noticed wisps of white hair sprouting among the curls of his tousled beard. "How you feeling?" he asked.

"Me? I'm just fine . . ." He peered out into the mist. "Anything happening out there?" he asked.

"No, nothing special . . . a few shepherds coming back from the valley, that's all."

"I hope Jalal's keeping his eyes open."

"No doubt of that." Leonard was tired and hungry and he could smell the steaming soup that Barrett and Mackintosh were cooking on the camp stoves in back of the cave, but he decided to wait and smoke a cigarette with Glenn. He lit himself one and offered another to Dyer. They smoked in silence for a few minutes, then Dyer asked: "Do you reckon we're going to make it out of here?"

"You heard the message . . ."

"It sounded crazy to me."

"It's not as crazy as you might think. About a year ago I saw a demonstration. A joint NASA/Lockheed production."

"Did it work?"

"Yes, it sure did."

"Jeez!" Dyer seemed to have lost some of his normal high spirits. "Just a thought," he said. "Why can't they send in a chopper, for Chrissake? Or why don't we find ourselves a landing strip?"

"We'd never make it."

"I didn't think you agreed with Arik on that."

"I do now. He's right. According to Jalal the valley's crawling

196

with gendarmes and revolutionaries. We wouldn't stand a chance down there . . . no chance at all."

"And how's Jalal going to explain it to all those crazies?" asked Dyer, throwing away the burning butt of his cigarette. It landed on the wet ground with a hiss and went out. "Those guys will take revenge on him and his people, won't they?"

"I doubt it. He reckons a full-scale Kurdish revolt could break out any day now and that'll put a stop to any persecution. Anyway"—Leonard stood up and stretched—"if this evacuation goes according to plan, how can they ever prove we were here at all?"

Dyer thought for a minute. "I guess not—wait, what about the parachutes we left behind?"

Leonard chuckled. "Oh, didn't you see? Jalal came by with the cuttings last night—it seems some shepherd friends picked them up yesterday and wanted to know if they could use them to make clothes. I doubt they'll be recognizable as Kurdish shirts and blouses!" He turned and walked back into the cave, passing Janet who sat wrapped in a thick woolen blanket beside the smoldering embers of a little fire. She smiled faintly at him. *I'd be interested to know how she fits into all this,* he thought, studying her scratched and bruised face. *How did she ever get mixed up with Khorasad? Must be his mistress,* he decided.

"How do you feel?" he asked.

"Fine."

"Have you eaten yet?"

"Yes, thank you. The main thing is I've grabbed some rest . . ."

"Are you worried?"

She smiled. "After everything we've been through these last few days, I don't have any worry left." She laughed, but her blue eyes were frightened and uneasy. "We will get out of here, won't we?"

"Don't worry," he said, "everything is going to work out fine, just fine."

"Leonard! Over here, quick, Neptune's on the line!" He winked at Janet and joined Arik and Khorasad who sat beside the radio. The red control light was flashing. He put on the headphones, punched out the prearranged sequence of numbers and pressed the transmit button.

"Swordfish here, calling Neptune. Receiving you, over."

"Neptune here, guest and consignment arriving oh six hundred local time. Is that understood, over?"

*That's short and sweet,* thought Leonard. He replied at once, "Swordfish here, understood. Oh six hundred Lima Tango, welcome. Any further message, over?"

"Neptune, over and out."

He took off the headset and switched off the mike. "They're sending someone," he said, "tomorrow at six A.M. He's bringing a consignment."

"The equipment," said Arik. "Excellent!"

"I still don't understand how this thing works," complained Khorasad. He scratched his stubbled chin, sighed and spat out the cigarette that Leonard had given him with an expression of disgust.

Arik glanced around the cave which was steadily growing darker. Doctor Amiri snored softly under a pile of blankets. Shraga, Yosi and Walter stared moodily into space while Mackintosh and Barrett were busy preparing their soup. Janet sat apart from the rest.

"Do you think those two will stand up to all this?" Arik asked Khorasad.

"Who?"

"The doctor and the woman."

Khorasad roared with laughter. "She's as strong as a Belgian mare!" he said. "Muscles of steel, believe me! As for the old man," he added, frowning, "he's just a lousy lump of shit. You can do what you like with him. I don't care!"

"Is she connected with you?" asked Leonard.

"Why?" The general smiled. "Are you interested in her?"

"I'm just curious."

"Well," Khorasad said, "she was Yasarian's woman."

*"Redwood?"*

"Yes." Khorasad's face darkened. "The one who dragged Dariush into the canyon."

Arik leaned forward and stretched his limbs. "I don't know about you," he said, "but I'm going to find a quiet corner and snatch some rest. We've a long day ahead of us tomorrow."

A few minutes before six o'clock the next morning they heard the big Ellison engines of the Hercules. Arik and Walter stood leaning on a big rock in jump suits and snow masks. A low cloud ceiling hid the plane entirely from view. "There it is!" cried Leonard, crouching on the ground beside the radio receiver. They heard the plane pass above them and move on; a few seconds later they heard a sharp rustling as four large containers, attached to red parachutes, dropped out of the clouds and landed on the frozen plateau about two hundred yards from where they stood. There was a brief pause, then the same sound, closer this time, as a parachutist appeared and landed with a soft thud. The stocky man rolled over on the hard ground, released the straps of his chute and sprang briskly to his feet. He took off his snow mask and smiled.

"Schneider!" cried Leonard. "Good God, it's Jack!" He switched off the radio and ran to meet Schneider with Arik and Walter following close behind.

They exchanged handshakes and Jack quickly inspected the terrain. The visibility satisfied him for now, but he peered anxiously at the sky. "If that cloud cover comes down below five hundred feet we'll have to postpone," he said, "and the fog won't help any . . . Jesus, you've picked yourselves a real hole . . . it couldn't possibly be worse!"

"Don't blame us," muttered Leonard. "This crazy scheme was your idea . . ."

"Sure," Jack chuckled. "It's cold, goddam it!" He put his snow mask back in place and walked across to where the big containers lay under the deflated canopies of the chutes. Arik joined him.

"What have you got in there?" he asked, pointing to the

containers. "Wings?" He smiled, then added, "Tell me something, Jack, do you really believe this is going to work?"

Schneider glanced at him quickly. "Listen," he said, breathing hard, "if I had any doubt, the slightest atom of a doubt, I wouldn't be here. Me and George can think of better ways of spending our time."

"Who's flying the plane?" asked Leonard, switching on his walkie-talkie to call out the rest of the party.

"A pilot from the Coast Guard and George. That's why I dropped by to visit you guys, I didn't feel much like sitting up there doing nothing and anyway"—he smiled to himself under the mask—"I'm the only one who knows how this fucking equipment works . . ."

Beside the containers they gathered up the big chutes and then detached the cables. "The boys will be along to help," said Leonard. "I asked them to bring Jalal, too."

Arik nodded. "That's good," he said. "We've got to remind him to hide as much as he can afterward and burn the rest." He helped Jack open the nearest container whose metallic cover was marked with a big letter $A$. Schneider pushed up his snow mask. "The ground station first," he said. "Come on boys, give me a hand!"

They dragged out a big aluminum crate wrapped in waterproof canvas and helped the pilot position it some distance from the containers and the chutes. Then they returned to the container and brought out two smaller crates. Jack set to work. Arik and Leonard looked on in astonishment as he assembled around him a series of electronic gauges, then inflated a small helium balloon. When he released it the little sphere rose rapidly into the grey sky, carrying beneath it a narrow gondola laden with gadgets and antennas. He took off his gloves, cursing the cold as he adjusted the controls, then flipped a series of switches. The instruments came to life and digital information flashed up on the tiny luminescent screens. Arik stared at the balloon hovering above them and when he looked down he saw his men approaching from the direction of the shepherds' village, among them the tall figure of Jalal.

"What altitude are we?" asked Jack. "I need to know precisely."

Arik glanced at his altimeter. "Three thousand, one hundred and ninety-seven feet," he said, "at this exact spot."

"Fine!" The pilot nodded his big head with an air of satisfaction. "Cloud ceiling eight hundred feet," he said, "wind's good ... perfect ... let's hope it stays that way for another"—he glanced at his watch—"another two hours. Hell, that's all we've got!" Then he stood up and asked, "Do you guys know this goddam place? I studied every detail on the map and the photos but all the same ... the boys up there have minimal freedom of maneuver, they're flying on instruments."

"We know it," said Arik.

"Okay ..." Jack inspected the equipment at this feet. "Help me set up the rest of the gear," he said. "I'll mark the spot where each item has to go ... without them George won't be able to get close enough."

"What height has he got to fly?" asked Leonard.

"Five hundred feet. One-fifty-two meters to be precise, no more no less ... and then he'll pick you up at a height of four-forty-five feet ..."

"Jesus!" murmured Leonard. "How's he going to get into this valley, through the clouds?"

"He will." Jack nodded. "I won't bore you with technical details, but just one small mistake and he'll come down, no ... he'll crash, maybe right on top of us!"

"That's encouraging," muttered Arik.

"How many passengers do we have?"

"Ten, aside from you ..."

"Okay." Schneider smiled. He stared at his charges, trying to guess their feelings. "Don't worry," he said, "I'm sure it's going to work."

"Your confidence is killing," grumbled Arik. He turned and glanced at the approaching group. "Two missing ..." he said.

"Nero and the woman have stayed back in the cave," said Leonard. "They'll join us later."

"Right . . . let's sort out the gear!"

Shortly before eight o'clock they stood ready beside the containers. Doctor Amiri, though, sat wrapped in a blanket on the ground, head slumped, face a livid shade of blue. Foam flecked his thin lips. Once or twice he muttered incoherently to Farha who stood close beside him.

Out in front Jack held a strap harness that was attached to a nylon cable. "I'll strap you up," he said, "one at a time, then I'll send up the balloons. All *you* have to do is stand still . . . you won't feel anything much, just a tug . . ." He looked at Arik and added, "Less than a tug of a chute when it opens."

"What then?" Arik's voice was tense.

"The plane passes above the balloon, a hook catches the cable and you're pulled inside . . ."

"God Almighty!"

"This is worse than Houdini!" cracked Dyer. "Whose idea is this for Chrissake?"

Jack laughed. "It isn't that bad . . . the Fulton Company and the Coast Guard say the system works. It's been tested thoroughly. If we had time to explain the method to you . . ." He paused and looked at the men. Jalal was staring at him with an expression of blank amazement. "I don't believe it," he said. "I never heard of anything so crazy."

"Come on, we're wasting time." Jack looked at his watch. "Half an hour til the plane arrives . . . who's going to be first?"

"I can't do it!" whispered Janet. "Oh Jesus, I can't do this."

Khorasad approached her. "Listen," he said. "there's no other way . . . just relax and get a grip on yourself!"

"I can't!"

He slapped her.

"Hey!" shouted Walter. He sprang forward, ripping the snow mask from his face. "Jesus Christ, General, that wasn't necessary."

Khorasad looked at the American with a trace of scorn. "This is no time for chivalry, gentlemen. You can argue . . ."

"Enough." Arik cut him off with his scowl. "Enough talk."

Khorasad shook his head and stomped away.


George was uncomfortable in Jack's copilot seat. Every now and then he gave a glance at the Coast Guard captain, a thin young man with a close-trimmed moustache and cold green eyes. He did not like flying copilot but also knew that in this operation the laconic young captain was the expert, leader of the special rescue team of the HC130H, ten experienced aviators who included, aside from him and the captain, a navigator, a radar officer, two flight mechanics, two load masters and two escape-and-rescue technicians. He inspected the instrument panel and then leaned forward and checked out the gray sky all around and the clouds beneath. *Another hour,* he thought, checking the instruments and the map. The captain smiled at him. "We'll begin descent soon. When do you think we'll hear from your man?"

"Soon . . ." He looked at the instrument panel. The signals on the radio compass showed that Jack's ground station was operating. "Not long now," he said. "If anything had gone wrong we'd have heard . . ."

"You know this goes against everything in the textbooks," said the captain thoughtfully.

"Yes."

"They'll write about this operation in the professional journals"—the captain smiled—"if we succeed."

"No they won't," said George.

"Why not?" The captain looked at him in surprise.

"They won't," he repeated.

Now the plane began losing height. Rapidly they approached the endless white carpet beneath them. George and the captain ran through procedures calmly, expertly . . . *like a routine flight,* thought George. Hundreds of times he had flown into clouds and through them, in zero visibility, but then he had relied on tried and tested aids, not some minicomputer set up by Jack somewhere in an unknown and invisible mountain range. He watched as the radar officer operated a complex system of screens and receivers. Groups of numbers flashed up on the panels as computers interpreted data relayed from the ground.

"Thank God . . ." he said.

"What's up?" The captain glanced at him with a hint of surprise and immediately looked back at the instrument panel.

"Just admiring your technology, boss. This bird of yours is a goddam miracle!"

"If it wasn't we'd never have taken on this mission," replied the captain drily. "Concentrate on your instruments, man."

At that moment they plunged into the cloud. George braced himself in his seat as cold sweat trickled down his cheeks. *God,* he thought, *Jack made the right choice to jump . . .*

"Height two thousand feet," said the radar officer. "Stay right on this bearing, Captain, no adjustments."

"Speed?" asked the captain.

"Steady, two-nine-five knots and falling."

"Height?"

"Reduce by five-oh feet . . ."

George read the DME apparatus measuring the range to Jack's radio beacon. Now the control of the Hercules demanded all his concentration and he spoke only when repeating the pilot's instructions. The distance registered by the DME grew smaller, the VOR needle tuned in to the ground station showed an adjustment to the left of ten degrees. The next set of figures flashing up on the DME gave a range of twelve miles. As they sank deeper into the cloud, Jack's call sign came through on the headphones: "Romeo One calling Romeo Two, cloud ceiling eight hundred feet . . ."

He tightened his grip on the controls. The air speed fell steadily. They were flying at one thousand feet and he knew they'd entered on the final phase. Any minute now they would see the ground. The slightest deviation would lead to collision on the wall of rock that enclosed the valley. "Eye contact with ground!" said the captain. They came out under the cloud and settled into a level flight above a grey plain littered with boulders and shrubs. On both sides rose abrupt foothills. He glanced quickly at the panel map in front of him and then at the range on the DME. "Any second," he murmured, "any second . . ."

"Eye contact with balloon!" said the captain. Ahead he spotted the red-and-white-speckled balloon, the nylon cable. The balloon shifted slightly in the wind. Now the party on the ground came into sight.

"Height five-one-oh feet," shouted the captain. "Too high, we'll have to come around again!" He pulled back the controls and the Hercules climbed steeply, above the balloon and plunging back into the clouds. It banked and returned in a broad arc to the start of the approach run. Now the cargo ramp was open, all team members in position. Under the nose of the plane the recovery yoke glinted; on both sides, like a thin moustache, stretched the protective cables designed to prevent tangling or snaring of the balloon cable in the event of error. Again they went through the approach procedure, constantly checking instruments as they descended. Again they settled into a level path above the plateau. Height 495, speed 153 . . .

The captain sat tensed in his seat, eyes fixed on the balloon. "Prepare to rescue!"

"Speed one-five-one knots . . ." George saw the big balloon directly ahead of them.

The captain adjusted the angle with a barely perceptible movement.

Arik make an effort to suppress his mounting apprehension. He stood harnessed to the long nylon cable which ran up from a strap at the back of his neck to the base of the balloon. Jack stood beside him. "Don't worry," he said, "you won't feel a thing. The whole mechanism's designed so you can't hit the body of the plane. There's nothing to worry about!"

205

"You've said that now a thousand times!" Arik looked over at the others. Leonard was chatting with Janet, Doctor Amiri still crouched pathetically on the ground, the others sought signs in the sky or sorted through the equipment that was to be left behind in the care of Jalal and Farha. The rest was being stowed in one of the containers, which would be hoisted into the plane once the rescue was complete.

"They're getting close," said Khorasad, pacing toward Arik slowly, hands deep in his pockets and collar turned up against the wind. He gestured upward with a jerk of his head as the sound of the engines grew stronger.

"Yes." Jack looked up at the gray sky. He tried hard to show confidence. The unfamiliar voice of the Hercules captain came crackling out of the radio set. "Eye contact with balloon . . ."

The plane appeared out of the clouds, slowly and noisily. They could see the shining disks created by the spinning propeller blades and the complex mechanism of hoists and cables. "Hold tight!" Jack shouted to Arik, stepping back, but as soon as he spoke the black nose rose up and the Hercules roared away, its cargo ramp wide open. He could make out the profiles of the pilots in the cockpit and a figure in a red flying suit standing close by the loading bay.

Arik opened his eyes. "What now?" he shouted, "what now, goddamn it!" His whole body ached from the strain of his tensed muscles.

"Relax . . . he came in too high . . . he'll be back . . ."

"Hell!" Arik heard the Ellison engines receding in the cloud, echoing round the valley, then approaching again. The plane returned, and this time he kept his eyes open. He heard Jack's warning cry, looked up at the balloon and felt a sharp tug hoist him off his feet. The ground fell away rapidly as he was dragged, swinging, into the cold air, dangling like a worm on the end of the line. The wind was fierce, the noise deafening. He was hovering now under the belly of the aircraft; he tried to focus his eyes on the cable but his vision blurred. He felt faint from the pressure of the harness on his shoulders, hips and back. *Oh God,* he thought, *I'm going to pass out!* He saw above him the huge tail piece, then the gaping black cavity of the cargo hold, then the hoist lifted him inside the aircraft, straight into the arms of the rescue technicians. Someone propped him up against the fuselage, while skilled hands dismantled the harness straps. He looked up and saw the smiling face of a young man in headphones. He tried to stand but the plane lurched suddenly and his knees gave way. "Shit!" he mumbled, then staggered to his feet and made his way into the interior of the plane, helped by the young man. Now, for the first time since he stood in the field waiting for the Hercules, he became aware of the intense cold. "God Almighty!" he exclaimed as he climbed unsteadily to the flight deck.

"Gabriel!" shouted Schneider. "Your turn!" He inflated another helium balloon, detached it from the gas cylinder and released it, watching the nylon cable unwinding and stretch upward. "How do you feel?" he asked.

"Okay." Walter flexed his limbs, feeling the tight pressure of the harness. He shrugged and pulled the snow mask down over his face. "Cold up there, isn't it?"

"Like a deep-freeze," murmured Jack. He looked across to the others. Barrett was helping Doctor Amiri to his feet while Leonard talked earnestly to Janet. He turned to Khorasad.

"What are we going to do with the woman?" he asked. "Looks like she's not convinced yet . . ."

"She'll be all right." Khorasad grimaced and spat.

Jack smiled. "It isn't that complicated," he said, "with modern technology . . ."

"You don't need to calm *me* down! I'd do anything to get out of here. I have to . . ."

Now the plane was approaching again and seconds later Walter was dangling in the cool morning air, then disappearing into the belly of the aircraft.

"You're next, General," said Jack. "Ready?"

"Yes." Khorasad put on his harness and watched with interest as Jack inflated another balloon. "Don't forget," he said, "give her a shot if she won't go willingly."

"Okay."

"I just can't do it," wailed Janet at that moment, her body trembling. "I just can't!"

Leonard laid a heavy hand on her shoulder and made an effort to smile. "Listen," he said, "Khorasad's right, there's no other way. You've seen how it works. It can't fail, believe me!" She shook her head. Her face was as pale as plaster and her eyes were red. He made a final attempt to reassure her. "Try not to be afraid," he said. "Listen, if you can make it we'll have ourselves a great party . . . dinner in Rome, d'you hear me? Rome, that's my regular base."

The plane returned and as it flew above them the broad body of Khorasad jerked off the ground and into the air, hovering in space, then disappearing after the plane into the cloud. The noise was deafening and she stopped her ears, collapsing into Leonard's arms. "No!" she cried. For a fraction of a second they stood locked together. "You must," he said softly. "Remember Rome!"

"Mackintosh!" shouted Jack. "Hurry up! You're next. Then Dyer. Move it! If the wind changes we'll be stuck in this fucking hole!"

The two young men left the others and hurried toward Jack.

Arik approached the pilot's seat and leaned against the cockpit fuselage.

"Sit down, damn you!" roared the captain. "Sit down and strap yourself in!"

Nobody looked at Arik. He saw George's hand on the throttle, saw the radar officer bending over his screens and heard him reading out data. He felt all the movements of the plane as it rose, turned, dived and banked in a broad arc. His face was covered with sweat. He stripped off his snow mask and tossed it away, then his gloves. His heart still pounded but gradually he began to relax.

With trembling hands he rubbed his shoulders, still aching from the pressure of the harness, then tried to restore the circulation to his legs. He felt a barely perceptible jolt, then the plane was climbing again. A pair of headphones lay on the arm of the seat. He put them on and heard George's voice: "Height eight-five-oh feet."

"Now for the third," replied the captain.

"Keep on this bearing," said the radar officer. "Keep on this bearing, Captain!"

"Okay, okay, height?"

"Seven-three-oh feet."

"Fine, here we go again!"

Leonard and Barrett led Janet to where Jack was waiting. The tall woman's legs betrayed her and she had to lean on Leonard's shoulder. Her mouth was dry and the blood pounded in her temples. She tried to resist when they put the harness on her but then stood motionless, breathing hard. Her eyes scanned the faces around her, the gray valley and the dark boulders. She saw Jalal and Farha by the pile of equipment and Shraga and Yosi supporting Doctor Amiri. Suddenly she let out a short laugh, her shoulders shook and Leonard looked at her with surprise.

"Everything all right?" he asked.

"I'm scared shitless . . . what about Amiri?" She looked again at the little scientist and saw Farha waving to them. Saying goodbye? To her or to Leonard? She waved back.

"Remember!" said Leonard. "Dinner in Rome . . ." He took off his snow mask and put it over her head, covering her face . . . in his eyes a familiar mischievous gleam . . . when had she last seen such a look? Khorasad?

"Now!" shouted Jack.

"No!" She took a step toward Leonard but was held by the taut nylon cable and at the same moment she felt the tug and heard the roar of the engines. "No!" Her body was swept up into the air and she lost consciousness.

Jack and Leonard watched her go while Barrett waved to Jalal and Farha. "My turn now!" he shouted. "Good luck to you and go easy with those medicines, I don't want you to poison yourselves!"

Schneider helped him on with the harness and a few minutes later he stood ready, stroking with his right hand the strap that held the nylon cable at the back of his neck. "Everything all right?" he asked.

"You'll find out soon enough," replied Schneider. "The old man's the problem . . ." He glanced anxiously at Amiri.

"He won't jerk out of the harness if that's what you're worried about. Still, he's a sick man. I gave him a shot . . . looks to me like something's wrong with his heart."

"Well, if we get him up, it'll only be a few hours to Tatvan. Anyway, enough of that. Are you ready?"

Barrett was dispatched, then Leonard.

"Now for the old man," said Schneider. He smiled at Jalal and Farha who stood watching the proceedings with a mixture of awe and incredulity.

"Sure you wouldn't like to join us?"

"What?" Jalal grinned. "Not that way! I wouldn't do that for the Peacock Throne in all its glory . . ." He turned and watched Yosi and Shraga, half leading, half dragging Doctor Amiri toward Schneider. The old man was deathly pale. A strange light shone in his eyes and his lips were turning blue. His tiny body was pathetic under the heavy flying suit they had dressed him in. He neither resisted nor cooperated as they tied on the harness. Yosi, speaking to him in a soft reassuring voice, came to the conclusion the old man could not hear anymore. They held him upright and watched as the Hercules approached. They released their hold less than a second before the big black nose missed the balloon cable by a couple of yards. The cable swung and hit the lines which then deflected the cable and carried it under the wing out of range of the propeller blades. The helium balloon swayed crazily and the plane disappeared in the clouds.

"What happened?" shouted Obis. He gripped the controls forcefully and scanned the instrument panel. The altitude rose sharply.

"We missed, fuck it!" replied the captain. "We'll have to go around again!"

Again they banked and went into a dive. This time the exercise worked and seconds later Amiri was dangling in the air, trailing behind the plane before being hoisted into the cargo hold.

"How many more?"

"Three plus equipment . . . four more runs . . ."

"Okay." The captain's face streamed with sweat. He wiped his stinging eyes with his hand and looked out. "Cloud ceiling falling," he said. "We'd better move it!"

Schneider dispatched Yosi, then the equipment and finally Shraga. Now only he was left, alone in the harness. Jalal and Farha stood a little way back, watching. "Give my regards to the general," shouted Jalal. "Tell him not forget us. *Sarabaste!*"

*"What's that?"*

*"Sarabaste!"*

*"What?"*

"It doesn't matter." The giant smiled. "Here he comes," he said, pointing to the sky. "Good luck!"

"Arik!" shouted Farha, waving the submachine gun that Leonard had given her. "Regards to Arik!"

The Hercules came in for its final run, settling into a horizontal flight. *Less than 500 feet,* thought Jack, *speed 150, maybe 160 knots.* He looked up and adjusted his stance. "Hail Mary full of grace . . ." he murmured. He felt the tug and was swept up into the cold air. His eyes closed and when he opened them he saw the ground far away and Jalal and Farha like two black dots.

Leonard climbed up to the flight deck and sat down heavily on the crew rest bed as the Hercules climbed with all the power of its engines. He looked at Arik who had released himself from the safety belt and was approaching him against the side of the cockpit.

"Lucky Strike?" offered Leonard.

"Sure."

"You look pale."

"You don't look like you've just skied in Saint Moritz either."

They laughed and smoked in silence. "We've done it," said Leonard at last. "Jesus, we've done it!"

"Yes . . ." Arik look a lungful of smoke and coughed lightly, then looked across at the pilots' seats. Obis turned to face them, grinning broadly. He gave a thumbs-up sign with his gloved hand, then put a finger to the tip of his thumb. "Okay!" he cried, "Okay!"

Arik nodded and leaned back. He closed his eyes and shook his head, then looked ahead again. Now they had risen above the clouds and the cockpit was full of light. He saw Khorasad climbing the flight-deck ladder, swaying slightly, his face calm. Walter Gabriel followed. The two men came and sat down beside them, crowding together on the broad bed. Arik closed his eyes again. He wanted to get up and look out the windows, but he knew he'd see nothing but the carpet of clouds.

"It's a wonderful device," he said at last. "I never believed it was going to work."

"Yes," Khorasad agreed. He was silent for a moment, then added. "Interesting, very interesting . . ."

A tall young man in a red flying suit, one of the rescue team, came into the cockpit. He wore headphones and as he entered he plugged the lead into a socket on the wall and said something to Obis and the Coast Guard captain. They turned. Obis pointed to Arik and the man in the red suit took off the headphones and walked toward them.

"The old man," he said. "There was nothing we could do."

"What happened?" Arik sat up.

"He's dead. He was dead before he got to the plane . . . I'm sorry . . . His heart was too weak."

Khorasad smiled, then changed his expression to a grimace. "Oh God," he said. "What a waste . . ."

"What's up?" said Leonard anxiously.

"Nero's dead," said Arik.

"What a waste," repeated Khorasad. "The operation was a success but the patient's dead. What a waste, Dariush."

# Afterword

Arik heard the light squeal of tires as the airport taxi drove off down the oily sidewalk into the evening traffic. He glanced quickly up at the building. The shutters of his room were closed. For a moment or two he hesitated, then he picked up his case from the sidewalk and walked to the door of the cafe.

Fishel, behind the display cabinet, peered at him through the empty bottles, dirty glasses and bread baskets. A broad smile broke out on his face. "At last! You're back at last, kid! I was worried about you!"

Arik smiled. He was tired and in an ugly mood, but he forced himself around the cabinet and into a hug with the little old man. "What's new?"

"Business as usual . . ." Fishel shrugged. "What about you?"

"Nothing special . . . I'm back."

"You look tired."

"Yes."

"A plate of soup?" The little man beamed. "I've got fine chicken soup here, the best in town!"

Arik chuckled and glanced around the cafe. Two elderly drivers in dark blue overalls sat grumbling by the window, and a plump little woman bent over a steaming plate by the kitchen door. "Why not?" he said.

He went to the table at the far end of the cafe and sat down, leaning his back against the wall. The radio played soft music and from the street came car noise and the sound of distant sirens. The dockyard, he thought. Home.

He lit a cigarette and watched Fishel limping toward him with a china bowl and a big spoon.

"There was message for you," he said, laying the bowl on the greasy table, "a phone call. Eldad . . ."

"Yes?"

"Some relation of yours arriving tomorrow, a lady. I don't remember the name . . . from Turkey, I think. Mean anything to you?"

"Yes." He stubbed out the cigarette and took a mouthful of soup. It was hot. "Hell," he murmured. He heard a snippet of the radio news. "Hey, Fishel," shouted one of the drivers, "turn up the volume!"

"In Sanandaj fighting has broken out between Kurds seeking independence and supporters of the Ayatollah . . ."

Arik took another spoonful of soup, warm and tasty.

"The fighting has spread to Mehabad . . ."

He coughed and smiled. "Jalal, you bastard . . ." he murmured.